BOOKS BY TINA FOLSOM

Samson's Lovely Mortal (Scanguards Vampires #1)
Amaury's Hellion (Scanguards Vampires #2)
Gabriel's Mate (Scanguards Vampires #3)
Yvette's Haven (Scanguards Vampires #4)
Zane's Redemption (Scanguards Vampires #5)
Quinn's Undying Rose (Scanguards Vampires #6)
Oliver's Hunger (Scanguards Vampires #7)
Thomas's Choice (Scanguards Vampires #8)
Silent Bite (Scanguards Vampires #8 1/2)
Cain's Identity (Scanguards Vampires #9)
Luther's Return (Scanguards Vampires #10)

Lover Uncloaked (Stealth Guardians #1)

A Touch of Greek (Out of Olympus #1)
A Scent of Greek (Out of Olympus #2)
A Taste of Greek (Out of Olympus #3)

Lawful Escort
Lawful Lover
Lawful Wife
One Foolish Night
One Long Embrace
One Sizzling Touch

Venice Vampyr – The Beginning

Copyright © 2012 by Tina Folsom
Previously published under the title Edge of Passion.

Published in the United States

Cover design: Damon Za
Author Photo: © Marti Corn Photography

Printed in the United States of America

LOVER UNCLOAKED

STEALTH GUARDIANS #1

TINA FOLSOM

1

Aiden launched his dagger at the demon, aiming for his forehead, but the weapon missed its target as the bastard spun with superhuman speed. Whirling to the left, Aiden avoided what was coming next: an ancient blade flying in his direction, leaving the demon's deft wrist just as fast as the underworld vermin had turned on his heels. The sharp edge of the knife passed by him not an inch too close. Forged in the Dark Days, the weapon could kill even him, an immortal Stealth Guardian. And he wasn't here to die. He was fighting evil to save his charge, the human woman he'd been assigned to protect from the influence of the Demons of Fear, the greatest enemies of mankind.

Aiden watched in horror as the three demons collected their powers and projected a vortex of black fog, engulfing the entrance to a rundown apartment building, its tendrils reaching the feet of his charge as she took another step toward it as if pulled by invisible strings.

Sounds akin to a tornado deafened his ears, and his screams were swallowed up by it just as Sarah would be sucked into its depths. Seduced by the demons' promises of power and riches, she advanced toward the dark portal that would take her into their world and turn her into one of them.

"Sarah! Noooo!"

She turned her head as if she'd heard him over the din in the alley. But her eyes were empty. As if she didn't even see him.

He knew the only way to get her to stop was to destroy the portal, which meant killing the demons who'd created it. In a flash, he turned to retrieve the knife the demon had thrown at him. Just as such a weapon could kill him, it could kill a demon. They were as vulnerable to tools forged in the Dark Days as Stealth Guardians were.

Aiden glanced down the narrow alley toward the intersection, but none of his brothers was coming to his aid. When he'd realized that he was outnumbered, he'd immediately called for his second,

Hamish. But his fellow Stealth Guardian was nowhere to be found. As if he'd vanished into thin air.

Their code of ethics dictated that a Stealth Guardian's second would be close at all times to respond quickly in situations like these—situations of life and death. Aiden had often been second to Hamish, and even though the term implied rank, a switch between sentinel and second occurred assignment after assignment. It assured a constant honing of their skills, of being as comfortable with issuing orders as with following them without question.

They were brothers, if not in blood, then united by a common goal: to protect the human race from the influence of the Demons of Fear and to further the good in this world.

From the corner of his eye, he perceived a movement and realized instantly that two of the demons had left the protection of the vortex, clearly to finish him off in close combat.

Aiden expelled a bitter laugh. They were in for a surprise. Killing up close and personal was his specialty.

"Come and get me," he taunted them, opening his arms in invitation. A gust of wind blew through his coat, causing its tails to flap wildly behind him.

The mocking laughter of the demons droned over the noise, and for a moment, it was all Aiden heard. His pleading look toward Sarah disappeared into her barren eyes. She moved her head slowly from side to side as she took another step forward. She was merely a weak human, the influence the demons exerted over her too strong for her to resist.

Gritting his teeth, and gripping the ancient blade tightly in his fist, Aiden leapt at the first demon, a creature humanoid in appearance, yet with glaring green eyes, the telltale sign of the malevolence inside. He bumped against his opponent, who was built as massively as a tank. It didn't dissuade Aiden in the least. While he was not as strong as the demon, he was more agile and faster. It was his advantage in close combat.

Snarling like a beast, the demon drove a dagger toward his chest, but Aiden sidestepped him in the blink of an eye and catapulted behind him. With one clean swipe, he ran the knife along the demon's neck, cutting it open from left to right. Amidst the surprised gurgles of the dying creature, green blood spurted onto the street. Aiden thrust his knee into the expired demon's back and tossed him to the ground.

But he didn't get a chance to breathe. With a ferocious growl, the second demon jumped him, tackling him. The impact squeezed all air out of his lungs, for a moment immobilizing him.

As he lay on the damp surface, the massive creature pinning him, he chanced a look at the vortex. Sarah was almost upon it, her steps less hesitant now. Aiden could fairly hear the seductive whispers of the third demon who was coaxing her to come to him. And weak as she was, she approached.

Yet Aiden wouldn't allow it. Collecting all his strength, he freed one leg and kicked it hard between the demon's thighs. Luckily, demons too had balls. And by the sounds the son of a bitch was making now, they were just as sensitive as a human's.

With a shove, Aiden pushed the hurting demon off his chest. His eyes searched for the knife he'd dropped when the prick had forced him to the ground. As he did so, the demon regained his strength and rose, his arm clutching the dagger as it whipped toward Aiden's neck. He rolled to the side, avoiding the deadly blade by a split second, and shot to his feet in the same instant.

But the demon was just as fast and threw his leg against him, catapulting him into the wall behind him.

A rib cracked, but the power coursing through his body made sure Aiden felt no pain. As an immortal, his tolerance for pain was many times that of a human, even if his body was entirely human in appearance. Beneath the skin and muscle, though, lay the collective experiences of all Stealth Guardians that had ever walked this earth. *Virta* they called it, and it lent them the power to fight demons and cloak themselves and humans from their view as if they'd thrown an invisibility cloak over them. They'd been bestowed with powers that defied physics—powers humans would deem supernatural—if they knew Stealth Guardians existed. But their existence had been hidden for centuries. Since their beginning in the Dark Days.

Just as Aiden scrambled to his feet, his hand brushed the dagger he'd tossed at the demon's forehead earlier. He gripped it and lunged forward again, barreling against his attacker, thrusting the knife in the lowlife's stomach.

As the Demon of Fear's eyes widened in disbelief, Aiden drew the dagger upwards, slicing him open like a pig. Guts and green blood spilled from him, the stench filling the crisp night air, before his body collapsed.

Not losing a second, Aiden turned and ran toward his charge. In a desperate attempt to pull her back, his body coiled in tension, his long, black trench coat flapping at his sides, blown back by the force of the swirling air and fog. Reaching his hands forward to try pulling her toward him, he concentrated all his energy on one thought: to save this human from the clutches of evil.

Anger boiled in him like in a caldron about to overflow. He couldn't allow the demons to take her. Every soul they brought to their side made them stronger. Soon, they would rise again from their lairs deep down in the netherworld and dominate mankind once more. The bleakness of this prospect made him shudder to his bones.

A scream from behind him caused him to spin his head around, making him lose his concentration for a moment. He spotted a woman with a toddler in her arms, frantically ringing a door bell at one of the apartment buildings, her eyes wide in horror.

Shit! He didn't need any witnesses to what was happening here. But there was nothing he could do now. His first priority was to save Sarah.

Collecting the ancient power that was within each Stealth Guardian, he allowed it to surge through his body and recharge his cells. He lurched forward, electrical charges dancing on his palms like little flames, and reached for her.

She pushed him back, anger glowing in her eyes. Behind her, he glimpsed the third demon as his hand reached forward through the vortex, a dagger in his palm. Whispering something to her, the demon pressed the ancient weapon into her hand.

With dread, Aiden noticed how she accepted it and flicked her wrist as if she'd been trained to do so. The demon was controlling her body now.

All Aiden could do was spin to the side to avoid the blade.

Then Sarah's eyes turned green. By giving in to the demon's demand, she'd become one of them.

Another scream pulled his attention to the woman behind him. What he saw turned his stomach. Sarah's dagger had hit the child in the head. Blood seeped from the gash onto the tiny white sweater and onto the hands of the mother who was trying desperately to save her baby.

God damn it! He should have killed Sarah the moment he realized that she couldn't be saved. Now she'd killed an innocent. And he was to blame, because he hadn't acted fast enough. He'd let her live because he'd hoped he could save her.

He'd failed again. Feeling his past reach for him, he forced the painful memories of his first and only other failure down and concentrated his energy on his erstwhile charge. Without hesitation, he aimed. The ancient dagger lodged in Sarah's neck, arresting her movements. Blood spurted from the fatal wound as she fell into the vortex.

The demon's cries of frustration filled the alley, and charges of light illuminated the dark night. A moment later, the air and fog stopped churning, and everything went quiet, except for the sobs of the woman whose child lay dead in her arms.

Aiden glanced at her, his eyes filling with moisture as he felt her pain. "I'm sorry," he whispered, his heart full of compassion.

When he walked to the spot where Sarah had fallen, it was empty. The vortex had swallowed her up. Only his bloody dagger was left as evidence that he'd killed her. He'd had no choice but to do so. It was better than allowing the demons to use her. Better for her and this world. It was the reason he couldn't regret his action. He only regretted that he had delayed the inevitable and not acted sooner.

Never again would he hesitate to kill a human he had reason to believe had been compromised already. It was better for one human to die than for the demons to capture another soul or for an innocent to suffer, as this child—and its mother—had. Next time, his dagger would find its target the moment he suspected that a demon was influencing his charge. He wouldn't hesitate again.

Humans were weak. They should be eliminated as soon as they represented a danger. The Council was wrong to try to protect them when clearly they would turn against their protectors, against the Stealth Guardians who only wanted their best. Sarah wasn't the first one who'd proven that to him.

Old memories, yet fresh as ever, reminded him once more that he could never be allowed to waver again. His hesitation had cost him too dearly many years ago. As a result, his entire family had suffered; they'd lost a loved one, and it was his fault. His heart clenched painfully as guilt about his past mistake resurfaced. He could never make the same mistake again. Evil had to be

Tina Folsom

eradicated swiftly, no matter in what form it presented itself: demon or human.

2

Leila lifted her head from the microscope when she heard an urgent knock at the door to her lab.

"Dr. Cruickshank? Are you still there?"

She smoothed her lab coat down and caught her reflection in the glass cabinet over the work bench she was hunched over. Her ponytail was still holding back her long, brown hair, but several strands had struggled free and now curled around her face. It looked almost as if a hair stylist had taken great pains to arrange her hair like that. Of course, that wasn't possible. She hadn't been to a hair salon in months. How could she waste precious time worrying about her appearance when she had such important work to do?

Over the last few months, she'd made huge progress. The clinical trials were promising, and it appeared that there was only a little more fine tuning necessary until the drug would do exactly what she wanted it to do: stop Alzheimer's Disease, a disease both her parents were suffering from, in its tracks. The drug even appeared to show some promise of being able to reverse some of the effects of the disease, even though chances of eradicating all damage Alzheimer's had already caused were slim.

For her parents, it was a race against time. There were times when they seemed perfectly well, yet at other times, their memory lapses were glaring, and she could sense them slipping away. If she didn't finish her research soon, the damage to their brains' neurons would become too severe for even her wonder drug to reverse it. The earlier the drug was administered, the higher the chances of some recovery of brain function. Even though she realized that her parents might never fully recover, she clung to the hope that at least some of their brain function could be restored to their former states.

At thirty-six, she should have children and a family of her own, but there had never been anything else but her work. After finishing medical school, she'd wanted to go into plastic surgery, lured by the high income the specialty offered. However, when first her father and then her mother had shown early signs of the disease, she'd quickly switched tracks.

Leila had suddenly realized that all her parents' money didn't mean anything when they were losing what they loved most: each other. After her fellowship, Inter Pharma had shown interest in her research and offered her a job. Now she headed her own lab, supervising three lab assistants and two young researchers.

She loved running her own lab; the order of her work appealed to her senses. Everything had its time and place. It was how she managed to deal with crisis: by keeping things in order and always knowing what came next, always having a plan. It gave her security, something she'd craved ever since her parents had fallen ill. And that need for security permeated throughout her work.

While her lab team would execute many different parts of her research, Leila was the only one who had access to the full set of data and the complete formula of the drug as it existed right now. Keeping her data secure was paramount to her.

It was one of the reasons she didn't use the networked computer Inter Pharma provided her with, but used her own encrypted laptop, backing up her data to a memory stick that hung, disguised in a diamond studded pendant, on a necklace around her neck wherever she went.

There'd been earlier incidents where another researcher's data had been stolen by an employee and later resurfaced at another pharmaceutical company, which then beat them to the discovery. A new drug meant vast amounts of money to Inter Pharma, but to Leila it meant getting her parents back and seeing recognition light up their eyes again before it was too late and they were gone forever.

"Dr. Cruickshank?"

Leila shot up from her chair and went to the door, unlocking it. She'd gotten used to locking the door whenever she was alone in the lab. As she opened it, she looked at the flushed face of the CEO's personal assistant, Jane.

"Oh, good, you're still here. I wasn't sure," she babbled.

Leila nodded, preoccupied. Her staff had already left for the night, but even though it was past eight o'clock, she wasn't ready to leave. There was always more data to be analyzed.

"Jane, is there anything you need?" she asked, hoping all the ditsy secretary wanted was an extra packet of sweetener or a teabag because she'd once again forgotten to order supplies for the executive offices.

"Mr. Patten sent me. He asked if you could spare a minute to talk to him."

"Now? I thought he would have gone home long ago." It was rare that anybody but she and the security guy worked this late.

"I wish. But he had a late meeting, and it only just ended. Of course, he made me stay." Jane blew out an annoyed breath. "So can you? I mean see him in his office?"

Leila nodded absentmindedly even though she hated the interruption.

"Oh, and would you have any sweetener left? I ran out."

Well, that explained why Jane hadn't used the phone to summon her to the office.

Leila turned quickly to snatch a handful of packets from the bowl on top of the refrigerator and pressed them into Jane's outstretched hands. Making sure the door locked behind her, she walked down the long hallway, flanked by Patten's assistant.

The key around her neck jingled against her pendant, making an eerie sound in the empty corridor.

"I've always admired your necklace," Jane chatted. "Do you remember where you bought it?"

"It's custom made," Leila said, ignoring the sudden prickling on her nape. She quickly cast a look over her shoulder, yet saw nothing but the gleaming linoleum floor and the sterile white walls.

"Custom made?"

She nodded back at Jane. "Yes, I had a jeweler make it for me." To conceal her sixty-four gig memory stick and keep her research close to her heart, literally. But nobody knew that. Maybe it was paranoia or perhaps it was simply common sense, but she wanted to ensure that none of her data would ever be lost.

"It's beautiful. Where's his shop? I would love to have something similar."

"He went out of business, I'm afraid," Leila lied and forced a regretful smile.

She wouldn't reveal the jeweler's name just in case he'd let it slip that the pendant was hollow inside and the perfect size for a memory stick. Nobody was supposed to know she carried her data with her. Already, not saving her data on the networked computer in her lab had raised a red flag and earned her a meeting with the CEO. However, once she'd made her case that she was worried about research being stolen, Patten had conceded to a compromise: each night when she was done with her research, she would back up the data on an external disk drive that she then placed in a safe. Only her own thumb print or that of Patten could open the specially designed piece, thus assuring that nobody unauthorized could access it.

It appeared that her boss was nearly as paranoid as she was. And why shouldn't he be? Pharmaceutical research was a cutthroat business. The first company to develop a new drug had an enormous head start no other company could compete with. To be first was everything in this business.

Her laptop was armed with a special software that would initiate a sequence to destroy all data on the hard drive should anybody tamper with it. It was failsafe.

"...so I went with the red one instead. What do you think?" Jane pointed to her fingernails, which were painted in a ghastly orange color. Clearly, the young woman was colorblind, even though colorblindness was a male phenomenon.

"Cute," Leila managed to say, wondering what else Jane had been prattling on about while she'd had her head in the clouds again. It happened so often lately: she would space out thinking about one thing or another and not even notice that other people were around her or even talking to her.

At the next bend of the corridor, they turned left. Leila pressed the button at the elevator bank. The doors instantly parted, and she stepped inside, followed by Jane. Her colleague pressed the button to the executive floor, and the doors started closing. Just as they were halfway shut, something beeped and the doors opened again.

"What the hell?" Jane cursed and pressed the button again. "I can't believe these stupid elevators. Half the week they're out of order, supposedly getting fixed, and the other half of the week they're on the blink again."

Leila shook her head. "I wouldn't know. I normally take the stairs."

"Well that's easy when you're on the third floor, but try the eighth, and you'll be out of breath in no time."

Leila couldn't stop herself from glancing at Jane's three inch heels.

Yeah, or break an ankle.

But she refrained from making a comment. It wasn't her business that Jane was out of shape. She herself ran at least four times a week, trying to stay healthy and fit. As well as slim. She'd noticed how much weight her mother had gained when she'd broken a leg a few years ago and hadn't been able to move much. Leila knew she had her mother's physique—petite and solid, rather than tall and lean—and knew that if she let herself go, she would balloon one day. Hence, she ran and climbed the stairs whenever she got a chance.

When they arrived on the eighth floor, Jane turned toward the kitchen, instructing Leila in leaving, "Go right in to see him. He's expecting you."

Leila pulled her lab coat straight and brushed a hair off the white fabric. Clearing her throat, she lifted her hand and rapped her knuckles against the door.

"Come." The order was instant and spoken with unmistakable authority.

She didn't lose any time, opened the door and entered Patten's office. The room was shrouded in semi-darkness. Patten, a man in his late fifties, graying at the temples and balding on top, sat at the wide desk, which was illuminated by a large halogen light. Yet the overhead fluorescent lights were off.

"Come in, come in, Dr. Cruickshank. Excuse the lack of lights, but they burned out just when my visitor was here earlier. Darn embarrassing, too. Better get maintenance on that right away."

"Evening, Mr. Patten," she answered simply, knowing he didn't expect a reply to his rant about the lights. "You wanted to see me?"

"Ah, yeah. That's right." He brushed a strand of gray hair back behind his ear, making her aware that just like her, he needed a haircut. He appeared somewhat disheveled.

Now that she looked at him more closely as she approached and took the visitor seat in front of this desk, she noticed that his face looked gray and tired. As if he'd been burning the candle at both ends, just like somebody else she knew: *yours truly.* Well, he

was probably not the only workaholic at Inter Pharma. Nobody got
to the top without sacrificing something for it.

"Sit down… Ah, you're sitting… good, good…"

Leila crinkled her forehead in concern. She'd never seen her
boss this flustered. She hoped he wasn't having a stroke, because
despite having a medical degree, she was ill equipped for dealing
with a medical emergency. The last time she'd seen a patient was
during her residency at Mass General, and that seemed eons ago.

"Are you feeling all right?" she felt compelled to ask, her
nurturing side rearing its head.

His eyes suddenly focused, and he appeared as clear as he'd
always been. "Of course, why wouldn't I? … Well, I wanted to
speak to you because I've had a visit from a shareholder."

Leila sat forward on her chair, uncrossing her legs. Why
would Patten want to talk to her about a shareholder? She wasn't
involved in the company's finances. Apart from being responsible
for her own lab budget, everything else she did was pure research.

A shot of adrenaline suddenly coursed through her. She knew
that the share price had recently dipped. Could this mean that the
shareholders were unhappy and wanted to cut programs? Possibly
eliminate her research?

"My budget is already tight as is." The words were out before
she could think any further. Darn! The way she acted, she would
have never made it in the diplomatic corps. And if she continued
with blurted-out statements, her career as a researcher with her
own lab could soon land on a slippery slope, too.

Patten gave her a confused look. "What?"

"I'm sorry, go on; you were saying a shareholder visited you."

"Yes. It appears Mr. Zoltan has purchased a large amount of
our shares when the market dipped. He now owns 36% of our
stock, and while that doesn't give him absolute control over the
company, it makes him the largest individual shareholder—"

Leila lifted her hand from her lap. "Uh, Mr. Patten, as you
know, I'm not involved in that side of the company. My
research—"

"I'm getting to it, Dr. Cruickshank."

She nodded quickly, not wanting to upset him any further.
Something clearly had rattled him today, and she wasn't interested
in getting caught in the crossfire. It was better to keep her mouth
shut and let him talk. Maybe he simply needed to vent to

somebody, and apart from Jane and the security guard in the lobby, she was the only one left in the building.

Leila sighed inwardly. *Great!* Now her boss was offloading some useless stuff on her when she could utilize the time much better and finish analyzing the data that she hadn't gotten to yet.

"As I said, Mr. Zoltan now owns a vast amount of this company and that gives him certain powers. You probably understand that it would be unwise to anger such a man and deny him what he wishes." Mr. Patten wiped a bead of sweat off his brow before he continued, "He could force a vote and practically reshuffle the board, boot me out... uh, as you see, I really don't have much choice in the matter."

His eyes glanced at her nervously. In turn, the same nervousness spread to her, making her skin tingle with unease and her palms turn damp. On edge, she shifted in her seat but refrained from saying anything, realizing that he wasn't done talking.

"He is merely making sure his investment is safe, you see. It's not any different from a new owner inspecting his factory and watching over the production process. Right, that's how we have to look at this."

Watching over the production process? Was he saying what she thought he was saying? He couldn't possibly allow... no, that would never happen.

"Mr. Patten, I... I," she stammered, her mind in too much uproar to be able to form a coherent sentence.

"Mr. Zoltan will be returning on Monday to sit in with you."

"Sit in?"

Patten nodded, avoiding her gaze, and instead stared at the darkness beyond his window. "He's requested to learn about your research. My understanding is that he has a medical degree as well and wants to assess the viability of the product you're working on."

Leila jumped up. "You can't allow that. My research... it's secret. No outsider can—"

"Mr. Zoltan isn't an outsider. He practically owns this company."

Disbelief welled up in her, making her knees wobble. "But you said he only owns 36% of the shares, that doesn't mean he owns us."

"In the corporate world that gives him sufficient power over us to force practically anything he wants. We don't even know what other resources he has at his disposal. For all we know, he can buy another fifteen percent, giving him full control."

Leila leaned over the desk. "Please, Mr. Patten, you have to stop this. I can't have a stranger looking over my shoulder. This is sensitive work. If somebody gets hold of my formula, they can steal it. It's not safe to have somebody in the lab who might—"

"I understand your feelings, Dr. Cruickshank, but I have no choice. My hands are tied. Your research belongs to this company. It's not your property. If I tell you that you have to allow someone access to it, then you'll do as I say," he ground out between clenched teeth. "Do we understand each other?"

Leila pulled back, disappointment flooding her veins. "I understand." Her jaw tightened. "Is that all for tonight?"

He nodded, a tired look crossing his features. "Go home, Dr. Cruickshank. You'll eventually see that things aren't as bad as you might think."

She turned without another word and walked back to her lab, holding back tears of frustration until the door latched behind her. Dropping into her chair, she covered her face with her hands and let the tears come.

This wasn't fair.

She'd worked so long and hard for this, and now some rich shareholder with a medical degree would swoop in and nose around in her work. What if that wasn't everything he wanted to do? What if he was intent on taking over the research and taking credit for it? She'd seen things like that happen before, where one researcher was booted out in the middle of the project and some newbie had taken over, getting credit for the ultimate result.

Or what would happen if he was incompetent and destroyed the progress she'd already made? If that happened, her parents would never get better.

She couldn't allow this to happen. Nobody would ever find out enough about her research to be able to take over. This was her life's work!

"You can't take this away from me, Patten," she mumbled, wiping the tears off her cheeks.

As she pushed back the chair, it scraped against the floor, the sound echoing in the empty lab. Her legs carried her to the wall safe. She pressed her thumb against the touchpad that activated the scanner. Then she heard a mechanism click. A beep accompanied by a green light told her that her authorization had been accepted.

Leila pulled the thick door open and peered into the dark interior. She had to do what needed to be done.

3

Aiden burst through the door of the compound. There was no need to open it. His body simply dematerialized as he passed through the solid material and rematerialized beyond in a process too fast for the human eye to analyze. All it would see was a man walking straight into a door or a wall, the process behind it remaining a mystery. It was a power unique to Stealth Guardians; no demons known to them had a similar skill.

He charged down the hallway. The massive building consisted of three stories above ground and two below. Its walls were thick, like those of an old English castle, build the way their ancestors had built their own strongholds. Their past was imprinted on the structure: ancient runes decorated the walls and floors, and charms to ward off evil hung over each door and window.

There were many Stealth Guardian compounds dotted all over the world, places where the brothers, and the few sisters, lived together. All compounds were protected by the collective power of the Stealth Guardians, their *virta*, and might as well have been invisible. An ancient hypnotic-like spell ensured that the buildings went unnoticed by humans.

Inside, no humans were allowed. Not even the charges of Stealth Guardians could be trusted to keep its location secret. There was always a chance that one of them would turn against them and eventually betray them to the demons.

Within the walls of the compound, Stealth Guardians could recharge their energy after each mission, energy they expended as they cloaked their charges from detection by demons.

Weapons long forgotten were stored in the vast underground vaults, weapons that could kill even an immortal Stealth Guardian. While no human weapon such as a gun or a knife could permanently injure Aiden or his brothers and sisters, any weapon forged during the Dark Days had the power to kill Stealth Guardians and Demons of Fear alike.

As Aiden rushed into the large kitchen that was the center and indeed the hearth of the house he called home, his eyes scanned the assembled quickly. Manus was busy raiding the refrigerator, clad only in a pair of tightly fitting leather pants, his scarred chest bare, while Logan poured himself a drink. His dark hair hung loose over his shoulders and it looked as if he'd just only risen.

Enya, the only female in their compound, lounged in one corner of the large couch in the adjacent great room. Her long blond hair was braided and pinned up in circles on the back of her head. She rarely wore it open, and Aiden could only suspect that it had grown down to her waist by now. Instead of watching the football game that blared from the giant TV mounted on the wall, she had her nose stuck in a book.

Aiden cursed. "Where the fuck is he?"

Heads turned toward him. Manus slammed the fridge door shut and placed a bunch of plastic packages of cold cuts on the kitchen counter.

"I'm afraid that my mind reading capacity isn't worth shit, so toss us a name, will you?" Manus exchanged a look with Logan who kicked back his drink in one gulp.

"Somebody's in a pissy mood today," Logan added as if wanting to provoke him.

Aiden felt his temper flare and squared his stance.

"Manus kinda has a point," Enya suddenly interjected not even looking up from her book.

"I'm talking about fucking Hamish!" Aiden felt the air rush out of his lungs, the anger about his second's failure to back him up growing with each moment.

Logan grinned and lifted the whiskey bottle once more. "Had no idea you guys were *that* close! But hey, if you wanna fuck Hamish, go—"

Aiden had Logan by the throat before he could finish his sentence and slammed him against the oven door. "I'm not in the mood for your fucking jokes. I'm asking again: where the fuck is Hamish?"

His captive pushed against him, shaking off his hands with more grace than a man of his massive build seemed capable of. As Logan carefully straightened his T-shirt and rolled his shoulders, he lashed an angry glare at him.

"I haven't seen Hamish in two days. He was supposed to be with you. So piss off, and let me enjoy my game."

Logan turned and walked to the couch, plopping down in the corner opposite to Enya. When the weight with which he'd let himself fall jolted her and almost made her lose her grip on her book, she only raised an eyebrow.

"Testosterone," she mumbled under her breath.

Logan narrowed his eyes. "And you know exactly what to do about that, don't you? But no, you're not gonna spread your legs for any of us, are you?"

"Shut it!" Manus's response came before Enya could even reach for the dagger that always sat at her hip, even when she was relaxing.

"Asshole," she hissed.

Manus glanced at Aiden. "As for Hamish. If he isn't with you, maybe he got ambushed."

"Then we should trace his cell and find him," a voice from the door added to Manus's sentence.

Aiden whirled his head to the new arrival: Pearce.

"It's not like him to neglect his duties," Pearce continued as he stepped fully into the room.

Aiden nodded. Pearce was right.

"I was outnumbered."

A soft hand touched his arm. His head snapped to the right. Enya had approached him without him noticing. "What happened today?"

Aiden braced one hand against the kitchen counter. He squeezed his eyes shut. "I called Hamish, but he didn't show. I couldn't hold them off any longer. I killed two of them, but the third stayed within the protection of the vortex. He was too strong. He had complete power over her." So much so that she'd tried to kill him, and instead... "My charge killed an innocent child. I had to terminate her."

"Fuck!" Manus cursed.

"Not another one!" Logan added.

"Damn it, what the fuck did you do, Aiden, sleep on the job? Why wasn't she cloaked?" Manus ground out between clenched teeth.

Aiden allowed the fury to blaze from his eyes as he faced Manus. "I protected her as best I could!"

"If you'd cloaked her properly, she wouldn't be lost now!"

"What are you saying?" Aiden bit out.

"You know what I'm saying!" Manus countered and moved in. "If you wanted her properly cloaked you should the fuck have been touching her the entire time."

Aiden knew exactly what Manus meant. He and his fellow guardians had two ways of cloaking humans: by the power of their minds, or by touch. The first needed more energy, but just as a cell phone signal could be intercepted or interrupted, it was possible to break the connection and inadvertently uncloak a charge. The second brought with it other problems. A Stealth Guardian's touch could be perceived as intimate even when it was not intended as such.

"Like *you* touch them? Like you pretend to feel something for them so they trust you? That's not protecting them! It's against every single rule in the book," Aiden snarled.

"I don't care about the fucking rules. Rules are for people who can't think for themselves."

"And you break them all." Aiden felt his chest heave. He couldn't be like Manus, who pretended to love each woman he had to protect, so he'd have a surefire way of making certain the woman was at all times cloaked. He, on the other hand, preferred not to touch humans when it could be avoided. Other than having the occasional one-night stand with a human woman, he wasn't interested in them. Not anymore. Not after what a human had done to his family.

"You fuck them so you don't have to expend any extra energy!"

The accusation only earned him a smirk from Manus.

"I wouldn't exactly say that. I'm expending plenty of energy doing that."

Before Manus could turn away, Aiden landed a punch in his face, wiping the grin right off it.

Damn, it felt good to hit someone!

It felt cathartic to beat the crap out of Manus, to unleash his anger and frustration on him. Maybe it would dull his mind.

An uppercut to his chin whipped Aiden's head back. He tasted blood an instant later, but ignored it to answer Manus's blow. Leveraging his right leg against the kitchen counter, a bar stool crashed to the floor as Aiden swung against his fellow Stealth

Guardian. The strike knocked Manus against the fridge, which groaned under the impact.

"Jerk!" Manus spat. "This isn't about what rules I've broken. Don't pretend you haven't thought of it yourself... how sweet it is to break a rule once in a while." He gave a devilish grin.

"Fuck you!" There were plenty of willing women in the bars Aiden frequented. He didn't need to screw his charges. Sex was sex—and as long as the woman was reasonably hot, what did he care who she was? He had no interest in getting involved with a charge. He kept his distance from them, emotionally and physically, knowing that the day might come where he'd have to kill one of them, just like tonight. He couldn't allow his emotions to get in the way.

"And stop blaming me for your failures! I'm not playing scapegoat today," Manus growled, interrupting Aiden's thoughts and making him focus on the issue at hand.

He had only himself to blame for what had happened tonight. Well, himself and Hamish. But once he tracked down his errant second, there'd be hell to pay.

Beating Manus to pulp wouldn't bring his charge back, wouldn't make it undone.

"Ah, shit!" Aiden cursed and lowered his fist. "I failed." He raised his eyes to meet Manus's gaze, but instead of a mocking glare, he recognized a flash of compassion.

Manus pushed himself off the fridge and brushed past him. "Get used to it. It'll happen more often now."

Aiden grabbed his shoulder and turned him around. "What do you mean?"

"Haven't you seen the reports from the other compounds?"

"And when do you think I would have had time to read stupid reports?" He'd been on this assignment for several weeks and barely had time to rush back to the compound for urgent updates.

Aiden wiped the blood from his mouth and looked at the others in the room.

Pearce cleared his throat. "The demons are getting stronger. The other compounds are reporting more and more... losses."

Aiden shook his head in disbelief. "How?"

"They somehow seem to know where our charges are. Despite them being cloaked, they find them."

"That's not possible," Aiden protested and looked at Logan and Enya. "They don't have those capabilities. They can't sense our charges when they're cloaked."

Enya nodded solemnly. "That's right, but what if they don't need those senses? What if they have another way of knowing where our charges are?"

Not wanting to follow Enya's thought process, Aiden took a steadying breath. "You can't mean that."

Logan huffed. "And why not? Our own emotions aren't that different from those of the humans we're protecting. So what makes you think all of us can resist temptation?"

"But that's what we're trained for..." Aiden's voice died. He swallowed past the dryness in his throat. His next thought came out of nowhere. "But Hamish. You can't mean that he... and the demons..."

"He wasn't there to back you up. And how did the demons find your charge anyway when you say you cloaked her?" Logan asked.

"Who better to know where you are at all times than your second," Manus added.

"A traitor? You think Hamish sold me out to the demons?"

When the words left his lips, his heart clenched painfully. Aiden sought support from the kitchen counter, his knees buckling under the strain. It couldn't be possible. Hamish was like a brother to him. A brother he occasionally butted heads with, but a brother nevertheless.

"We have to find him." Aiden glanced at Pearce. "Find his cell. Maybe he's hurt somewhere."

He put all his hopes into his last words. It was better that the reason why Hamish hadn't come to his aid was because he was hurt. The other possibility—that he had joined the demons—was too awful to contemplate.

4

Barclay dropped the gavel and called for order in the council chambers. The mumbling of his fellow council members tapered slowly. When it finally died, he gazed into the faces of the men and women who sat around the table, which was built in a half circle. All of them were experienced Stealth Guardians, seven men and two women with great knowledge and skill, who'd been serving their people well for many centuries. They had been hand selected to serve on the Council of Nine, the ruling body of their ancient race. Judge, jury, and executioner in one, the council bore a heavy burden. Yet each member wore their duty with pride.

Surrounded by ancient runes engraved in the stone walls of the chambers, and protected by the collective powers of the Stealth Guardians, this was the inner sanctum, a place where few other guardians were allowed to set foot. Important decisions were made within these walls, decisions that could mean life or death for humans and Stealth Guardians alike.

Whenever he sat at the center of the table, Barclay, as *primus inter pares*, the first among equals, felt the weight of responsibility on his chest. He sensed the winds of change, and he knew their world was at the edge of something new—something that would change all their lives for the worse if he and his fellow Stealth Guardians couldn't stop it. If only he knew what it was.

Barclay cleared his voice and rested his eyes on the tall man, whose hazel eyes looked anxious and whose dark brown hair looked more disheveled than usual.

"Geoffrey, you called this meeting. The council is eager to hear your report."

Geoffrey stood. "Brothers, Sisters, Primus—" He nodded toward Barclay. "—I have received disturbing reports from our *emisarii*. Information has surfaced that the demons have discovered a serum that may make humans more susceptible to their influences."

A collective gasp rippled through the assembly. Barclay sucked in his breath, the thought of such a thing being possible shocking him to the core. Was this the change he'd been sensing lately?

"Demons aren't capable of witchcraft," Finlay protested loudly.

"Never heard of such a thing!" Riona, one of the two female council members, interjected throwing her hands up in a dramatic gesture. "Besides, the witches are *our* allies, not theirs."

Barclay pounded the gavel on the table. "Order! Order!"

His fellow council members fell silent as he lashed an angry glare at them. Then he cast his eyes toward Geoffrey. "Continue with your account."

Giving a pointed look to Finlay, Geoffrey parted his lips. "Witchcraft no. *That* we agree on, my friend."

Barclay was fully aware that Geoffrey and Finlay rarely saw eye to eye on anything. He'd had to mediate many a fight between the two guardians, who were as stubborn as they came. For once, he hoped that no such fight broke out at this meeting. Circumstances were too dire to waste time on a useless display of excess testosterone as if the two were green teenagers and not the hardened men who had fought by his side for centuries.

"However, I'm not talking about witchcraft. I'm talking about science."

"Science?" Finlay echoed, clearly stunned.

A grim nod marked Geoffrey's reply. "Pharmaceutical science. Dr. Leila Cruickshank—" He passed a picture around. "—is a talented researcher for Inter Pharma. Over the last few years, she's dedicated her life to finding a cure for Alzheimer's."

"Very admirable. But what has that got to do with us?" Wade interrupted, threading his fingers through his dark blond hair. "Besides, many others have tried before her, and nobody has succeeded."

"Has this Dr. Cruickshank?" Finley asked, waving his hand at the picture that reached Barclay at this moment.

Barclay's gaze fell on the young woman's face. The picture had been taken through a window from a fair distance. Despite that fact, the lens had been able to capture her essence: her pleasant, yet determined features and her straight nose and piercing eyes underscored what Geoffrey had said. Wearing a white lab coat, she sat at a computer, gazing into the screen in fascination. Her long dark hair was pulled together in a haphazard looking ponytail, strands of it having escaped, framing her classic features, softening them.

"Our *emissarius* reports that she is at the edge of a breakthrough. According to lab reports he was able to get access to, early clinical trials suggest that the serum seems to be... unlocking the mind."

"Unlocking?" Barclay echoed. "Explain."

"With Alzheimer's, neurons and synapses in the brain are destroyed, shutting off the mind, locking away memories and experiences, making people not even remember their loved ones. If this serum does what we think it does, then it seems to reverse some of these effects."

"Well, that's a good thing then," Deirdre agreed and pushed her long blond hair behind her back. "So I'm assuming you want her protected?"

Geoffrey shook his head and gazed into the round, his expression solemn. "On the contrary. I want her eliminated."

Finlay shot from his seat. "What?"

"We've sworn to protect humans and help further the good in the world," Deidre added, placing a hand on Finlay's arm and urging him to sit back down. "And you want to do the opposite?"

"You'd better have a bloody good explanation for that," Wade bit out.

As Norton, Ian, and Cinead, the three council members who'd so far remained quiet, cleared their throats, Barclay stood and motioned everybody to be silent. Then he turned to Geoffrey.

"I too would like to hear your reasoning behind this. Alzheimer's has plagued mankind for many years, and to deny humans a cure for this ailment..." He shook his head. "Speak."

Geoffrey's cheeks appeared heated as he continued. Clearly, this subject was dear to his heart. "Just as the serum may halt Alzheimer's and reverse some of its effects by repairing some of the damaged neurons and allowing memories to flow freely again, it will unlock the mind to allow demons easy access. The natural resistance humans possess to withstand the influence of the Demons of Fear will be melted away. There will be no block, no gate. A human mind will be as open as a school gate on graduation day. And if Inter Pharma decides to not only use this drug to treat current Alzheimer's patients, but to use it as a vaccine..."

Geoffrey didn't have to finish his sentence. Everybody in the room knew what this meant. From an early age, all humans would be walking invitations for the demons to take over their minds and control them to do their bidding.

"Nobody would be able to resist," Cinead said in a gravely voice, rising. He nodded toward Barclay. "May I speak?"

Barclay showed his agreement with a wave of his hand. Cinead, the Scotsman who'd been on the council longer than any of them, yet had never accepted a nomination as Primus, was the wisest among them, always looking at all sides of an issue before making a decision.

"Geoffrey, you say your *emissarius* has seen lab reports. Are those available for our review?"

"I can procure them, if you don't believe my words." He appeared miffed at Cinead's request.

"I would like to see them and study the data myself. We cannot callously eliminate a human solely based on the report of one *emissarius* who might not have the relevant knowledge it takes to assess this issue. We've never acted on rumors or assumptions. There's no need to start now."

Geoffrey huffed. "I'll get you the bloody report, but I'm telling you, there's no time to lose. If the drug is allowed to be brought to market, it has the potential to annihilate the human race and us in the process."

"I agree," Riona said. "At the very least, access to it has to be restricted until we know more. If the demons get a hold of it, they may well be able to reproduce it and distribute it among the human population."

"It would still have to be administered by injection, I assume?" Norton asked, his eyebrows pulling together into a deep frown.

Geoffrey shrugged. "Not every vaccine is delivered with a needle. Should the demons get hold of it, who says they can't infiltrate the human food or water supply with it? They have to be stopped before they get that far. We have to destroy all traces of Dr. Cruickshank's research and all samples of the drug."

"If the drug truly does what you say," Norton conceded. "However, until then, I am with Cinead: we will not interfere until the facts have been confirmed."

"The facts seem pretty clear to me," Ian voiced. "Her research is dangerous. It needs to be taken care of now. Every minute we sit here discussing this, the demons get closer to her, if they haven't already found her."

"So this is how much you value a human life," Riona remarked. "What if it were your life?"

"I'm immortal," Ian ground out.

"Even you can be killed," Riona pressed out under her breath, "with the right weapons."

Barclay ground his teeth, not keen on listening to more bickering between the two. "Either keep your remarks to the subject at hand, or take your disagreements outside. What is it to be?"

At his stern look, both of them pressed their lips together.

Wade lanced a look at the two, then straightened in his seat. "If what Geoffrey says is true, I believe the human race is in grave danger. And there's really only one way of dealing with a threat like this. We're not simply guardians, we're also warriors; collateral damage is expected."

Barclay clenched his jaw. Wade had always erred on the side of striking first and asking questions second, and in this instance it didn't appear any different. Barclay gave his fellow council member a tight look. A shrug was Wade's answer.

Geoffrey shot Barclay a pleading look. "Primus, I appeal to you. We cannot let this continue. The danger is too immense, the consequences could be disastrous."

Barclay steepled his fingers, blowing a breath against them. For a moment, he closed his eyes. This was not his decision to make, no matter how much he feared that Geoffrey was right. A drug that turned a human mind into an all-you-can-eat buffet for the Demons of Fear would herald a wave of evil sweeping over this world. With more and more humans acting on the evil influences of the demons, wars would ravage the earth, misery and pain would spread. Fear would escalate, and the demons would feed on all of it, particularly the fear. And they would grow stronger with every human they brought into their fold.

Soon, the world would be overrun with evil: even more people would die of disease and hunger. Every country would be rife with war and conflict; there would be no peace keepers, no law enforcement, no organizations delivering humanitarian aid. Everybody would be out for themselves. Armageddon.

Barclay lifted his lids. "A vote then. Those of you who believe the woman should be assigned a Stealth Guardian for protection for now, say 'aye'; those who want to eliminate the threat by eliminating the scientist and her research, say 'nay'."

One by one 'ayes' and 'nays' bounced against the wall of the chambers.

Barclay held his breath until everyone had voted.

~ ~ ~

Aiden paced in the long hallway that led to the council chambers, casting a look at the closed door every few seconds. It seemed as if the council members had been in there forever, or maybe it was simply because he felt anxious to get this over with. Already the council wouldn't be pleased with the outcome of his last mission, but having to accuse a fellow Stealth Guardian of treason in the same breath, would not endear him to anybody.

His friends at the compound had warned him about making the accusation and suggested he let the council draw their own conclusions, simply presenting the facts that he and his brothers had discovered when looking for Hamish. But Aiden knew himself too well. He was as much a hothead as Logan, even if he didn't flaunt breaking the council's rules the way Manus did. Most of the time, he followed them. Not doing so would earn severe punishment from the council.

The only reason Manus's transgressions hadn't reached the council's ears yet was because their compound was particularly close-knit. Nobody wanted to be known as a snitch. Their unspoken rule was to sort things out between themselves without involving the council.

While Manus had no qualms about seducing the women in his care, Aiden didn't enjoy the bitter aftertaste such an affair left behind. Yes, he sought sexual adventures outside the compound, with mortal women, but without pretense, never sleeping with the same woman twice, confining himself to one-night stands in order not to lose focus on his mission or get emotionally involved.

He rarely had any downtime during which to involve himself in a relationship that went beyond the usual *wham-bam-thank-you-ma'am* method. Not that he was complaining. He wasn't interested in a relationship. And sex? He could always get sex when he really needed it, but lately even the thrill of a quickie with a virtual stranger couldn't chase away the emptiness he'd started feeling in his gut. He wondered whether it was the coming change that caused these odd sentiments. He was nearing his two hundredth birthday, and with it what Stealth Guardians called *rasen*, mating season. His hormones surged to find a mate, yet there were few choices.

The reason so few female Stealth Guardians were available for mating was the dominant male gene, which favored producing males rather than females of their species, tilting the equilibrium in their world. For centuries now, male Stealth Guardians had to look in the human world for their mates. The entire undertaking was fraught with danger: should a Stealth Guardian choose a human as his mate, rather than one of the few female Stealth Guardians, they were both in danger of losing their lives. Only a love pure of heart made a union between a Stealth Guardian and a human possible. Aiden didn't believe such love existed. Could a Stealth Guardian ever love a creature so inherently weak?

And if the love wasn't true and pure, the ritual mating, which bound the two lovers together, would rob them of their lives. Their death wouldn't be instant, but knowledge of it would be. A Stealth Guardian's immortality would drain away like sand in an hourglass. Just like his mate, he would wither away in a few short months, enough time to regret his actions and see his own death coming. Hamish had almost entered such a union, and only by sheer luck found out in time that his intended mate had been a plant by the demons.

The success rate for finding a mate was thus low, with few single female Stealth Guardians available. He'd practically grown up with Enya, who lived in the same compound with him, and he regarded her as a true sister. There was no physical attraction between them. He knew most of the other female Stealth Guardians in the US, because they were rare, but none stirred him the way a woman should tantalize a man. Maybe he was simply not meant for a relationship.

Aiden knew what was expected of him, and he didn't want to disappoint. But pleasing his mother and father as well as their community wasn't in the forefront of his thoughts. He was a guardian first and foremost; finding a mate and helping his race procreate was a distant second. Maybe he could suppress the urges *rasen* forced on him. He was strong-willed—those damn hormones had nothing on him.

"Guardian," a voice called him. "The council will see you now."

The attendant, who seemed to have appeared out of nowhere, stood in front of the door to the council chambers.

"One moment," he requested, "please place all your electronic devices here." He pointed to a carved out indentation next to the door.

Aiden did as he was asked and then allowed the attendant to swipe a wand up and down his body. It was a security measure so that no recording devices could be smuggled into the council chambers since all undertakings within were kept secret.

As Aiden finally walked inside, the door closed behind him with a loud clunk.

"The council welcomes you, Guardian," Primus's voice greeted him.

Aiden looked straight at him to acknowledge his welcome. He bowed his head. "I thank the council for receiving me, Primus."

With the formalities behind him, it was time to give them the news. He couldn't stall any longer. "I bring bad news. My last assignment ended in a loss. My charge succumbed to the demons. I had to eliminate her."

Low mumbles went through the assembled.

"As much as we regret this incident," Geoffrey piped, "it is hardly a matter to bother the council with. You're not the only one who's lost a charge in the last few weeks. Reports have—"

"I've heard of the reports," Aiden interrupted impatiently.

When Geoffrey and several of the other council members gasped, he knew that he'd acted against protocol by interrupting him. However, enough time had already been wasted. He couldn't stand on ceremony.

"And what I have to tell you might be related to it."

When Geoffrey tried to speak, Primus held up his hand. "Let him talk."

Taking an extra breath, Aiden recounted what had unraveled at their compound.

"Hamish has disappeared. At first we thought he might have been ambushed, but then we traced his cell phone and found his things."

"Meaning what?" Primus asked curiously.

"We found his cell phone in a dumpster, together with all this clothes. Neatly folded."

Several eyebrows rose. Deirdre spoke up. "What are you alleging?"

Aiden swallowed away the bitter taste in his mouth. "When I was on my last mission, outnumbered by the demons, I called for Hamish. He was my second. He didn't show. I have reason to believe that he deserted us." The next words hurt to speak, his heart clenching painfully at the loss he experienced. "I believe he's joined the demons."

He wished he was wrong, but everything pointed to it.

Outraged gasps filled the council chambers.

Cinead rose from this seat. Aiden had always liked the Scotsman and knew he could expect a just ruling from him. "Those are serious allegations, Aiden. Hamish is a valued member of our society, a fierce fighter. I don't believe him capable of treason. He's strong of mind, one of the least likely guardians to be influenced by the demons."

"Then explain to me why he didn't come to my aid, why we found his clothes and cell phone. He got rid of everything that would have made it possible for us to trace him." Aiden lashed an accusatory glare at Cinead. Maybe the council member didn't *want* to believe that a fellow Scotsman was capable of such thing. "Why did the demons find my charge when I had cloaked her? Only Hamish could have known where we were."

Ian raised a hand. "Ah, not entirely true, I'm afraid."

Aiden lifted an eyebrow in question as several heads turned to the council member who'd spoken.

"As you all know, everybody who sits on this council is aware of any assignment that is handed out. Each one of us could have known the whereabouts of your charge. Are you calling us traitors, too?"

"No, of course not!" he hastened to answer.

"Then you might grant your fellow guardian Hamish the same courtesy. There could be a myriad of reasons why he disappeared. Maybe he was captured."

"Since when do assailants fold clothes they strip off their victims?" Aiden grumbled under his breath. Only Hamish himself took such care of his beloved designer clothes.

Cinead nodded at Ian. "We'll send out guardians to search for him." He waved toward Geoffrey. "Can you notify the *emissarii*? They might be able to help."

Geoffrey gave a nod.

"I want to be on the search team," Aiden requested.

"I don't believe that's wise. You're too emotionally involved," Cinead declined.

Aiden shot a pleading look at the head of the council. "Primus, I appeal to you."

The slow shake of his head quashed any hope that he could get to Hamish before anybody else and wring the truth from him.

"Father, I implore you," he insisted, hoping by emphasizing that he was not just his Primus, but more importantly his father, he could be reasoned with.

He and his father exchanged a long look. The older man's dark hair showed a few errant strands of silver, and his angular face was full of laugh lines. Brown eyes studied him from beneath dark lashes. Aiden knew that he'd inherited many of his father's features, and side-by-side, many would have thought them brothers rather than father and son.

Like all Stealth Guardians, his father aged only fractionally compared to humans. While the offspring of Stealth Guardians aged in the same way human children did, once they reached their twenty-fifth birthday, their aging slowed to the speed of a snail. Even the oldest man of their species, a Stealth Guardian of over 1,500 years of age, looked like a man in his late fifties. Time was good to their kind.

Finally, Primus shook his head. "I'm afraid, son, that's not possible. You're needed elsewhere. We have an assignment for you."

5

In his cloaked state, Aiden paced outside of Inter Pharma's facility. After leaving the council chambers, he'd looked at the manila folder containing the details of his assignment and read it cover to cover. He'd formed his opinion on this case by the time he reached the last page, secretly questioning the council's decision. Given the details laid out in the report, he would have decided on eliminating the human in question. It would be the safest and only reliable way of ensuring that the demons wouldn't gain access to this dangerous drug.

However, when he'd pulled out Dr. Cruickshank's picture, which had been tucked into an envelope and placed in the back of the file, his gut had instantly made a curious flip. He'd expected her to be different… older… and not so… beautiful. But it wasn't only her beauty that created such a physical reaction in him. It was the determined look in her eyes the camera had managed to capture. What he read in them attracted him most of all: strength. A human woman who was strong and determined, not weak and impressionable, not easily seduced. Would she be strong enough to resist the demons once they found her?

He turned, annoyed at himself for letting a picture sway him in his conviction. What she looked like didn't matter. It would not influence at all how he treated her: with utter professionalism. Just as he treated all the others. And should it become necessary to kill her, he wouldn't hesitate.

Aiden's gaze drifted down the street. The area was a mix of residential and commercial buildings. The shops had long closed, but a couple of the restaurants farther down the street were still open. Some of the windows in the nearby office buildings were illuminated, and in the apartment buildings he saw people go about their lives, cooking dinner, watching TV. He always felt like a thief when he watched others like this. Yet it had become second nature. All Stealth Guardians did it.

Curiosity had always been one of his traits. Even early in his training, he'd liked to watch humans, observe how they lived. In many ways it was so different from his own life of duty and service. Inside those apartments he gazed up at, people loved and lived. They raised children, had careers, shared laughter and tears. And one day, they died. A strange yearning came over him each time he thought of their lives.

While his life at the compound afforded him the same comforts humans lived with, life was very different there. For starters, he spent very little time at the compound, and it was rare that all inhabitants were there at the same time. One or the other was always on assignment. Birthdays weren't celebrated, neither was Christmas, Easter, or any other holiday. Every day was the same. There was no weekend where people relaxed and unwound. Demons didn't rest on Saturday or Sunday, and neither did Stealth Guardians. Danger was always awake. It never slept.

Aiden tore his gaze from the apartment building and continued surveying the area. Few cars passed. A bus stopped on the next block, dropping off a woman with a small child. In the distance, a door closed and another opened. Normal sounds of a neighborhood.

But his senses were only partially engaged, his thoughts going back to his new charge, Leila. He would follow her home tonight and assess where she was most vulnerable to an attack by the demons. Not that he believed that they would mount an outright attack: they wanted what she had, the drug. They were more likely to find something in her life to make a bargain with.

The sound of distant footsteps and voices, carried to him by his preternatural senses, made him turn his head back to the building Inter Pharma occupied. Through the floor-to-ceiling windows that encased the lobby, he saw Leila crossing to the door, exchanging a few kind words with the night watchman. The photo he'd been given didn't do her justice. In reality she looked even more enchanting than on the black-and-white picture. His stomach tensed at the sight, giving him a visceral reaction he was unaccustomed to when dealing with a charge. She was so unlike anybody else he'd ever had to protect.

Aiden attributed his reaction to the fact that this woman was extremely dangerous: if the demons were to ever seduce her over to their side, they would have a brilliant scientist working for them. He'd gathered that much from the dossier on her. Who knew what other little serums she could invent, maybe one that rendered Stealth Guardians powerless? Yes, he reasoned with himself, what he felt in his gut now had everything to do with the knowledge that a brilliant mind like hers was trapped in a human body that would eventually succumb to the demons, because despite the strength he'd seen in her eyes, she would never be strong enough to resist them.

And his reaction to her had nothing whatsoever to do with the fact that he found her more intoxicating than any woman he'd ever met.

Leila smiled at the security guard before exiting into the crisp night air. It was September, but the day had been overcast, and it was colder than normal for the season. She turned left and walked down the block.

Aiden followed her, remaining in his cloaked state, and mindful that even though his body was invisible, he could still be heard. His breathing, his footsteps, none of it could be disguised by his cloak. It was one of the reasons, he and all his fellow Stealth Guardians wore specially designed soft-soled shoes when on assignment. They absorbed nearly all of the sound of his footsteps on the pavement. In addition, he'd learned to tread lightly like a cat, or like a thief. If he stayed far enough back, his charge would never notice him.

Yet, he broke protocol and approached, walking a mere step behind her, close enough to touch her should he desire to. A faint smell of roses surrounded her. It was so exquisite that for an instant it made him forget why he was there.

She wore a short jacket over her blouse. Her delectable behind, encased in those tailored slacks, swished from side to side in a tantalizing rhythm that could make any man turn soft in the head and hard in other places. Her hair was kept in a tight ponytail, and he wondered what it would feel like to release it from its confines and bury his face in it. Soaking in her scent, feeling the silken softness of her tresses, all while she writhed underneath him in obvious ecstasy.

He exhaled sharply at the unexpected thought.

An instant later, Leila spun on her heels. He would have crashed into her were it not for the preternatural speed his species was graced with. He rocked to a halt and held his breath.

Her eyes peered into the darkness, tension lines forming on her forehead, her lips slightly parted. He noticed the pulse in her neck twitch. Her hand reached into her shoulder bag, clearly gripping something tightly in her fist. A knife? A gun? But she didn't pull it out, her eyes and her face relaxing slowly as she scanned the area. Her shoulders dropped, and she turned back, continuing in the same direction as before.

Aiden started breathing again. It was best not to concentrate on Leila's enticing body, or incidences like these would keep happening. And next time, she might crash into him and realize something was amiss. He couldn't risk that, even though he wouldn't mind knowing what her body felt like pressed against his, and feel her curves yield to his hard muscles.

Shit, why was he focusing on that rather than on the fact that she represented a danger to humanity? He wasn't so starved for sex to forget that getting involved with a charge would only give rise to lots of problems. He had more control than that!

His eyes fell back on those curves she so innocently flaunted right in front of him without even knowing what she was doing. Would she curtail those swinging hips if she knew the effect those movements had on him? Or would she continue taunting him with her sinful body? Because taunting she was.

A flash of light suddenly made him jerk his head away from her backside. With horror, he witnessed a car barreling toward her at the intersection she'd just reached. About to step into the crosswalk that showed a 'go' signal for her, Leila jolted backwards but her heel caught in a storm drain.

Aiden lunged forward, grabbed hold of her and yanked her out of the path of the out-of-control vehicle. Losing his balance, he tumbled onto the sidewalk, rolling into the doorway of a shop with Leila in his arms. His heart hammered in his chest, and his instinct kicked in, uncloaking him in a split second. Her surprised cry was muffled against his coat.

"Are you okay?" he managed to say as he caught his breath and tried to sit up without releasing her.

This incident clearly counted as an emergency, and revealing himself to her was therefore necessary. It didn't mean she had to know who he was. She would never need to find out that he wasn't human, and that he possessed powers that would scare the living daylights out of her. It was best for her not to know, because he didn't know how she would react.

Leila seemed dazed and made no attempt to free herself from his embrace. Her body so close to his felt intoxicating. She smelled like a ripe fruit ready to harvest, her curves exhibiting the perfect combination of yielding softness and firmness that stood its ground. He savored the moment, knowing that once she'd recovered, she would push him away. After all, he was a stranger, it was dark, and there were few other people around. Instinct would tell her to be cautious, despite the fact that he'd saved her from being run over by a car.

Aiden glanced toward the intersection, but the car hadn't even stopped. A drunk driver, most likely. Nevertheless, he couldn't shake off the thought that this was no coincidence. He'd long stopped believing in things happening at random.

"I'm fine," she mumbled, her hand pushing against him to steady herself.

As she managed to sit up and lift her head, she looked at him, assessing him as if to figure out if he could be trusted.

"Thank you. I didn't see... the car ran a red light."

He nodded. "I'm glad I was there."

"I didn't see you," she said, her voice a hotbed of caution as she eased farther away from him now. "There was nobody behind me. I would have heard you."

Perceptive human. "I was just crossing from over there. The car's headlights probably blinded you, so you didn't see me."

He rose slowly and reached a hand out to her.

Leila gave him a doubtful look. "Thank you." She made a motion to get up, declining his hand, but the moment her right foot touched the ground, her knee buckled and she cried out in pain.

Aiden didn't hesitate and supported her by putting an arm around her waist, making her lean against him. Heat from her body seeped into his, igniting his cells instantly.

"Brace yourself on my shoulders," he instructed as he crouched down. Her elegant hands dug into his shoulders.

He reached for her foot. "I'm going to check if it's broken, okay?"

"Okay," she whispered.

Slowly, he stroked his hands over her ankle and tested her range of motion. She winced immediately.

"Ouch!"

"I'm sorry. It'll be just a second," he assured her as he allowed his supernatural senses to penetrate her skin and reach to the bone. It was intact. There was no break, merely a sprain. Relieved, he exhaled. "It's not broken."

"How do you know? Are you a doctor?" With curiosity in her eyes, Leila looked down at him.

Aiden released her foot and rose, making sure he kept supporting her weight. "No, I'm not a doctor. But your ankle is just sprained. You're very lucky."

"Thank you again."

"You should put some ice on it right away."

"I'll do that when I get home."

"No, I mean right now. Even a half hour delay can make it worse." He pointed toward the end of the block where the lights of an Irish Pub flickered invitingly. "They should have some ice down there."

What the hell was he doing? He shouldn't engage any more with her than he already had. If he were smart, he'd leave her now. But apparently tonight his mind was occupied with other things, lust being one of them, the inexplicable need to get to know her being another.

"That won't be necessary. I'll just get a cab to take me home."

He glanced up and down the street. "You won't find a cab around here this time of night. We can call one from the pub—after you've put some ice on your ankle."

And thanked your rescuer.

He could vividly imagine what kind of thanks he'd prefer: a kiss from those pert lips. The thought jolted him. He'd never before hoped for any kind of thanks from his charges, no matter how many times he'd saved their lives. It was what he did, what he was called to do. No payment of any kind was ever expected.

"Okay, I think I can walk that far," Leila finally conceded.

"Walk?" He shook his head. Not as long as he was here to lend a hand. "I don't think you should walk."

Ignoring her protest, he lifted her into his arms and strode toward the pub.

"But..."

When he looked into her ocean-blue eyes, her eyelids suddenly fluttered, and she lowered them quickly. Color flushed her cheeks.

With every step, her body rubbed against his, and despite the clothing that separated them, he felt a rush of excitement course through him. The contact was intense and real, the payoff torturing, as the bulge in his jeans could attest.

He noticed how she studied his neck and the muscles that flexed underneath his tight tee. It seemed she didn't want to lift her eyes to peruse his face so openly. Not that he would mind being studied by her. Hell, there wasn't anything he could think of right now that he would mind her doing.

With his foot, Aiden pushed the door to the pub open and was glad to see that it was half empty. Ignoring the inquisitive stares of the few patrons, he lowered Leila to a bench next to the window and lifted her leg onto it.

"Stay here, I'll get some ice," he instructed and went to the bar.

The bartender looked first at Aiden, then past him. "Something wrong?"

"My friend twisted her ankle. Could you spare some crushed ice and a clean dish towel?" he asked and put a twenty on the counter. "And two Jamesons, neat."

"Yep, women and their heels," he responded and took a towel from behind him, filling it with ice.

"Her heels weren't to blame. A car ran a red light and nearly killed her." He shuddered as the words left his lips.

"Fuckin' drunk drivers," the bartender hissed. "Tell ya one thing, when I see one of my regulars having too much, I confiscate their car keys. Don't care how much they curse me for it." He handed him the towel. "Here. I'll bring the Jamesons to your table."

"Thanks."

Aiden took the ice-filled towel and walked back to his charge who was sitting up straight, leaning against the wood-paneled wall, her leg stretched out over the bench. He sat down at her feet.

"This should make you feel much better soon."

He rolled the towel into a long tube and snaked it around her ankle, tying it at the ends so it held in place. When he looked up, he collided with her gaze.

"You've done this before," she approved.

He winked at her. "I used to get into a lot of scrapes when I was younger."

Stealth Guardian children didn't heal automatically like adult Stealth Guardians did. They needed to be tended to in the same way human children did. They were, however, immune to human diseases such as measles and mumps, but broken bones, cuts and bruises would leave their mark the same way they did on mortal children.

"Here are your two Jamesons, neat," the bartender announced and set two glasses with amber liquid on the small table next to them. "Cheers."

Aiden nodded to him then looked back at Leila, motioning toward the whiskey. "To wash away the shock."

6

Leila took the glass her rescuer handed her and hesitated. Was this a wise decision? She was a lightweight when it came to liquor, and this man was a complete stranger. *A very handsome stranger*, she corrected. One who had saved her life by the looks of it. Had he not pushed her out of the way so quickly, the car would have hit her full on and she would have been tomorrow's headline. *Promising Researcher Killed in Hit-and-Run Accident*. She shuddered inwardly.

Maybe she did need a drink now that reality hit home.

"My name is Aiden," the hottie said. A name that suited him.

"Leila."

He clinked his glass to hers. "Shall we drink to good luck, Leila?"

"To good luck." She sipped from the whiskey. As it made its way down her throat, her skin began to burn, but it wasn't unpleasant. Warmth spread in her body, making her instantly feel better despite her throbbing ankle.

When she bent toward the table to set her glass down, Aiden took it from her, his fingers brushing against hers in the process. She caught him looking at her at the same time. His gaze was intense, his dark eyes seeming even darker than when he'd returned from the bar with the towel in hand. Odd, how a person's eye color could change like that.

At the same time, she was unable to break the contact. Her mouth went dry as her gaze fell onto his parted lips. She'd never felt so aware of another person. He was right there, yet too far away to touch him, while he could put his hand on her leg at any time if he wanted to. Would he? She shook off the errant thought. What was wrong with her? Clearly, the shock of nearly being run over by a car had scrambled her mind. Otherwise why would she suddenly fantasize about kissing a stranger?

And why was her heart beating faster, her chest heaving and her tongue snaking out to moisten her dry lips? As if anticipating a mouthwatering treat. Her stomach clenched in concert with her breaths, likewise expecting something delicious. Her palms felt sweaty, but she refrained from wiping them on her pants, not wanting to draw attention to their traitorous state. If she didn't know any better, she'd say she was behaving like a high school girl who'd just seen the quarterback of her football team stepping out of the locker room in nothing but a towel wrapped around his hips.

Aiden was fully dressed, yet he had the same effect on her. Her reaction to him was unusual for her. She'd never been one to see any appeal in a one-night stand, but with this man, she would throw caution to the wind, just this once.

"Thank you again," she said quickly, not wanting the silence between them to stretch even longer and turn to awkwardness. It was bad enough that she was drooling all over him. As if she'd never been out with a handsome man.

Handsome? Make that sinfully gorgeous, she amended.

His dark hair was short and straight. By the looks of it, it was thick, and she was sure she could confirm her assumption if only she could thread her fingers through it. Maybe at the same time, she could test how soft his lips were and what it felt like to rub her fingers over the scar above his brow or over the stubbles that graced his chin.

"It looks like you're getting your color back."

He glanced at her cheeks, and she realized how flushed she felt. Was she blushing? At her age, she should be past such sophomoric reactions, but a quick peek to catch her reflection in the window revealed that her face looked indeed a little red.

She found a scapegoat very quickly and had no problem passing blame. "The whiskey." Leila pointed to the glass on the table. "I'm not used to it."

"I should have asked you if you wanted something else, but considering the shock you had, I figured whiskey would do the trick. Always helps me." Aiden took a sip from his glass, clearly savoring the taste before swallowing.

"Yes, the shock," Leila agreed hastily.

Her hand was still shaking when she smoothed a strand of hair behind her ear that had loosened from her ponytail, but she already felt better. The ice had a numbing effect on her ankle. Unfortunately, the handsomeness of her companion had reduced her brain's speech center to producing only simple, short sentences. She couldn't allow this to continue. It was ridiculous. She was a doctor, an intelligent woman and more than capable of speaking to a handsome man in complex sentences. She just had to pull herself together, be her usual confident self again.

"I was working late," she mumbled then cleared her throat to lend her voice more strength. It worked. "Well, I work late most nights." What else would she do? She had practically no social life.

"You shouldn't walk home alone at night. There are all kinds of things that can happen."

She shrugged, surprised at the concerned look on his face. "I was only walking the few blocks to the subway."

"The next subway is five blocks from here—five *long and pretty deserted* blocks, if I may add." He clicked his tongue. "That's risky."

"I'm not worried. I'm armed." She'd grown up in the city and knew to be prepared.

He raised a surprised eyebrow. "Gun?"

She dug into her shoulder bag and pulled out her weapon of choice, waving it triumphantly. "Mace."

But Aiden seemed unimpressed, shaking his head in apparent disapproval. "You know how easy it is for a man who knows what he's doing to rip this out of your hand and use it against you?"

She waved him off. "I know how to use it." She'd been carrying the spray for years.

"Do you?" There was an odd glint in his eyes when he made a sudden movement. Before she could react, he snatched the mace out of her hand and held it up.

Shock coursed through her, and from the corner of her eye she saw the bartender stop in mid-movement. A sense of panic gripped her even though there were other people in the bar.

"See?" Aiden asked. "See how easy it was for me to disarm you?"

Her heart still pounding, she stared at him with widened eyes. This had not been on her predictability list. "But... but I wasn't prepared in here. We're in a bar."

He shook his head and placed the can of mace back in her hand. "It can happen anywhere. You'll always have to be prepared."

His voice carried a heavy dose of insistence as if he wanted to make sure she didn't forget the lesson he'd taught her.

She'd always thought she was prepared, but this stranger had just proven to her that she was nowhere near close to dealing with the unpredictable. She made a mental note to work on that, how, she wasn't quite sure. "You had an advantage because I showed it to you."

She felt the need to defend herself, not wanting to come across as a weak woman who needed a man's protection. Particularly not in front of Aiden. When she looked at him, she felt the strange need to show him that she was strong, that she needed nobody—as if to prove something to him, even though she didn't know what.

He smiled and put his hand over hers. Instinctively she tightened her fingers around the can.

Aiden nodded approvingly. "Good, you're learning. Because anybody could be an attacker."

"Even you? Even though you saved my life?" She had no idea why she asked him that, her lips forming words without her permission.

He briefly squeezed her hand, then severed the contact, a strange look on his face. "You have nothing to fear from me."

Leila lifted her chin. "So you're telling me I can trust you?" Could she trust him? Or was she letting herself be fooled by his handsome face?

He leaned closer and reached for her free hand. His eyes penetrated her as if he was trying to see deep into her. When his lips parted, he did so only to whisper so quietly she barely heard it, "Maybe you shouldn't."

Then he pulled her hand to his lips and pressed a warm kiss on the back of it. When he let go, a smile played around his lips. Her belly fluttered excitedly in response. Now she understood. It had all been a joke. He'd just pulled her leg.

She drew in a breath of relief. As she exhaled, a chuckle rolled over her lips.

He stared at her in surprise. "What's so funny?"

"You. You were trying to scare me, but you couldn't keep a straight face. Do you always do this to charm women?"

"I was charming you?"

She preferred not to answer that question.

Aiden smirked. "I guess you found me out." For a moment, she could see the little boy in him that he must have once been. "A woman's intuition?"

She tilted her head, studying him. "Maybe."

Nervously, she reached for the glass again, but he anticipated her move and handed it to her. When she took another sip, another wave of heat spread in her body, but she wasn't certain whether it was the alcohol causing this reaction or the fact that his eyes were pinning her. Returning his intense gaze, she suddenly realized that she was flirting with him. Everything feminine in her bloomed in an instant.

"And what else is there to know about you?" she asked before her courage could desert her.

"I'd hate to bore a woman by talking about myself."

"So you prefer to remain mysterious," she countered.

"Is that what I am to you, mysterious?" His eyelashes lowered a fraction, heat blazing in his eyes. "Good mysterious or bad mysterious?"

She swallowed quickly. "I haven't decided yet."

"What will help you make that decision?"

"I'd have to know more about you."

He let out a hearty laugh. "That defeats the purpose of remaining mysterious. If I tell you all about myself, there'll be nothing mysterious left about me."

"Would that be so terrible?"

"You'll find me boring and uninteresting."

She chuckled. "I doubt that very much." She paused for a moment, her eyes suddenly homing in on the scar above his eyebrow. She pointed to it. "Tell me how you got this scar."

He rubbed his finger over it. "This? That's an old one. I was a boy."

"And?" She motioned for him to continue.

"You really want to know?"

Leila nodded.

"My twin sister and I were little hellions. We were always roaming through the woods, disappearing for hours on end. We were driving our parents nuts."

She smiled. "Roaming in the woods? My parents would have been beside themselves with worry."

He grinned. "We were ten, and trust me, my parents were glad to have a few hours to themselves. They had their hands full with us."

"I believe it," she murmured, noticing the excitement that gleamed in Aiden's eyes.

He looked mock-surprised. "I wasn't the problem! My sister was. She was the wild one."

"Sure." Leila chuckled to herself, enjoying him reliving his childhood adventures.

"I heard that." He winked. "Julia always thought she could do anything. But... she slipped and fell. There was a cave, and she was dangling there, about to fall into it."

"Oh my God, how deep was the cave?"

"Deep. I was horrified, but I reacted out of instinct. My hand went around her wrist, holding her while I braced my feet against a massive root that was anchored in the ground. I pulled her out, but the moment she was safe, the root snapped under our weight and hit me. Narrowly missed my eye."

Leila let out a breath. "You saved your sister."

He nodded, a sad look crossing his face. "That time, yes." Then he smiled, changing the subject. "So, how's your foot feeling?"

She looked at it. "Actually, I haven't even been thinking about it in the last few minutes. You're a miracle worker."

"Hardly."

"Thanks for helping me."

"It's all in a day's work."

She studied his face. "But you said you're not a doctor."

"I'm not."

Surprised that he didn't take the lead-in to talk about his job, something most men liked, she dug deeper. "So if it's not medicine what do you do?"

"Security stuff."

"You mean like a security consultant?"

"Not exactly."

"Military?" God, she hoped not.

He hesitated as if contemplating what to tell her.

"If you don't want to tell me, that's f—"

"I'm a bodyguard."

Of their own doing, her eyes instantly roamed his body. Yes, he was tall, and when he'd carried her, it had seemed without effort. She'd felt his muscles flex beneath her. Yet he wasn't just muscle and strength. He had speed, too. The quickness with which he'd grabbed her and moved her out of the way of the speeding car, had been unreal.

Excitement and disappointment collided inside her. He was a man with a dangerous job, somebody so very different from herself, from her ordered life. A man not to get involved with no matter how hot he was and how much she owed him. She didn't need to add another person to her life whom she would worry about. She worried enough about her parents. That took all her energy. There was nothing left for a man who would be gone for days on end, likely without a word. No, she would never be able to do that.

The one-night stand she had contemplated only minutes earlier lost its appeal. She didn't want to be tempted to want more. Because things happened, and what if a one-night stand turned into two nights, a week or a month? It was the same reason she never dated a policeman, fireman, or anybody who was in the military. A bodyguard fell into the same category.

With regret she allowed her lips to form her next words. "It's getting late. I should call a cab."

He seemed jolted by her answer for a moment. Then he emptied the last of his drink and looked into his glass. "I'll make sure you'll get home safely."

7

Aiden insisted on waiting for the cab with her. As he helped her into the taxi, his mood was gloomy.

Why did it bother him that Leila had suddenly cut their impromptu evening short? He should be relieved. But after telling her about Julia and their adventures together, he'd felt a strange sense of wanting to open up to her, when he rarely talked to anybody about his sister.

Why Leila's mood had suddenly changed when he'd told her he was a bodyguard, which came pretty close to the truth, he had no idea. Her rejection should suit him fine, but for whatever reason he didn't like it. Intellectually, he knew that the more distance he could keep between him and her, the better for everybody involved. They weren't friends, and she should never make the mistake of seeing him as such. Neither should he want anything from her but her compliance, so he could protect her. End of story.

No, it's only the beginning, his inner voice insisted while his heartbeat accelerated in agreement.

Not wanting his thoughts to go farther down that road, he watched the taxi disappear around the next corner and pulled out his cell phone. He dialed Manus's number and started walking in the direction where his car was parked.

"Yeah?" his second answered immediately. Of all people, the council had assigned Manus to him.

"I need you to check on a license plate for me. My charge was nearly run over by a car tonight."

"No shit."

"Could be a coincidence…"

Manus snorted. "Since when do you believe in coincidences?"

Manus was right. He didn't.

"What's the plate number?"

Aiden recited it from memory. "I didn't get the last number. There was some dirt on the plate, obscuring it." He'd only had a split second to read the plates as the car had whizzed past him. But his preternatural senses had picked up what they could anyway.

"What kind of car was it?"

"Toyota, looked like a Corolla." A very indistinct car, like millions of others.

"Give me a few hours. I'll text you what I can find."

"Good, I'm going to Leila's place now—"

"Ah, it's Leila now. Interesting."

Aiden's hand tightened around his phone, anger surging. "Dr. Cruickshank's apartment," he corrected through clenched teeth.

"What's she like?"

"Not your type," Aiden bit out, his hackles rising once more. It would be a cold day in hell if he ever allowed Manus to guard her in his stead. She was his assignment. His responsibility.

"Ah, so it's like that now."

"What the fuck are you talking about?"

"You want her—Leila, is it?—for yourself," Manus guessed.

"Bullshit! She's my charge, that's all. I don't get involved with my charges." He obeyed the rules. Even if his body wanted something different this time. Something that would not only break the Stealth Guardians' rules but his own code of ethics.

"You'll see the light one day, believe me."

"Just do your job!"

Aiden disconnected the call and looked down the dark alley at the entrance of which he'd parked his black Ferrari. It was the same type of alley where only days earlier he'd lost a charge. Shaking off the unpleasant memory, he unlocked the car and slunk into the driver's seat.

The engine howled seconds later, and the car shot into the street. Traffic was light, making it easy to slip back into his thoughts even though he didn't want to.

He forced his thoughts away from Leila and back to his best friend. Best friend? He had no best friend anymore: Hamish was gone, by the looks of it seduced to the dark side by the demons. Was that what had happened? Had he turned bad? If that was true, then next time they met, it could be as enemies, clashing swords.

It was a gruesome prospect, one that for a moment even drowned out his thoughts about Leila. Aiden felt the blade that was lodged in the side of his right boot, a dagger forged in the Dark Days. Would he have to use this weapon against Hamish one day? He felt his heart contract painfully at the thought of it, but he knew it had to be done.

As a Stealth Guardian, Hamish knew too much. He was aware of the portals that connected all compounds with each other. Like worm holes, they allowed their kind to step into a portal at one compound and emerge, seconds later, at another, even if it was thousands of miles away. It made travel between their strongholds child's play. But should demons ever get wind of the location of their compounds and therefore the portals, they could destroy the Stealth Guardians from within. A frightening prospect, and the reason why no charges were ever allowed inside the walls of any compound, even though it would be the safest place for them.

Aiden pulled the car to a stop opposite the small building Leila lived in. Her apartment was on the second floor and faced the street, making it easy to watch from the outside. The lights in two rooms were on, the living room and her bedroom. Earlier, before he'd gone to Inter Pharma, he'd entered her apartment, passing through the locked door as if it were air, and had scoped out her place. He'd found nothing amiss, no traces of demon activity, nothing unusual.

Her bookshelves were stuffed full with medical textbooks, her coffee table littered with medical journals, and her refrigerator bare. He knew that Inter Pharma had a canteen, and he assumed she ate there rather than cooking at home. The apartment was neat, yet it lacked the frills he'd encountered in other women's homes.

His sensitive hearing picked up the ping of a microwave, and moments later he saw Leila limping back into the living room, plate in hand.

Aiden drummed his fingers against the steering wheel, contemplating whether to go up there and sit with her. He knew it wasn't necessary, because from the short distance he was at, he had no trouble cloaking her with his mind. She would be invisible to any demon in the vicinity. Yet, something inexplicable made him want to draw closer.

The decision was made for him when he heard a doorbell ring in Leila's apartment and saw her rise. His gaze shot to the front door of the building, but there was nobody.

He catapulted from the car and raced across the street, bolting through the door and up the stairs. He turned the corner after the first flight of stairs and looked up to the next landing, just as Leila opened the door to the young man who hovered there.

"Hey, Jonathan," she greeted him with a tired smile, but a smile nevertheless.

Who the hell was this guy? Her boyfriend? Aiden perused him quickly: tall build, slim, short blond hair, his arms behind his back, dimples in his cheeks when he smiled. Which he did now. He positively grinned back at her.

"Hey, Leila. I heard you come home. Didn't want to miss you."

Aiden noticed how she leaned against the door jamb, her injured leg slightly lifted off the floor. Darn, this guy shouldn't keep her. Didn't he see that she was tired and needed to rest?

"I was just about to turn in..." Good, it seemed she wasn't in the mood to talk to this interloper.

He brought his hands to his front, and Aiden instantly went on alert, in case he was about to touch her. Yet, his hands held a square box about ten inches long on each side, wrapped in colored paper, a ribbon and a bow around it.

"Just wanted to be the first one to give you a birthday present."

"Ohh," she cooed. "You shouldn't have." Yet she took the box from his hands.

Now get lost, Aiden wanted to growl.

Jonathan raised his finger. "But you're not allowed to open it until tomorrow. It's not your birthday yet."

She smiled back. "Promise." Then she paused. "I'd invite you in, but..."

No!

Aiden took a few steps up toward them to interfere if necessary.

"No, no, don't worry, I can see you're tired. We'll hang out some other time." Then he bent toward her and kissed her on the cheek. "Happy Birthday!"

Piss off!

"Good night, Jonathan, and thanks again."

She turned and disappeared back in her apartment. Aiden watched as Jonathan waited until the door closed behind her, then walked up a flight of stairs. So that jerk lived in the same apartment building. This wasn't good. It meant he had to stay with

Leila day and night, there was no way around it. He couldn't allow this guy to slip past him.

He put Jonathan on his mental list of people to check out. For all he knew the guy could work for the demons. He was clearly human, but that didn't mean a thing. The demons had plenty of humans on their payroll—humans who didn't even know who they were working for.

The asshole had kissed her, only on the cheek, but nevertheless it was a kiss. Leila hadn't seemed surprised by it either, as if he'd done it before. Had he?

Aiden looked down at his hands that had balled into fists, as if wanting to hit someone, preferably Jonathan. What the fuck was making him so aggressive?

He knew he couldn't jeopardize this assignment and draw attention to himself, so he forced himself to relax and unclench his fists. If the council got wind of his erratic behavior, they'd take him to task. Not even his status as the son of the current Primus would help him then. Not that it had ever helped him before: now that he thought of it, he'd never received any preferential treatment because of it. On the contrary, sometimes he felt that he was being treated harsher just because he was Primus's son. Well, he didn't care. Whatever they threw at him, he could handle it.

Without another thought, he entered Leila's apartment. Whatever was driving him, he didn't care to analyze.

8

Aiden smelled her arousal.

Leila had taken a brief shower after finishing her dinner, a shower he had forced himself not to watch. It was inexplicable enough that he lusted after her. Watching her as hot water ran down her naked body would have snapped his control like a twig in the path of a herd of elephants. Merely imagining pearls of water trickling over her lush flesh made him wish for a dip into a frozen lake to cool down his overheated body.

Now she lay in bed, naked, the covers pushed to the side.

He glanced at her face, but her eyes were closed. She wasn't sleeping yet and she wouldn't for a while, because he knew what was coming next. Anticipation made him hard and battled with the guilt that he felt rising in his chest. Because what he was doing was dishonorable. He should give her privacy, but he couldn't tear himself away. A better man would have left her bedroom and gone into the living room, guarding her from there. Maybe he was just as depraved as Manus. Wasn't that what his second had alluded to a few days earlier? That given the right woman, he would disregard the council's rules the same way Manus did?

Or maybe *rasen* was controlling him, despite the fact that he was fighting its influence.

Aiden allowed his hungry eyes to travel over Leila's nude form: from her graceful neck and the little indentation at the base of her throat, alabaster skin stretched over well-toned muscles down her strong biceps to slender wrists. The curves that made up her luscious torso were more than just a little enticing. Despite the warmth in the room, those dark nipples that sat on perfectly round breasts were beading. Hard and demanding, they topped beautiful mounds of flesh and fairly screamed to be caressed.

As his gaze descended, sliding down through the deep valley between her magnificent breasts, he salivated. From farther south, where a dark canopy guarded a treasure he wanted to taste, her aroma drifted to him more intensely now. Without having to look, he knew she was wet there. If she spread her legs, he'd see sweet honey glistening on her rosy flesh.

At the juncture of her thighs, strong legs met, legs that could envelope a man and make him forget everything. Those toned legs could cross behind his back and tighten so she could pull him closer to her as he thrust into her. With her strength, she could force him to go deeper, take her harder, faster.

Aiden wiped pearls of moisture from his brow, but couldn't take the deep breath he needed. Leila would hear him otherwise. Only shallow breaths entered his lungs, and they did nothing to alleviate the heat in his body or calm down his racing heart. All he could do was admire her. She was perfect, her body that of a goddess.

When her hands moved, he widened his stance, giving his ever growing appendage more space between his legs. It felt like a release, but he had no time to enjoy it, because Leila's hands were now on her breasts.

With languid strokes, she massaged them slowly, her fingers circling her erect nipples. They seemed even harder than before. If he could swipe his warm tongue over them, he could find out exactly how hard.

No! He shouldn't think of this. He should leave the room now, give her the privacy she deserved and stop watching what he had no right to see. But as much as he tried to command his legs to move to the door, they remained frozen where they were. He had no control over his body. As if something or somebody was controlling him. Was it *rasen* that had taken over his body, or was it simply the desire he felt for her? A desire so unreasonable and yet so powerful that he didn't know how to combat it. This wasn't him: he wasn't a man who sought this kind of forbidden thrill. On the contrary: he prided himself on his honor, his ethics and the emotional detachment with which he treated his charges. Why couldn't he do the same with Leila?

Again he tried to make his legs move toward the door, but his silent command remained unanswered.

Instead, he looked back at her. Her lips parted and issued a soft sigh as if she'd waited for a while to do this. Did she touch herself like this every night? Was this what she did to release the stress of her work? And as her protector, would he be tempted to witness this night after night? Would he have to go through this torture every night, where one part of him urged him to grant her privacy and the other forced him to watch?

When she tweaked her nipples, she moaned again, this time louder. At the same time, her legs fell open and for the first time, he saw the pink flesh that was hidden there. The little light beam from a streetlamp that drifted into the room from underneath the curtains was sufficient to illuminate what he wanted to see, and his superior night vision did the rest.

Aiden took an instinctive step closer, unable to tear himself away from the tantalizing sight. The scent grew more intense as he approached, and it only heightened his hunger. Almost as if she was drugging him with her aroma.

With rapt fascination, he watched as her hand wandered down to her stomach and reached between her legs, while her other hand continued kneading her breast.

Her body twisted and flexed with every move of her fingers, while her moans cut through the silence in short intervals. When her second hand joined the first, she spread her legs even farther, giving him a view that nearly catapulted him over the edge. She dipped one finger inside her glistening channel while her thumb stroked the engorged bundle of flesh at the base of her curls.

Her soft sighs and moans filling the room, he closed his eyes for a moment, shocked at the intensity of emotions that overwhelmed him. This wasn't the first time he'd seen a woman pleasure herself, but this was the first time it aroused him to the point of pain. Keeping his control had never been this hard. But he couldn't allow himself to act on his desire. She was his charge, he reminded himself. He should leave the room now and forget what he'd seen.

Her rhythm sped up, and he could feel how her breathing turned into short bursts. "Oh, Aiden," she murmured unexpectedly.

Her words made his heart stop as a shock wave rippled through his body.

Did she know he was there?

His gaze shot to her face, but her eyes were closed, and she was too engulfed in her own emotions to sense him. But if she didn't know he was in her bedroom, then why had she called out his name? Had he misheard because he so much wanted her to call out to him, to scream his name as she came?

"Aiden," she whispered again.

This time he heard it clearly: his name. She *was* calling for him. It could only mean one thing: as she pleasured herself, she was fantasizing about *him*! But then why had she rejected him earlier? Was it simply because she didn't trust him? He was a stranger to her, but plenty of women went to bed with strangers, and he'd seen interest in her eyes at first.

Another moan pulled him from his musings, making him snap his gaze back to her hands that so eagerly caressed her sex. Her finger plunged deeper inside her, and her other hand rubbed her clit faster and faster.

"Inside... yes, take me... make me come..." She expelled the words in short, breathless huffs, her skin now covered with a light sheen of perspiration, the scent of which drove him nearly insane.

When his knees knocked against the mattress, he realized he'd crossed the remaining distance between them. From the foot of the bed all he needed to do was slide onto it and he'd be lying between her legs, his mouth at her sweet pussy. He could lick her and take her over the edge, feel her succumb to her orgasm, a pleasure he would give her.

Do it!

His hands fisted at his sides, his throbbing erection urging him to take what he wanted. She would never know it was he. All she would feel was his touch, his fingers, his mouth, his tongue. If he kept it light enough, maybe she would simply assume her fantasies were more powerful than ever, more real. And even if she suspected somebody was in her bedroom, she would see nothing, just air around her. He would be a vivid dream to her as long as she didn't touch him and realize that there was an invisible body in her bed, because even while invisible, his flesh would feel as real as ever.

Nobody would ever find out. But *he* would know, and he would hate himself for it. When he touched her, he wanted her to know it was him, to call out his name, to look into his eyes. Still, his mouth watered, imagining what she tasted like, how sweet her honey was and how soft her flesh.

As if she knew that he stood there, fighting his inner self, she whispered, "Yes." Her hands continued teasing her sensitive flesh, and from her choppy breathing, he realized that she was close.

His hand reached out.

A loud bang sounding like an explosion stopped his action. His head whipped toward the door.

Shit! He rushed to the door just as Leila reared up from her supine position, equally shocked.

Then the smoke detector started beeping.

"Oh, no!" she cried out.

Aiden passed through the bedroom door without opening it. From the hallway that led to the kitchen and living room, a cloud of smoke billowed beneath the ceiling, and coming from the kitchen he saw flames shooting through the open door. A violent fire was raging there, and he knew enough about fires to realize that this one would spread quickly.

Behind him the bedroom door opened.

A startled scream nearly pierced his eardrum. He turned toward Leila, who stood in the door frame, nude.

She stared right at him, eyes wide, her lips readying themselves to scream once more.

She saw him! *Shit!* In his panic, he'd inadvertently uncloaked himself.

"How did you get in here?" Her hands scrambled to cover her nudity, but it was to no avail; her small hands couldn't cover her plentiful curves.

"Leila, I can explain. Later. The fire, we have to get out of here." He shot a worried look toward the kitchen, where the flames were engulfing the entire door and were working their way into the corridor, the smoke cloud underneath the ceiling growing larger.

Only now her look seemed to drop to his pants where his erection created a visible bulge.

Her eyes widened, and true fear shone through her irises. "Oh, my God, you came to rape me!" She shot back into the room and slammed the door. He heard the lock click shut.

Fuck! He'd screwed up royally! But there wasn't time for any explanations now. The fire was approaching quickly, consuming anything combustible in its way. Already now, the hallway was impassible and they'd have to find another way out.

There was no time to plead with her to open the bedroom door, no time to waste on kicking it in. They would need that door as a barrier against the fire. Realizing he had to expose himself for what he was, he passed through the door.

A shriek greeted him, her hand barely holding onto the receiver she was punching a number into. 9-1-1 he guessed. He snatched it from her hand and pressed the off button before tossing it into a corner.

Her face blanched. "What are you?"

9

Leila hit the back of her knees against the bed frame and automatically snatched her pillow to press it against her front.

As if that gave her any protection!

But covering her nudity wasn't her biggest concern. What she'd just seen couldn't have happened. Aiden, if that was really his name, had passed through the locked bedroom door as if it were made of air and not of solid wood. A sideways glance to the door confirmed that it was still closed and locked.

She shook her head. Was she having a nightmare? No! That was impossible. She knew she was fully awake. In fact, she'd never gone to sleep. Then it came to her in a flash.

"You drugged me at the bar!" she cried out. That's why she was hallucinating. "You followed me."

"No, Leila, that's not true."

She didn't believe him.

"I'll explain everything later." He took a step toward her. "But we have no time now."

Of their own volition, her eyes drifted to his jeans. The bulge was now markedly smaller, but he still sported an erection.

"Get away from me!"

"You need to put some clothes on, now." His eyes searched the room and fell on a pair of jeans and a sweater. He took them from the chair they lay on.

As he approached her anew, she tried to back away from him, but with the bed at her back, she had nowhere to go.

"Now, Leila," he said in a voice that brooked no refusal.

Coward that she was, she took the clothes he handed her. When she tried to put on the pants while shielding herself with the pillow, he pulled it from her hands and dropped it on the bed behind her. Heat suffused her cheeks.

"Damn it, Leila, there's no time for modesty. The fire..." He pointed to the door, where smoke started creeping in from the top.

She dressed more quickly than she ever had, fear giving her wings. This couldn't be happening to her. Not only was he here to rape her, he'd also set her place on fire so he could abduct her. And she couldn't even protest: it was either go with him or die of smoke inhalation. She had a medical degree; she knew how quickly that could happen.

"Please don't hurt me," she begged.

There was a flash of disbelief in his eyes. He stared at her, seconds ticking away. "I would never hurt you. I'm here to save you."

Then his arms pulled her to him and all strength left her. She couldn't do anything to protest. "Let me go." But her demand was a mere whimper.

She didn't do danger and panic very well. This was a situation she wasn't prepared for, one that didn't fit into her orderly life.

His hand connected with her cheek, but the touch was caressing, his knuckles brushing lightly over her skin. "Never, Leila. I'm here to protect you."

Oh, God, no! He was an obsessed stalker. For all she knew, he'd been following her even earlier in the night, before they'd ended up in the bar.

From the corner of her eye, she saw the paint on the door blistering. The smell of smoke was getting stronger by the second as it crept through the crevices along the door frame. She knew it was only a matter of time until the door gave way, allowing the fire into her bedroom. It made the decision for her: she would go with him for now, but as soon as she had escaped this inferno, she'd scream for help and flee.

She nodded and saw him exhale with relief.

"We have to go out the window."

She stared at him. "I can't jump down there. It's too high." Her ankle was sprained. There was no way she could land on it. Most likely she'd sprain or break the other leg too, trying to absorb the impact of the fall with it. Landing awkwardly could result in all kinds of injuries.

She tried to pull from his arms, but he didn't let her go.

"You won't jump. I will."

Her forehead creased. "But how will I…?" Would he leave her here after all, to perish in the flames?

Aiden released her and pushed the curtains to the sides, yet he didn't open the window.

"We have to get out before the fire consumes the door," he explained.

"Oh, God," she whispered, horror making her blood freeze in her veins.

When she felt Aiden's arms around her, she almost felt safe: exchanging one evil for another. He pressed her to his front, his body warm and strangely comforting.

"Wait! My bag." She pulled from his arms and grabbed both her handbag and her necklace from the nightstand. Her necklace was one thing she couldn't let perish in the fire. No sooner had she shoved the pendant into the pocket of her jeans and slung her bag diagonally across her body, did Aiden draw her back to him.

"Wrap your arms and legs around me," he ordered.

Fear made her comply without protest. She clung to him like Velcro, his breath hot at her ear.

"Don't lose your hold on me. I'll jump, and I promise you, you'll be safe."

Something in his voice settled her pounding heart and slowed her breathing. For a moment she remembered him telling her how he'd saved his sister when he was a boy, and it gave her comfort. Or had the story been a lie? But oddly enough, she thought she'd heard tenderness in his words. She must be out of her mind if she assumed that.

Leila buried her face in his neck when she felt him kick the window out with one foot.

Simultaneously, the flames broke through the door, the force of the blast catapulting them outside. She prepared for the inevitable hard impact on the sidewalk, but it never happened. Either she was dead or Aiden had landed on his feet.

"You can open your eyes now."

Hesitantly, she peeled her face from his neck and blinked. As if nothing had happened, they were suddenly standing on the pavement in front of her building, not a scratch on them. She had to be still drugged, because a landing like this was impossible, particularly after practically being tossed out of the window by the flashover.

"How—?"

But she didn't get to ask her question, because his lips prevented her from speaking. As if he'd done this a hundred times before, his mouth slid over hers. His kiss was one of pure possession, exploration, and desire.

To her surprise, she responded to him without thought. She blamed the fact that she'd just escaped a burning apartment. Or the drugs he'd somehow managed to spike her drink with at the Irish bar. Perhaps she was in shock. There was no other sane reason why she would kiss back a man who'd clearly broken into her apartment, set it on fire, and was about to kidnap her.

Right, no sane reason, other than the fact that he tasted so male and so virile. His hands on her back pressed her against his rock hard chest where she felt his heart beating as fast as hers, while his tongue foraged into her mouth, ravishing her as if he hadn't kissed a woman in years and was starving for a taste. Maybe as starving as she, for she couldn't stop stroking her own tongue against his, dueling with him, exploring him like he explored her. It was madness, and wrong on so many levels.

But her body didn't listen to her brain, which tried to tell her to push him away. On the contrary, just as she'd felt aroused when she'd fantasized about him earlier, liquid heat now pooled at the juncture of her thighs. And he could probably feel the heat through his clothes. It was madness.

The distant siren of a fire engine brought her back to her senses and made her pull her head back, severing the contact. He stared at her, his eyes hooded, his lips red and moist from the passionate kiss they'd shared.

Then he suddenly turned his head as if he heard the siren only now. "We have to go."

Above her head, she glimpsed the flames shooting from her apartment window. She tried to free herself from him, dropping her legs to the ground and pushing against him, but he was stronger. "Let me go," she begged.

He shook his head, his expression dark. "No. Twice somebody tried to kill you tonight. I'd be crazy to let you out of my sight."

What had he said?

"Kill me?" was all she could echo, darting nervous looks around her, desperately hoping for the fire engine to shoot around the corner, so she could find help from them or the police that would surely arrive instantly.

"I'll explain everything later, but we'll have to leave now. You're not safe here. They know where you are."

Ignoring her protests, he carried her to a parked car across the street. A click and the car lights flashed briefly, indicating that the doors were now unlocked. Without ceremony, he dumped her into the passenger's seat and slammed the door shut behind her. In the darkness, her fingers fumbled for the handle, her shaking noticeable now. Before she could open the car door, he was already in the driver's seat and yanked her hand toward him.

His dark eyes bored into her. "You might not trust me right now—God knows, the circumstances don't speak for me—but if you want to live, you have to stay with me."

Without waiting for an answer, he engaged the engine and pulled the car into the street. In the back mirror, she saw the fire engine careen around the corner. They'd finally arrived to save the building from total destruction, but it was too late for her. She was at Aiden's mercy now. And who knew what his plans were.

Leila glanced to her side, her eyes falling onto his groin once more. The bulge in his pants was barely noticeable now. Not that it was any consolation. Once he brought the car to a stop somewhere, once they'd arrived at whatever destination he had in mind, he would do what he'd planned all along. Force her...

Would she react the same way she'd reacted to his kiss? Would she simply let it happen without mounting any resistance? Would she allow him to take her without putting up a fight? Hell, she'd allowed the kiss; not just allowed, she'd participated with more enthusiasm than she'd ever kissed a man before. It could only be the drug that had made her react like this, dulled her defenses so he could do with her what he wanted.

"What did you drug me with?" Maybe if she knew what it was, she could somehow fight its effects.

He didn't take his eyes off the street as he weaved through traffic. "I didn't drug you."

"The drink at the Irish pub," she insisted.

He shook his head. "It was pure whiskey. The bartender poured it for you. You saw it. He brought you the glass. I couldn't have put anything in it even if I wanted to." He paused and gave her a sideways look. "Which I don't. I want you in possession of all your faculties."

So she would feel pain? Humiliation? "Why are you kidnapping me?"

"I'm not."

"Could have fooled me," she mumbled under her breath, her lips trembling nervously.

"I heard that."

"Where are you taking me?"

"To a safe place."

Suddenly he removed his hand from the steering wheel and clasped it over hers. Her entire body coiled in tension. Was he going to fondle her here in the car? Then maybe she could grab the steering wheel and cause an accident. It would give her occasion to escape.

Yeah, if you survive the accident.

Shit, why was she such a coward?

"Leila," he said so softly, she whirled her head to look at him, trying to make sure he was still the same man, because for all she knew, she could be hallucinating. As she had earlier when she'd thought she'd seen him pass through the locked door.

It looked as if he wanted to say something, but then he didn't. Instead, he pressed a button on his steering wheel. She heard a dialing tone, then the sound of a speed dial. The call was answered on the first ring.

"Aiden? What do you need?" A male voice came through the loudspeakers.

"My charge's apartment went up in flames," Aiden explained.

Charge?

"Shit!" the man cursed.

"Listen, Manus," Aiden continued, "I don't think it's a coincidence. Anything on the car yet?"

"Negative, Pearce is running the plates right now. Another half hour or so."

"Good. I need you to listen in on the fire department. They just arrived at the scene and are putting out the fire. I need to know what they think the cause is. My guess is arson."

Leila felt as if a fist clamped around her heart. Arson? Somebody wanted to kill her? No, that couldn't be true.

"I'm on it. Is she hurt?"

"No, thank God, I got her out in time."

He'd saved her, yes, he really had. Did this mean, he wasn't the one who'd set her apartment on fire? Could she trust what she was hearing now?

"Where are you taking her?"

"To a safe place."

"Call me when you get there," the other man said.

"Later."

He pressed a button, and the call disconnected.

"What are you? FBI? CIA?"

He gave a slow shake of his head. "Not exactly."

If he wasn't with the government, he had to be something else, something more dangerous. "Mafia?"

She knew her voice was laced with fear. Aiden had heard it too, because he gave her a long look before his lips parted once more to speak. "By the life of my parents, I promise you one thing: I'll never hurt you."

At his words, a single sob tore from her chest. She'd completely forgotten about her parents. Oh, God, what would happen to her parents if she was gone? Who would make sure they continued to receive the care they needed? Who would make sure the caregivers didn't mistreat them? She had to fight to get away. Her parents needed her. They counted on her, even though on their bad days they didn't always know who she was. Yet there was still a chance for them to at least gain back part of what Alzheimer's had robbed them of—if only she was able to finish her research in time.

She had to fight for them. Besides, she wasn't brave enough to face death. There was so much more she needed to do, so much more of life she hadn't experienced. No, she couldn't allow this stranger to kidnap her and take her away from everything that was dear to her. She had to bargain with him.

10

Behind a dumpster in a deserted alley, Aiden brought the car to a stop. Leila sat in the passenger seat, her body coiled in tension, her lips pressed together as if fighting against the urge to cry. Given the circumstances, she'd reacted with far less hysterics than he'd expected from anybody in her situation.

Aiden realized it had been wrong to kiss her after all that had happened, but he hadn't been able to stop himself. The fire had been so close, and fear had thickened his blood to the consistency of gel, making his heart nearly stop at the thought that she might get hurt. He'd never been so afraid for anybody else. Never feared losing anybody like he feared losing her. Even though he had no right to possess her in the first place.

But he'd needed that kiss. Needed it to make sure she was unharmed. Like a release, he'd craved it, and when she'd given in, he'd nearly come in his pants like a green teenager. The way she'd held him so tight and her tongue had played with his as if it were meant to be, had wiped every sane thought from his mind. Even now, he could still taste her like she'd imprinted her scent on him for eternity.

Gripping the steering wheel as if his life depended on it, he addressed her without looking at her, "I promise you, everything will be fine. Nobody will hurt you. I'll kill anybody who tries."

His words seemed to jolt her, because she lifted her head and turned it to look at him. When he glanced at her, he saw fear dominate her eyes.

"Please let me go. I'll do what you want. I won't fight you. But then please just let me go. My family…"

He barely listened to the rest of her words, because he wasn't quite sure he'd heard correctly. *She would do what he wanted? Did it mean what he thought it meant?*

"You really think I came to your apartment to rape you?"

And why wouldn't she think that? He'd broken in, for lack of a better word, and when she'd first laid eyes on him, he'd sported a hard-on the size of a baseball bat. Of course, she'd jump to that conclusion.

When she said nothing, but only looked at him with fearful eyes, he reached his hand to stroke hers but pulled back instantly when he realized what he was doing. Shit, he should keep his distance. Touching her would make things even worse.

"Leila, I'm your bodyguard. I'm charged to protect you. I was in your place to watch over you."

He ran his hand through his hair. How would he explain to her why she'd found him in an aroused state?

"My bodyguard? I would know if I'd hired a bodyguard."

He expelled a tense breath, uncomfortable that he had to reveal who he was. It was only done in the most dire of circumstances, which this situation probably counted as.

"I'm not the kind of bodyguard you can hire. I get assigned. I don't ask questions, I do my duty." Most of the time. With Leila, he'd done a little more than just his duty. Watching her masturbate and kissing her after he'd rescued her wasn't part of the Stealth Guardian's code of conduct. Nor his own personal code.

"I don't believe you."

That was to be expected. He nodded. "Do you remember that you locked your bedroom door after you ran into me in the hallway?"

"Yes." She thrust her chin up in a sign of defiance. Strangely enough, he liked that gesture. She was no pushover.

"A moment later, I stood in your bedroom. You saw how I entered."

She shook her head. "No. I was still half asleep. I was dreaming. It couldn't be."

Aiden focused on a strand of hair he wanted to push out of her face. She looked so much more feminine with her hair down rather than tied in a ponytail. "You weren't dreaming. You weren't even asleep yet."

She gasped, her eyes widening in horror.

Oh shit!

He hadn't wanted to let her know that he'd been in her bedroom earlier, that he'd watched her. It had simply slipped out.

Leila's mouth opened in disbelief as she scrambled toward the door to get as far away from him as possible. "You were in my bedroom?"

"Leila, I'm sorry... I didn't mean to... I... I'm sorry."

"Oh, God, no. How could you?"

He'd asked himself the same question, yet he still had no answer for it. He'd violated her privacy, and there was no excuse for it.

He turned his head and looked out into the darkness. Did she find the thought so utterly disgusting? "I didn't mean to... I..."

"You watched me? The entire time? All the while as I was..." She pressed her eyes shut. "You had no right to watch me!"

"No, I didn't," he said, sobering. "I'm sorry. I don't know what came over me. I have no excuses." And he wouldn't make any up now. He alone was to blame. He and his uncontrollable lust that even now was coursing through his veins.

When he looked back at her, she avoided his gaze.

"And I still don't believe your stupid 'walking through doors' claim. Why don't you just admit it: you drugged me, watched me... then set my place on fire so you could kidnap me."

"Fine. I suppose it takes a little demonstration."

He pressed the car's locking mechanism. "As you can see, I've locked the doors."

Then he concentrated and exited the car as if the door were wide open, allowing his body to pass through the glass and metal while remaining visible the entire time. There was no need to reveal to her that he could also make himself invisible. It would only invite more questions and stir up more doubts.

From outside the car he looked through the window and noticed Leila slamming her hand over her mouth, her eyes projecting a shocked stare. But he also saw acceptance there as it crept into her features.

He reentered the car the same way he'd exited, letting himself fall back into his seat.

"Do you believe me now?"

She nodded. Slowly, she lowered her hand from her lips. "What are you?"

"I'm an immortal, a guardian, a warrior who was sent to protect you."

"An angel?" she echoed.

He gave a crooked smile. "No, we're not exactly angels, least of all I." He was pretty sure angels didn't get hard-ons for their charges. "We're called Stealth Guardians, we're here to protect humans from the Demons of Fear."

He placed his hand over hers and felt her shrink back from his touch.

"Please don't touch me."

~ ~ ~

Mortified, Leila looked at him.

She'd seen him pass through the closed car door, and she believed him. It didn't mean she had to like it—or comply with what he wanted for that matter. On the contrary, there was something very disturbing about his words. He was still a stranger, one who had followed her, entered her home without her permission, and practically kidnapped her. That he was some kind of superhero didn't change that in the slightest.

He'd called himself an *Immortal Warrior*.

Aiden was a dangerous man with a dangerous job, even though *warrior* was probably not considered a job as such. His mere presence spelled trouble. What kind of trouble, she had no idea, but she sensed she was in a hell of a lot of it. Even if he was telling the truth and was really some sort of guardian or protector—which she wasn't at all convinced of—what did he want from her? The only protection she needed was somebody who protected her from him. Because he stirred a side in her she thought didn't exist. A side that craved excitement, passion, even danger. A side that frightened her to death.

But that wasn't all of it: he'd watched her pleasure herself. What this meant she didn't even want to begin to contemplate. No, she had to get her mind to focus on something else.

Shit, she was so totally screwed up. It was time to get her head around all this, find out as much as she could, assess the predicament she was in, and then make a break for it.

"Demons?" she asked. "Like in the Exorcist?"

"No. The demons I'm talking about are made of flesh and blood. They're close. They're watching, and they want to harm you. That's why I was sent."

Why would anybody want to hurt her? She had no enemies. She treated people politely, she paid her bills and her taxes, and she donated to charities. Didn't she have enough to worry about with her parents? She just wanted to be left alone with her research.

Instinctively, she pressed her hand over the pendant she carried in her pocket. It was still there, still safe. Whatever had burned in her apartment could be replaced. The item in her pocket could not.

"Looks like you're doing a bang-up job," she said, unable to keep the sarcasm from her voice. Since she'd met him, she'd been nearly run over by a car, and her apartment had gone up in flames. Maybe he was the one who brought danger with him. Maybe it followed *him*.

"I suppose this kitten has claws," he answered.

"I'm no kitten. I'm a respected resear—"

"I know everything about you, Dr. Cruickshank. There's no need to inform me." His voice was suddenly tight.

So, Dr. Cruickshank it was now? After watching her pleasure herself—God, what a horrifying and at the same time shockingly exciting thought—and kissing her, he found it necessary to be formal. Fine. She could be that way, too. It was better that way. As long as she could keep him at a distance, she might get out of this unscathed.

"What kind of danger am I in, *Mr. Stealth Guardian*?"

She noticed him shift his gaze away from her, a clear indication that he neither liked her question nor the way she addressed him.

"The kind that gets people killed."

She trembled involuntarily. "I can take the truth."

"Are you sure?" he asked. "Because there's somebody out there who wants a piece of you."

She shivered slightly, the predatory glare in his eyes indicating that *he* wanted a piece of her. And truth be told, in this instance she wasn't sure whether she would have the willpower to resist him if he took what he wanted. Her throat was suddenly dry as sandpaper. She swallowed quickly, taking in an extra breath of air. Her nostrils filled with his male scent, a scent so potent it would have made her knees buckle if she weren't already sitting. But she wouldn't give him the satisfaction of showing him the effect he had on her.

"I have a right to know."

Aiden gave her a long look. "I suppose you do."

Then he studied the area outside as if he could see through the darkness that engulfed them in the dark alley. His hand went to the ignition. "It's not safe here."

A moment later, the engine roared back to life.

"I'm not going anywhere with you if you don't—"

Her protest died when the swift acceleration of the sports car pressed her back into the seat. With a clear disregard for any rules of traffic, he merged onto the next street.

"You—"

He shot her a look that didn't bode well for her immediate future. "You'll get your answers when we've reached our destination."

She could only hope that their destination wasn't far, because she wasn't sure how long she could keep her tongue in check while her so-called rescuer behaved like a caveman. It riled her up to no end, making her want to fight him when she'd never been one for confrontation. But this was different. This oaf was trying to take over her life. Without even telling her why. It was unacceptable.

Whatever this stupid threat was, she was sure that the authorities could take care of it. As soon as she found out from him what it was, she'd ditch him and go to the police. Then they could handle whatever the problem was, and she could go back to her well-ordered life and continue with her research. This unpleasant interlude would become merely a faint memory as long as she didn't dwell on it.

11

Aiden didn't say another word until they arrived at their destination a few minutes later. He locked her in the car while he secured a room at a run down two-story motel in one of the shabbier parts of town, giving her no chance to escape.

As he now locked the door behind him, Leila perused the sparsely furnished room. Her eyes instantly fell on the bed: there was only one. Did he really think she'd share a bed with him? Instinctively, she crossed her arms over her chest. There was no way she'd stay here with him.

"Are you cold?" his gruff voice came from behind her.

Her shoulders tensed involuntarily. She ignored his question. "You were going to tell me what's going on."

The worn carpet swallowed the sound of his footsteps as he walked around her. He opened the bathroom door and peered inside as if to assure himself that they were indeed alone. When he turned back to her, he ran his eyes up and down her body. Then he pointed toward the bed.

"Sit."

"I'm not a dog," she snapped.

"Suit yourself."

What had she ever done to deserve this impolite behavior? "If I did what suited me, I'd be back home right now."

"Well, your home burned, so that's not an option."

He was right about that. But that didn't mean she had to admit it. "I'm still waiting for an explanation."

Aiden narrowed his eyes. "If you think you can handle it." He paused for a moment and ran his hand through his dark hair.

His eyes drifted to the window that was obscured by the heavy curtains he'd drawn upon entering. "There's evil out there. Things you can't even imagine."

"Try me." Leila steeled herself for his explanation.

He let out a bitter laugh. "I've been sent to protect you from the Demons of Fear."

She nodded. "You said that earlier. But that doesn't tell me anything." He would have to be a little bit more specific about the alleged danger she was in.

"They want to seduce you to their side, so you'll do their bidding."

"Excuse me?" She wasn't one to be seduced easily, and for sure was she never going to do some demon's bidding. Besides, "What do those so-called demons do?"

"What do they do? I'll tell you what they do: they spread mayhem in this world. They incite wars, they create discontent."

Still not enough information for her. Did he really think he could serve up a couple of lines, and she'd be happy with it? "What else is new? There are already plenty of wars."

"If you think what this world is going through right now is bad, if you think the atrocities that happened during World War II were bad, if you think what happened in the concentration camps in Germany was horror, or what Pol Pot did to his people in Cambodia was evil, you've seen nothing yet. The demons are capable of much more evil than that."

His words shocked her. "How? How do they do that?"

There was clear hesitation in him, just the way he'd hesitated back at the Irish bar when she'd asked him what he did for a living. He'd not lied to her outright then, but he'd only told her a half-truth.

"They approach the most talented and promising humans and entice them with things beyond their reach in exchange for their soul. Then they make sure whatever good those people were going to do is used for evil in their hands. And they're coming after you now."

Uneasiness crept up her spine. "Somehow I don't feel flattered by that."

"You shouldn't be. But you will. They all are eventually. And in the end, many give in to them. That's how the demons get stronger."

"By getting human souls? Sorry, but that's a little too abstract a concept. You can't separate the soul from the body. Scientifically that's—"

He took two swift steps to cross the distance between them, bringing himself entirely too close to her. "It's got nothing to do with science, at least not the science you know. This is supernatural, something you wouldn't understand."

Leila expelled an angry huff. He made her sound like an imbecile. "I'm not some stupid woman who doesn't have two brain cells to rub together, something I can't say for—"

He bared his teeth. "Say it and I'll bend you over my knee right now!"

Her jaw dropped at his ridiculous threat. Would he really do such a thing? Like she was some naughty schoolgirl! She planted her hands at her hips and realized too late that this action virtually shoved her breasts against his chest.

Aiden lowered his lids, and there was no doubt that he was checking out her boobs. Instinctively, she took a step back to bring some distance between them and to prevent her nipples from hardening if they rubbed against his hard muscles once more.

The jerk responded with a self-congratulatory smirk around his mouth. "Backing off, Dr. Cruickshank? That's so unlike you."

As if he had any idea what she was like! And he was still keeping up this ridiculous pseudo-formality of calling her *Dr. Cruickshank*, when she knew what he really wanted to say: *bitch.*

She thrust her chin up, ignoring his mocking expression. "What do those demons want from me?"

The word *demons* left a strange taste on her tongue. It felt so odd to say it when her brain couldn't wrap around this data. As a scientist, she needed more than just somebody's word. The existence of demons was highly unlikely and not supported by any testable evidence. Extraordinary claims required extraordinary evidence. Without evidence, all she had was a stranger's statement—or a lie.

"Do you really need to ask? I thought you were so smart," he continued mocking her.

She was about to retort when it suddenly dawned on her: there was only one thing precious enough that anybody could want to steal from her. Her research. Her chin dropped.

"Ah, finally," he said calmly. "Do you understand now why you have to stick with me? You're not safe on your own. I'm here to protect you from them."

"If you think I would ever give my research to some demons, you're sorely mistaken." She would guard her data with her life. For her research she was prepared to do anything. This was her life's work. There was nothing in this world anybody could possibly offer her to part with it.

"Everybody has a price. Even you."

Leila shook her head. "You don't know me. You don't know me at all."

"I know everything I need to know." He glared at her.

For a long moment, she faced off with him. As she stared into his chocolate brown eyes, a thought hit her out of nowhere. What if he was a demon himself, and under the guise of wanting to help her, he gained her confidence and thus access to her research? She'd seen his preternatural skill of passing through solid materials. For all she knew, he could be a demon and not the immortal guardian he claimed to be.

"What do these demons look like?"

Aiden shrugged. "They are humanoid in appearance; only once they use their demon powers will you recognize them by their green eyes."

She swallowed. This wasn't good. According to his description, anybody could be a demon, even he. She had to get away from him. Now.

"I need to take a shower."

~ ~ ~

Aiden watched as Leila wrapped her arms around her waist as if trying to cocoon herself, guard herself from the danger he'd warned her about. Maybe now she understood.

"You took a shower earlier," he said without thinking.

Her outraged look confirmed that he shouldn't have reminded her that he'd been watching her in her apartment. Another stupid move on his part.

With a clenched jaw, she glowered at him. "I feel dirty."

Great! How had he screwed this situation up so quickly? It had taken him all of an hour to turn his charge against him. That had to be a record, even for him.

But every time Leila had voiced a protest or asked another question, he'd felt like he had to defend his actions. Her combative nature was riling him up, and he felt unable to keep his temper in check when around her. It had started when she'd told him in the car not to touch her. Despite the fact that he deserved her rejection, her words had hurt him. He should have been able to let them wash over him like an insignificant wave, but her words had struck him as hard as if she had slapped him in the face.

"Fine. Take a shower."

As she slid past him, the aroma of her skin drifted into his nose. She felt dirty? He was in the right mood to show her what feeling dirty really meant. He clenched his fists so he couldn't reach for her and throw her onto the nearest flat surface to show her what he called dirty.

When she opened the door to the bathroom, remorse for his behavior filled him. He wasn't angry at her, but at himself, at his lack of control when it came to her.

"Leila, please, I'm—"

She slammed the door without listening. The click that followed confirmed that she had locked the door. Aiden let himself fall onto the bed, lacing his fingers behind his head as he stared at the ceiling. He dreaded the night ahead of him, a night he had to spend alone with Leila. As if being near her wasn't bad enough. No, if he wanted to make sure she was fully cloaked while he got a few hours of shuteye himself, he would have to keep her in his arms all night. During sleep, a Stealth Guardian's power to cloak with his mind ceased to function, and only his ability to cloak with his touch remained.

He hadn't even broached that subject with her yet. Because he could already guess her reaction. She'd fight him tooth and nail, question the necessity of it, the science behind it, the ins and outs of how it worked. Hell, he wasn't in the mood to give a lecture on the special powers of Stealth Guardians. In fact, he should tell her as little as possible. It was bad enough that he'd had to tell her about the demons and show her his power of walking through solid objects.

Anything else, and he might as well give her a tour of their compound and show her how the portals worked.

Fuck, he wasn't the right person for this job. Everything about this assignment was wrong. He was emotionally involved, and that was never a good thing. His conscience dictated that he hand the assignment over to somebody else who would deal with Leila in a more professional manner than he was capable of. She was getting to him, stirring a part of him that he'd rather leave hidden. She would be safer with somebody else. He was too distracted by his desire for her to be a good bodyguard. Eventually, he'd make a mistake. And then what? Would Leila have to pay the ultimate price for his failure? It was unacceptable. It was better if he took himself off this assignment and made sure she had a protector who wasn't as conflicted as he. Given the state he was in right now, he couldn't trust himself.

He pulled out his cell. When the call connected, Aiden took a deep breath. "Father, we need to talk."

"Aiden," his father replied in surprise. "I thought you were on your assignment."

"I am. That's what we need to talk about. I'm not the right man for this." Never before had he shied away from a challenge, but this was different.

"Aiden, you know we have faith in you. You were trained for this," his father's calm voice came through the line.

Trying to convince his father to let him off the hook wouldn't be easy. He would have to emphasize his shortcomings. "I lost a charge only a few days ago. I shouldn't be the one to protect this charge. This case is too important."

"Unfortunately, sometimes bad things happen. The demons are getting stronger. All reports indicate it. Even the best among us have lost charges, more than usual. Not even your near-perfect record could be upheld. That's why you need this now. You haven't had to deal with failure in a very long time. If you don't battle it now, it will grow in your mind and hinder you forever. You can't allow it to fester like an infected wound."

Replaying his last assignment in his mind, Aiden couldn't detect any obvious mistakes he may have made. As much as he blamed himself for his failure, there was nothing he would have done differently, except to kill Sarah earlier before she killed the innocent child.

"You don't understand." And how could his father really know what was going on inside him? That he couldn't protect Leila like he was supposed to because he wanted her the way the desert craved water.

"I'm sorry for your loss, Aiden. I know what it feels like to lose a charge. We've all been there, but you'll get past this. We've survived much worse."

Aiden shook his head, wanting to repress the bad memories that resurfaced at his father's words. He didn't want to be reminded of his greatest failure. "It would be a more efficient use of my time to give this charge to somebody else and let me look for Hamish."

"We'll handle Hamish. You concentrate on your job!" The order was clear.

Aiden reared up from his position on the bed, frustration surging. "Please reconsider."

There was a short pause, and he only heard his father's breathing. "What is this really about?"

Aiden rubbed his eyes with his free hand. "I don't think I can protect her." Not when lust controlled him like this. A woman like Leila deserved better.

"Are you saying you don't *want* to protect her?" his father shot back.

"Yes... no... I don't know. What I mean is, what if I fail like I have before? Or worse, what if can't do what needs to be done because I..." His voice trailed off. He couldn't tell his father. He couldn't admit to him that there was something going on inside him that bothered him. That it appeared as if *rasen* had taken hold of him and was making him unpredictable.

"You're questioning the council's decision to assign you to this case? Are you telling me that we were wrong to trust you with this?"

"Circumstances change."

"And what circumstances are those, Aiden?"

"You heard me earlier: I lost a charge. She killed an innocent child before I eliminated her. If I'd killed her earlier, it wouldn't have happened. We knew she was weak and susceptible to the demons' influence. We knew how much they wanted her for her skills. You should have voted to eliminate Sarah, not to protect her. Some humans are just not worth protecting. They represent too much danger. They'll turn against us and their own kind. They can be seduced too easily."

And they could do things that put Stealth Guardians in danger. It had happened before. But it was only half the truth, the other half, he couldn't confess to his father.

"That's nothing new. We've always known about the risks. So, why are you making this an issue now?"

Aiden shot up from the bed and paced to the window. "I'm out there every day. I see what's going on. You know yourself what's been happening at all compounds. More charges are being lost. The demons are getting stronger. I don't think we have the luxury of preserving one human's life if it means jeopardizing millions because of it. We have to adjust our thinking to that."

Yet even as he said it, he knew if he were given the order to kill Leila, he wouldn't be able to execute it. And that was the reason why he had to hand this assignment over to somebody else.

"You have to give humans a chance. Can they never redeem themselves in your eyes? Every life it worth saving," his father claimed.

Before Aiden could stop himself, the words were out. "So was Julia's."

At the other end of the line, his father pulled in an audible breath. "Don't bring your sister into this. This is not about her."

"It is. It's always been about her. Nothing has changed." Julia would be alive today if he hadn't failed. If he'd acted earlier. If he hadn't hesitated in killing his charge. He had his sister's blood on his hands. It still stained his skin even after all these years. And it haunted him day and night.

"Then I suggest you make an effort to change. It's time to move on and let the past lie where it belongs. We all grieved, but you're the only one who's never closed this chapter."

"And how do you expect me to move on? I'm responsible for her death." Aiden felt old pain well up in his chest. "I know in my gut that I'll fail her."

There was a moment of silence on the other end before his father spoke again. "Fail Julia or fail your charge?" His father sighed. "I think this assignment is exactly what you need. Don't fight it. Whatever your gut is telling you, follow your instincts. You won't fail her—neither of them."

Aiden opened his mouth to ask his father what he meant, but didn't get a chance.

"Good night, son."

The click in the line confirmed that his father had disconnected the call.

Why had he not had the guts to tell his father outright that he couldn't remain impartial when it came to Leila? Was it because deep down he didn't want to be pulled off this assignment after all? That he wanted to continue to protect her because he wanted to be near her? How would he make it through this night, let alone the assignment, knowing what his body craved yet his code of ethics forbade?

Like an electric shock, a thought suddenly jolted him. Lifting his head, he listened. The shower was still running. With a jolt, he moved to the bathroom door. He'd been to this motel before. It was old and run down, but it served its purpose. However, the water supply in this dive left much to be desired. Aiden glanced at his watch. She'd been in the shower for half an hour. There couldn't possibly be any hot water left.

"Leila." He knocked to be heard over the running water. "Are you okay?"

There was no reply. He strained to hear whether she might be crying, but apart from the sound of the water, his sensitive hearing couldn't discern any other noises.

"Leila!" he called out again.

What if she had hurt herself? Or had she overheard his conversation with his father? Damn it, he had to get in there and make sure she was okay. She'd probably be pissed at him for barging in on her, but he could live with that.

He passed through the door and stepped into the steam-filled room. His eyes adjusted instantly and homed in on the window above the toilet. It was open.

"Stupid, stupid, stupid!" he cursed himself and rushed out of the empty bathroom.

He'd fallen for the oldest trick in the book. And he only had himself to blame.

12

Leila had noticed a sign for a subway station when Aiden had driven up to the hotel. Her handbag clutched tightly to her body, her limbs shaking from the cold night air, she ran, or rather limped, toward the entrance as fast as her aching ankle allowed. She fumbled for some quarters and dropped them into the ticket machine. The clinking of the coins as they made their way through the machine echoed in the empty entrance area.

She cast a look over her shoulder, scanning her surroundings, hoping that Aiden was still at the motel, thinking she was in the shower.

Her eyes tried to penetrate the dark but couldn't. She saw nobody and hoped she was alone.

A coin dropped from her trembling fingers. She bent to retrieve it and inserted it into the slot. In the distance she heard a voice over the loudspeaker.

"Next inbound train in one minute. Platform two."

Leila hit the 'purchase ticket' button, but nothing happened. Frantically, she pressed the button again, but no ticket emerged from the slot.

"Shit, shit, shit!" she cursed.

Footsteps behind her made her reach into her bag and grip the can of mace she still kept there as she spun on her heel, ready to defend herself. Her heart beat into her throat, choking off the air to breathe when she saw a dark figure approach. As soon as the light from the station engulfed him, she released a shaky breath.

A tall teenager dressed in a hoodie and worn jeans, his posture slouching, entered the ticket area. He glanced at her before approaching the turnstile, then jumped over it, not even checking if a station clerk was watching or not.

As he sauntered toward the stairs, she focused her attention back on the machine. She'd put the correct amount of coins in, so why wasn't that damn thing spitting out her ticket? Angrily, she hit her foot against it, hoping to un-jam the darn machine.

Suddenly, all the coins she'd inserted landed in the little receptacle for change.

"Yo!" a deep voice behind her jolted her.

Leila pulled the can of mace from her bag in a flash and whirled around to her would-be attacker. She'd never felt so jumpy in her entire life.

A tall black guy the size of a football player took a deliberate step back, lifting his hands in the process. "Hey, sis, no harm." He motioned his head toward the machine behind her. "Fuckin' thing's broken again. Ride's free tonight."

Then he slowly walked toward the turnstile, watching her as he did so.

Leila lowered her can of mace, now breathing again, and watched him as he too jumped over it.

"Train approaching on platform two," the voice from the loudspeaker announced.

"Uh, screw it," she mumbled to herself and rushed to the gate, lifting herself over it much less elegantly than the guy before her had. She had no time to lose. If she didn't catch this train, who knew when the next one was due. For all she knew, it could be the last one for the night.

She ran down the stairs, using the handrail to keep the weight off her injured foot, and saw the train that had already opened its doors.

"Doors closing," the next announcement sounded.

"Hold it!" she screamed and ran as fast as she could, ignoring the pain shooting up her leg now.

Panicked, she saw the doors closing and lunged for them. A hand emerged from the train, pushing between the closing doors. Shrill beeps sounded as the doors reopened.

Leila hurtled inside, past the black guy who'd held the door open for her, the same who'd told her the machine was broken. As she took a steadying breath, she turned her head to him. "Thank you."

He simply nodded. "No prob."

She slunk into a seat next to the door, realizing only now that her heart was beating like a jackhammer and her breath had once more deserted her. But she'd made it, she acknowledged with relief. Now that she was on the train, she was safe.

For a few moments she relaxed and allowed the rumbling sounds of the train to lull her into a sense of security. The flickering lights as it changed tracks and moved from one tunnel to the next, felt almost soothing, comforting. It was something she knew, something familiar. Something so unlike what had happened tonight.

She wrapped her arms tightly around herself, trying to stop her body from trembling. Maybe she'd been in shock all this time, but suddenly things were hitting home: Aiden, a stranger, had followed her home and broken into her apartment. He'd watched her doing... that... and then kidnapped her. The things he'd told her about demons and guardians, supernatural beings and immortals seemed so surreal now, so totally unbelievable.

Yet, she couldn't deny that she'd seen him pass through the door of her bedroom and through the car. But that didn't mean that anything he'd told her was the truth. He could be a demon—the very thing he pretended to warn her of. She didn't know what to think anymore. If he was really an immortal bodyguard as he claimed, why hadn't he said so when they'd first met? Why had he snuck into her apartment in the middle of the night? Yet at the same time, she had to admit that he hadn't harmed her even though he'd had plenty of occasions.

But did that mean she could trust him? Or was it simply a ploy to gain her trust? And he was playing dirty, using the sexual attraction that sizzled between them to slip past her defenses.

Her cheeks still burned at the thought of him watching her. Kissing her. Oh, God, and she'd been so numb from the shock of having escaped her burning apartment that she'd responded to him like a common slut. This wasn't her. She wasn't like that: wanton, lusty, reckless. But this man, this stranger, had turned her into a person she didn't recognize. A person she didn't want to be.

Liar, a tiny voice in her head whispered. *You liked it.*

She tried to protest, but all strength seemed to have drained from her tired body and mind. Defeated, she lowered her head into her hands, trying to hide from the world, and more so from herself.

By the time she looked up a few minutes later, the train was approaching her stop. She was about to get up when she realized one thing: she couldn't get off here. Her apartment was in cinders, and there was no way she could stay there tonight. She slumped back in her seat. Where could she hide for tonight?

Her parents' home was on the outskirts of town, and there was no train this late at night. Without a car, she couldn't get there, not tonight anyway. It only left one place for her to hide out, a place with good security: her office.

Even though she realized that Aiden could walk through walls and doors, it wouldn't help him: Max, the security guard in the lobby of Inter Pharma would see him. There was no way Aiden could get past him, not with the security cameras that were mounted in every corridor. At least for tonight, she'd be safe. Tomorrow she would figure out what to do. Maybe after a few hours of sleep, her brain would function better, and she'd come up with a plan of how to proceed.

The police would think she was crazy if she told them about demons and immortals, and, who knew, they might just send her for psychiatric evaluation if she dished up a story like that. No, she had to get her story straight first before she went to the police and made a report.

Her hands played nervously with the strap of her handbag while the train proceeded to the next station, then another one. Finally, after what seemed like an eternity, it approached her stop.

She was the only one exiting the train. Paranoid that someone would follow her, she kept her hand around the can of mace as she left the station and limped the five long blocks toward Inter Pharma. The streets were deserted. Even the Irish pub was now closed. Leila hurried along.

When she spotted the light in the lobby of her building, she let out a sigh of relief. Through the glass walls, she saw Max sitting behind his desk, his eyes scanning the monitors in front of him.

She ran toward the door. Despite the security clearance she had, all external doors were locked after 9pm, and there was no other way in other than being let in by the security guard.

"Max," she called out as she reached the glass door and knocked.

Max's head spun to look at her, a surprised expression on his face. Then he smiled and got up.

A moment later he unlocked the door and motioned her inside, locking it behind her.

"Hey, Dr. Cruickshank. Some emergency?"

She forced a sweet smile onto her lips. "No, no, Max. But you know me. I couldn't sleep and I was just thinking about one of the experiments I was working on, so I figured, I'd come in and look at some of the data."

She knew he wouldn't find it too strange for her to show up so late. He knew she was a workaholic.

He shook his head in a slight reprimand. "You're working too hard. Mr. Patten better be giving you some raise soon. That man really doesn't know what he's got in you."

"I really don't mind. I love my work."

"Well, it's one thing loving your work, it's another having some time off."

"Once this part of the research project is done, I'll take some time off, not to worry," she pacified him and spied behind her, scanning the darkness beyond the building.

"If you say so."

"I'll just be going up to the lab. Oh, and Max, nobody's been here tonight looking for me, right?"

He gave her a confused look. "Looking for you? Why would somebody be looking for you?"

"Oh, nothing... Anyway, just wanted to make sure I'm not disturbed while I'm working," she waffled.

"No problem."

Relieved, she walked toward the elevator and stepped inside. By the time she reached the door to her lab, she felt better already. Max would make sure nobody could enter the building. Even if Aiden walked through the walls out of view of the lobby, in order to get to her lab, he would have to pass by several security cameras. Max would spot him on the monitors and activate the intruder alarm. The police would be summoned instantly. For tonight, she would be safe. She could sleep on the old couch in her little office just off the lab.

She reached for the keys in her handbag, grateful that she'd had the presence of mind to grab it when she'd had to flee from her burning apartment. Instinctively, her hand went to the pocket of her jeans where her pendant made a small bulge. Her research was safe. That was all that mattered. She pulled the necklace from her pocket and put it around her neck. When she felt the pendant against her skin again, a sense of relief flooded her.

As soon as she'd unlocked the door, she slipped into the dark lab. Only when she let the door snap in behind her, did she reach for the light switch, flipping it. The room was instantly bathed in the harsh tones of fluorescent light.

She took a step farther into the room and glanced around. Her gaze fell onto her work bench where her laptop lay—the lid was open. She was sure she'd closed it before leaving earlier tonight.

With an odd sense of foreboding in her gut, she approached the bench and looked at the monitor. On a black screen the curser flashed ominously. All it said was 'c:/'.

Her heart sank.

"Oh God, no!" she whispered to herself, knowing all too well what the flashing curser meant. But she didn't want to believe it.

She hit the enter key, but all the computer did was spit out another 'c:/'. And another. Sliding onto her chair, her fingers flew over the keyboard, entering all commands she was familiar with to try to reboot the system. Nothing worked.

It confirmed her suspicion: somebody had tried to access the data on her encrypted laptop, and the security system on it had initiated the self-destruct sequence and wiped the hard drive clean. Not a single byte of data was left on it.

She couldn't help but suspect that this incident was connected to the events earlier in the evening: the car, which had nearly swiped her, her burning apartment, the kidnapping. Somebody was trying to get at her research. There was no other explanation for it.

Had Aiden been sent by a rival pharmaceutical company to steal her data? Was that what this was all about?

She had to have certainty about it. Shooting up from her chair, she ran toward her office. If somebody had tinkered with her safe, then she would know for sure that this was what they were after, whoever *they* were.

"Demons, my ass," she mumbled. "More like industry spies!"

Leila threw the door to her office open and turned to her left, where her safe was built into the wall. She stopped in her tracks. The door to the safe was wide open.

She took a tentative step toward it. It didn't look as if anybody had broken the locking device or used explosives, no, the safe had simply been opened. And the only other person who could do that was Patten, her boss.

Why?

Had he been paid off by somebody to steal her data for another company? She shook her head, trying to shake off the disappointment that rose inside her. Her hand reached toward the safe as she took another step. Her foot stepped on something, making her move back instinctively.

She lowered her gaze and stared at the floor.

At her feet, a thumb lay in a small pool of blood, discarded like a useless tool.

Her mouth opened for a scream, but it never left her throat: a hand clamped over her lips to prevent her from giving voice to her panic.

13

Aiden held his palm over Leila's mouth, making sure she wouldn't scream. His other arm snaked around her waist, pulling her tightly against him.

It hadn't been hard to find her. She'd really had only two options: her apartment or her lab. Sure, she could have gone to any hotel, but knowing what he knew about her life, what he'd read in her file, he guessed she would choose a familiar place, somewhere where she felt safe. He'd figured she'd choose the lab for obvious reasons. One being that her apartment was uninhabitable right now, the other that she deemed her office to be safe from intruders. It wasn't.

He'd had no problem sneaking past the security guard. In his cloaked state, he was invisible to the unsuspecting man.

Aiden moved his mouth to Leila's ear, a strand of her hair brushing his cheek in the process. "Quiet, Leila."

He felt her body jolt at the realization that it was he who was keeping her captive once more. A muffled word he didn't catch bounced against his palm. Her warm breath nearly torched him, sending a hot flame into his groin.

"That's right, it's me. It was very stupid of you to run away. Didn't I tell you I'd protect you?" He felt himself getting angry again. "Will you remain quiet if I take my hand off your mouth now?"

She moved her head up and down in agreement.

Slowly he lifted his hand and turned her toward him in the same instance. Her lips instantly parted, her throat tightening. Clearly, she wasn't going to comply with his wishes. There was only one thing he could do now.

With a low curse, he yanked her flush against him and slid his lips over hers, capturing her mouth in a searing kiss, one he'd been craving all night.

Shit, this wasn't how this was supposed to play out. All he should do was to collect her insolent ass and haul her back to a safe place, watching her like a hawk. And what was he doing, idiot that he was? Kissing her!

And it was no ordinary kiss. He devoured her mouth, plundered her delicious cavern, tangled with her reluctant tongue until a sound—part sob, part sigh—escaped her. Still, he didn't stop. On the contrary, the little sound she'd made spurred him on even further, made him thread his fingers through her hair to hold her tighter to him. All the while her fists beat against his shoulders in a futile attempt to get him to stop.

Sliding his other hand to the sweet curve of her ass and palming it, he pressed her against his growing erection. He wanted to punish her for escaping him. Maybe this would teach her to listen to him. Because a charge who didn't listen to her bodyguard was as good as dead. And that was a prospect he didn't relish. At the thought of Leila been hurt, or worse, dead, an icy-cold hand clamped around his heart, squeezing the life out of him. He'd only once before felt like that: when Julia had died. He couldn't allow this to happen again. He had to find a way so Leila would trust him.

What if they'd met under other circumstances? Would she mold her sinful body to his, press her soft curves into his hard muscles with abandon as if they were lovers? The thought ricocheted in his mind. Could he ever make her understand him to the point where such a thing was possible?

Aiden released her, albeit reluctantly.

Leila glared at him, gasping for air. Her lips looked thoroughly kissed. Her eyes darted past him toward the door that he blocked, thoughts of escape so clearly etched in her face as if he were reading her mind.

"How dare you? How did you get in here?" Her clipped tone underscored her anger, and the way she wiped her lips with the back of her hand was so deliberate he knew the gesture was meant to tell him that his physical attention wasn't wanted.

"The way I always do, through the walls."

"The security guard will have seen you on the cameras. He will have alerted the police already."

"He didn't see me."

She took a slow step back and bumped against the open safe door behind her. His eyes were instantly drawn to the dark interior. He pointed to it. "What happened here?"

"Why don't you tell me?" she spat. "You opened the safe. You did this!"

He took an instinctive step in her direction, making her shrink back. "And when would I have done that, Leila? I was with you all night. You had an almost half hour head start on me. So tell me, how I could have broken into your lab when I arrived after you."

Her forehead furrowed as she pulled her lower lip between her teeth, chewing on it. And darn it, if that wasn't a gesture that made him want to pull her back into his embrace and assure her that everything was alright.

"Why should I believe you?"

Again her eyes darted past him. If she was still hoping for the police or the security guard to arrive, he'd have to sorely disappoint her.

"Because you're an intelligent woman." Maybe if he appealed to her intellect, he would get somewhere. "If you look at it logically, you'll see that it's impossible. I was with you the entire time until you went to take a shower in the motel." He scoffed. "Well, I guess I fell for that old trick. Nevertheless, do you really think I would have left you alone at the motel while I believed you were in the shower?" He locked eyes with her.

For a few seconds she stared at him, then she finally shook her head.

"Then who did this, if not you?" She pointed to the floor.

Aiden followed her outstretched finger and saw what she was looking at. On the floor in front of the safe lay a human thumb, a tiny pool of blood around it. He shot her a confused look. "What the fuck?"

Tears brimmed in her eyes now. She still pointed at the bloody human thumb, her voice trembling as she answered, "The only way to open the safe is with a thumb print, either mine..." Her voice broke.

Instinctively his eyes searched her hands even though he knew what he'd find: flawless, perfect fingers.

"Whose thumb?" he urged.

She swallowed hard. "Mr. Patten's. My boss. He's the only other person who could have opened..." A solitary tear rolled down her cheek. "Tell me you didn't do this. Tell me I'm not in the clutches of a madman," she begged through the sobs that now started.

He lifted her head with his thumb and forefinger. "I didn't do this. You have to believe me."

He fought against the urge to pull her into his embrace. There was no time for that now. He glanced past her into the safe. "The safe is empty. What do you normally keep in it?"

Leila hesitated, chewing on her lip once more. "A backup drive of my research data."

A curse left his lips. "The Alzheimer's drug?"

Her head shot up, her eyes widening. "How do you—?"

She sidestepped him, trying to get to her desk, clearly in order to bring distance between them.

"It doesn't matter. Was it the Alzheimer's drug?"

Her eyes darted to the door, hope that rescue was on its way fading in them. Reluctantly, she nodded.

"Fuck!" He ran a shaky hand through his hair. He'd been too late. "Now the demons have it. Please tell me the data alone won't help them recreate the drug." If it was all they needed, then he'd failed again.

"The demons?"

Was she finally starting to believe him? He hoped so.

"Why do they want my research? Why?"

He saw the horror in her eyes. "They need it to cement their power over humans. It'll help them gain the upper hand. The drug you've been working on will help them influence humans and pull them to their side."

"Oh God." Then she stared back at the safe. "It wasn't in there," she murmured so softly he almost didn't hear her. She sounded confused.

Maybe the entire night had been too much for her. After all, she was a human, and there was only so much they could take before they cracked. He should make allowances for that.

He gestured toward the open safe. "Well of course not, it's empty, they took it. The demons took it."

Leila shook her head. "It wasn't in there. The disk."

He focused his attention back on her words. "What do you mean?"

"A couple of days ago, I took it out and erased it."

Could he trust his ears? "You what?"

Her ocean blue eyes looked up at him, wide, beautiful, still glistening with tears. "I destroyed the backup drive. I had a strange feeling... I just felt it wasn't safe there. So I took it and erased the data."

"Where is the original data?" If this was only the backup, there had to be another drive. Had they gotten to that one instead when they'd realized that the safe was empty? If it was still here somewhere, there was only one thing to do now that the demons had gotten brazen enough to attack outright.

"Show me where it is. We'll have to destroy it."

~ ~ ~

Leila's heart stopped beating for a moment. "Destroy?"

She shook her head in disbelief. He couldn't mean that. She'd devoted years of her life to this and couldn't simply wipe out her work as if it had never existed.

When she'd seen genuine shock in his eyes the moment she'd told him that a backup drive with her data was kept in the safe, she'd realized that he wasn't the one who'd broken it open. But the revelation that he wanted to destroy her data didn't make the situation any better.

"You don't understand. This is my research. I'm going to cure Alzheimer's."

And she would get her parents back. They would have a chance to recover enough of their faculties to remember that they loved her and each other.

Aiden gripped her shoulders tightly. His chocolate-brown eyes bored into her. "I understand. But this is more important."

More important than curing a terrible disease? "No!" She shook off his hands and stepped back. He couldn't be serious. Instinctively, her hand shot up, wanting to touch her pendant. She forced it back down to her side, hoping not to have drawn attention to it. Protecting the last copy of her research data was vital now, because not only did the demons want it—she believed that much now—Aiden wanted to destroy it.

"If this drug is brought to market, it will open the minds of humans and make them more susceptible to the influence of demons. It'll be child's play for them to infiltrate their minds, play with them, manipulate them. Don't you see? Your drug will cause this. We can't allow this to happen."

Leila shivered at the determination in his voice. He wouldn't listen to her arguments. There was only one thing she could do: lie.

She nodded, pretending that she agreed with his reasoning. She'd given up hope that Max would come to rescue her. "The only other copy is on my encrypted laptop." She pointed to the door. "In the lab."

Aiden turned, and she followed him.

"Where?" he asked.

She passed him and went to her bench where only minutes earlier she'd confirmed that her laptop had been wiped clean. All she needed now were some acting skills to convince him that the last set of research data was destroyed, too. Maybe then he would leave her alone, thinking there was nothing else the demons could take. And she would get her life back.

"Oh no!" she cried out, hoping she sounded convincing.

She let herself fall into the chair and stared at the monitor where the ominous 'c:/' still pulsed in silence.

"What's wrong?"

She looked up at him, forcing tears to her eyes. "They tried to hack into my laptop."

"Shit!" he cursed. "Did they get in?"

Shaking her head, she continued her charade. "No, but they activated the self-destruct feature."

"What do you mean?" he asked, looking over her shoulder, hovering far too closely.

"I had a security program on my laptop. If anybody tried to access my data and there were more than two failed login attempts, the program would initiate, wiping the entire hard drive clean."

"You mean there's no data left on the computer?"

She shook her head. "None." Feeling that she should show despair about the loss of her research, she turned her face away and let out a sob. It's wasn't too hard to produce. The thought of the bloody thumb on the floor in her office gave her reason enough to cry her eyes out. It struck her out of nowhere: the pain her boss must have suffered.

"Oh, God! Patten. I must find him. He needs a doctor. Oh, God, those bastards!"

She jumped up and almost bumped into Aiden, who instantly steadied her with a hand on her hip.

"Where's his office?"

"On the eighth floor."

"Let's go," he ordered.

As they rushed to the door and opened it, a loud alarm sounded from the hallway. Strobe lights flashed.

Aiden tossed her a questioning look.

"They're locking down the building." And she could guess what that meant.

14

Aiden by her side, Leila raced toward the elevator, hitting the call button impatiently.

"Come on, come on," she coaxed it, shifting from one leg to the other, her concern for her own safety overshadowed by worries for her boss. She might have had a disagreement with him the last time they'd met, but that didn't mean she didn't care about his wellbeing. And she couldn't help but think that part of this was her fault.

Aiden grabbed her elbow, making her look at him. The grim expression on his face confirmed that he had the same suspicion as she and feared the worst. It didn't exactly calm her nerves.

A ping announced the arrival of the elevator. As soon as the doors opened, she squeezed inside quickly and hit the button for the eighth floor.

They didn't speak while the elevator ascended. Instead, Leila fixed her gaze on the display panel that showed their movement from floor to floor. It felt like it moved at a snail's pace. The local bus could have gotten them there faster.

"We should have taken the stairs," she muttered.

Then she felt Aiden's hand on her arm, squeezing it in reassurance. She glanced at him and noticed a flicker of compassion in them. It disappeared as quickly as it had appeared. Maybe she had simply seen what she wanted to see, even though she guessed the hard man next to her had no capacity for such emotion. Hell, he'd coldly demanded that she destroy her own research without as much as flinching. If somebody could do that, knowing he would deprive thousands if not millions of people of a cure for a devastating disease, what else was he capable of?

Leila let out a sigh of relief when the doors finally opened on the executive floor. She rushed out, heading for Patten's office. As she approached, she found the door wide open.

She stormed in, Aiden on her heels.

The room was lit, the fluorescent lights illuminating the space; the small lamp that normally stood on Patten's desk lay broken on the ground in front of it—next to Patten's body.

A choked cry tried to leave her throat but didn't quite make it. Her breath deserted her. But her feet carried her closer, almost as if some perverted part of her wanted to gorge itself on the sight. She needed to know how he'd died.

Leila stared at the lifeless form at her feet. Blood oozed from his neck, having soaked his shirt and tie. The wound looked straight and almost... perfect, as if the murderer knew what he was doing. Her gaze drifted to Patten's hands. And there, as if she needed a confirmation, a thumb was missing, cut from his right hand.

A sob worked its way up from her chest and past the lump in her throat that prevented her from speaking. She'd seen dead bodies before: in medical school, and during her time as a medical resident. But this was different. This wasn't clinical, this wasn't expected. This was a brutal crime.

All this so somebody could get to her research? Didn't that make it her fault?

Sounds from the corridor made her lift her head. Aiden's eyes bounced to the door, then back to her.

"Somebody's coming. Not a word, promise me, don't say a single word," he ordered.

She nodded automatically. As if she could say anything while she fought the bout of nausea that developed in her stomach as the metallic scent of blood drifted into her nostrils.

Aiden pulled her aside, away from the body, and she didn't have the strength to fight him this time. By now, somehow, her brain had figured out that he wouldn't hurt her, even though she knew she couldn't fully trust him—and could never tell him that a last copy of her research data still existed.

He pulled her closer to him as suddenly several people trampled into the room. The first one, she recognized instantly: Max. Behind him three other men barged in.

"Right here, Officer." Max pointed at Patten's body. "I was doing my rounds when I found him."

Police, she registered instantly, relieved that they had finally arrived.

As two of the men knelt down next to the body, the heavy set one Max had addressed, spoke. "Are you the only one in the building, Mr. Flanagan?"

Max shook his head. "No, Dr. Cruickshank is still working, too, actually... I should check on her in her lab, make sure she's alright."

Why would Max need to check in her lab when she was right here? Leila opened her mouth, wanting to speak up, but Aiden's hand clamped over her mouth to prevent her from talking. Before she could protest, his mouth was at her ear, his warm breath caressing her skin as he whispered to her so low she barely heard him.

"Don't make a sound. I'll explain later."

Confusion made her vocal cords constrict. Why didn't Max or the other people acknowledge her presence or the fact that Aiden was holding his hand over her mouth? Wouldn't that look suspicious to them? What kind of detectives were these people that they couldn't see what was right in front of them?

"Kowalski," one of the officers next to the body called out. "Looks like a clean cut through the throat. He was probably dead instantly."

"The forensics team should be here in a moment." Officer Kowalski's gaze swept the room, never pausing on the spot where Leila and Aiden stood, as if he didn't see them at all.

"Holy shit!" the other officer suddenly exclaimed. "Look at that." He pointed to Patten's hand.

Kowalski stepped closer. "Christ, the murderer cut off his thumb. What the—?" Then he turned to grace Max with a questioning look. "Do you know what that could mean?"

Max's face turned almost as white as a sheet as he clutched his stomach. Oh, God, if he started to puke, Leila wasn't sure she could tamp down her own nausea any longer.

"Oh, God, the safe. There's a safe in Dr. Cruickshank's o-o-office..." Max's voice stuttered to a halt.

Aiden's mouth was at her ear again. "Let's go. Now."

He yanked her toward the door, the brusque movement making her stumble over her feet.

"Did you hear that?" Kowalski asked.

"Hear what?" one of the officers replied.

Kowalski rubbed the back of his neck. "Nothing. So, you were saying something about a safe…"

Aiden guided her outside, the voices behind her drifting into the distance as they walked along the corridor.

"The stairs?" he whispered.

She pointed toward them. When they reached the door, he opened it and pushed her through, closing it silently behind them.

Numb with confusion, horror and nausea, she allowed him to drag her down the endless flights of stairs, the sound of her tennis shoes echoing in the stairwell. The sound was eerie and only added to her sense of devastation.

In the span of a few hours, her entire life had turned upside down: her apartment burned, her belief in the order of this world shaken, her research nearly destroyed, and her boss murdered. She didn't know if she could take any more. But somehow she knew this wasn't the end of it.

And why hadn't the police or Max seen her when she was right there in the same room with them? Why had they talked about her as if she wasn't even there? Something was wrong. Was she dreaming all this? Was she hallucinating?

Aiden pulled her toward the exit, pushing a door open, then another one, until the cold night air hit her.

Outside, police sirens blared and several police cars screeched to a halt, stopping next to the one that was already there. More police officers, some in plain clothes, some in uniform, jumped from their cars and headed for the building.

They all ignored her and Aiden and allowed them to pass when they should have stopped them, questioning them what they were doing there in the middle of the night.

"Why?" she mumbled.

Aiden dragged her around the next corner, then finally stopped walking and pulled her into the entrance to a coffeehouse.

She stared up at him. "Why didn't they stop us? Didn't… didn't they see us?"

He brushed a strand of hair from her face and pushed it behind her ear, a gesture so gentle, she must have dreamed it.

"I cloaked us. We were invisible to them."

"Invisible?" That was impossible. It was against the laws of physics. It couldn't be. "But—"

"It's one of the powers of Stealth Guardians. With our touch, we can make humans invisible to others. We use it to hide our charges from the demons. That's why they didn't see us. But they could still hear us. That's why I had to stop you from talking."

"It can't be. That's not possible. Physics... there's no such law... nobody can make..." This was too crazy, but it had to be true: neither Max nor the police had seen her. In fact, they'd looked through her as if she were indeed invisible. Besides, she'd seen Aiden walk through walls. Turning invisible wasn't any stranger than walking through solid objects.

"I was invisible," she whispered to herself.

He nodded. "Yes, that was the only way to get us out of there. We can't afford to get involved with the police. They won't be able to keep you safe. I will."

"They killed Patten."

"We have to leave, now." He cast a look in the direction they'd come from. "We're not safe here. The demons might still be in the vicinity."

For once, she had to agree with him. If these creatures were capable of killing Patten in cold blood and cutting off his thumb, they could do the same to her if they found her. Clearly, the security in the building wasn't enough to keep them out. Somehow they had gotten around Max, maybe the same way Aiden had. Now that she knew that he could both walk through walls and make himself invisible, there was no question how he'd gotten in. The demons could have done it the same way. She was better off going with him now. He was the only one who could keep her safe from the demons.

"Are you going to hurt me?"

His eyes widened and his lips parted. His breath ghosted against her skin. "Never."

15

Aiden's stomach twisted as he led Leila back to where he'd parked the car.

He'd told her that he would never hurt her. What a lie! If his mission demanded it, he would have to kill her. Should the council alter their votes and decide at a later time that Leila needed to be eliminated to keep humankind safe, he would have to follow their orders, knowing that if he didn't, two things would happen: he'd be punished for disobedience, and humans would be in a hell lot of trouble. The first consequence he could handle; the second one was unacceptable.

However, would he really do it? Would he be capable of driving his knife into her sweet body and draining the life from her, when what he really wanted was to see her live, laugh, breathe, and most of all, love? Would he waver in his duty in the end because she meant something to him?

He tried to shake off the thought, but it only pushed another problem to the forefront.

He'd told her that by touching her, he could make her invisible. He hadn't lied outright, but he'd simply omitted that he could also render her invisible just with the power of his mind. No touching would be necessary. He let her believe that if she wanted to remain invisible to the demons, she would have to allow him to touch her. He should correct his omission right now.

He hesitated for a moment. If she believed that she needed to remain physically close to him to be cloaked, at least it would be easier to protect her. She wouldn't bolt again. And it would save him from divulging even more information about Stealth Guardians than he wanted to give. But she had a right to know the truth. He would correct her assumption as soon as they were at a safe place where he had time to explain everything to her, lay out the ground rules, and answer the many questions she would surely have.

"Where are we going?" Her voice trembled as she rushed to keep up with his long strides.

"A safe house."

There were several in the city: inconspicuous and staffed with humans loyal to their cause, humans who owed them something.

Aiden pulled his smartphone from his jacket pocket and punched in a code. A moment later, an App loaded. He entered another code and allowed the system to calculate. While he knew each safe house in this city, since this was his home base, he didn't know if any of them were already taken. It would be against protocol to go to a safe house when another Stealth Guardian had already taken one of his charges there. It would only endanger others.

When a map pulled up, only one red dot blinked: the only safe house available to them. He swiped his finger over it to claim it and thus alert them to his imminent arrival. A bubble appeared on the screen, reading *Notify second?*. He pressed *yes*, then switched off the phone, so nobody else would be able to track him.

"Let's go."

He ushered Leila into the car, and she complied without protest. Maybe seeing her boss's dead body had finally driven reality home and made her understand that she had to trust him if she didn't want to meet with the same fate. Aiden turned on the engine and hit the gas, leaving Inter Pharma and the police in his rear view mirror.

"Tell me about the demons."

He tossed her a sideways glance, surprised at her question. He'd thought she would want to block out everything she'd seen and not talk about it. Apparently he'd been wrong about her. Maybe she was stronger than he suspected.

Easing the car into traffic, he thought briefly about where to start. "What do you want to know?"

"Everything: what they look like; their motivation, strengths, weaknesses, where they hide, how they operate—"

"Whoa, whoa, that's quite enough to start with. Besides, I don't have answers to all of your questions."

"How can you still hide things from me after all that..." She tossed a look toward the window, indicating what they'd left behind. "...that happened there?"

He looked at her, his heart rate spiking at her accusation. Why did he even care what she thought of him? Yet he couldn't deny that he did. He didn't want her to think of him as the enemy.

"I'm not. I don't have all the answers. Do you really think we wouldn't have taken the demons out if we knew where they were hiding?" He kept his voice calm despite the storm that was raging inside him.

"Oh." She wrapped her arms around her torso and looked straight ahead. "Then how about all the other stuff?"

He lifted a hand from the steering wheel and ran it through his hair. "They've been around since the Dark Days. Nobody knows how—"

"What are the Dark Days?" she interrupted.

He sighed. "I'm getting to it. Patience." When he looked at her, he noticed how tightly she clamped her arms over each other. Instantly, concern flooded his cells. "What's wrong?"

"What's wrong? Isn't that pretty clear? Demons killed my boss, and now they're after me. What if they catch up with us and see me? I'm not invisible anymore."

He opened his mouth to correct her, but before he could find the right words, she gave him a pleading look.

"Please." Her hand slid onto his thigh. "I need to stay invisible."

The warmth emanating from her palm seared his flesh. It felt good, way too good to admit now that she'd been cloaked all along, ever since he'd caught up with her at her lab. He should come clean right now and not leave her in this false belief, tell her that it wasn't necessary for her to touch him.

"Leila..."

"The demons..." she prompted.

Aiden cleared his throat, but he was unable to make a confession cross his lips. Was it *rasen* that made him react like this when he should tell her the truth about cloaking instead? Yet he couldn't. He admitted it to himself: he was weak. And when Leila touched him, he couldn't think clearly.

"The demons..." he answered instead, "they live in a place we call the Underworld for lack of a better term. They enter and exit it through portals, but we don't know whether these so-called portals are stationary or not, or where they are. We've only seen them when fighting demons, but we've never been able to go through one, and it seems that they vanish when the demons disappear."

He glanced at her, making sure he hadn't lost her with his talk. "Have you ever watched *Stargate*?"

She nodded.

"It's a little like that. The demons step through it, and they're gone. Presumably to their lair in the Underworld." He deliberately didn't mention a word about the fact that he and his kind also had portals. It was better that she didn't know about that. She would never get to see one, and there was such a thing as too much information.

"So they come out at will?"

"Pretty much."

"How do you fight them?"

"They're immune to human weapons," he continued and heard her mutter softly.

"Figures."

"However, the Stealth Guardians have weapons against them. Any weapon, blade, dagger, sword or the like that was forged in the Dark Days has the power to injure or kill a demon. It's the only thing they are vulnerable to."

From the corner of his eye he noticed her part her lips and instantly figured what she wanted to ask.

"The Dark Days? It was when Stealth Guardians came into existence. Our race is descended from a tribe in the Outer Hebrides, off the Scottish mainland. They were knights, warriors who protected their islands from intruders by shrouding them in a dense fog that no eyes could penetrate. Any would-be invaders simply sailed past them, never knowing there was any land in sight."

Leila sucked in an audible breath. "Is that what you do? Hide people in a cloud of fog?"

Aiden cast her a quick smile. "No. Our powers have evolved over the centuries. We no longer need the fog to hide ourselves or the people around us. We simply render them invisible."

And could do so selectively. If he chose, he could keep her cloaked from the demons, yet visible to humans.

"What do the demons want?"

He sighed. Leila was a veritable waterfall of questions. Knowing that she was a scientist, he should have guessed that would be the case. "What does anybody want? Power, domination, survival."

She made an impatient hand movement, dismissing his answer. "No, what do they really want? They must have an agenda, a mission."

"That *is* their mission: to gain power over humans, to seduce humans to do their bidding, to fuel the fear in this world, so they can feed off it."

"They feed off fear?"

"That's what makes them stronger. The more fear there is in this world, the stronger the demons. In times of war and uncertainty, they grow more powerful. During the Cuban Missile Crisis we had our hands full. Only the actions of a decisive leader were able to turn the situation around."

"The Stealth Guardians defused the crisis?" she asked.

"Only indirectly. We don't interfere in your world directly. We're only there to protect those humans who can in some way help their own race get stronger again. We protected several key figures in the US government, who were instrumental in reaching an agreement with the Russians to end the crisis. We made sure the demons had no influence over them."

"You mean you can somehow stop them?"

Aiden shook his head. It wasn't that easy. "All we can do is hide those humans who your race can't do without and help them achieve their purpose in life, whether that is to act as a peace keeper, a brilliant inventor, or a scientist. But the rest is up to the humans. We can only guide them on the right path; we can't force them to stay on it."

He glanced at her. Their gazes clashed, and he noticed that realization had suddenly sunk in.

"What happens when the human you're protecting can't fight off the influence of the demons?"

Aiden pressed his lips together. He hadn't expected her to ask him this question. And he wasn't prepared to answer it.

"Tell me. What happens to those who do what the demons want?"

Her eyes drilled into him, and he knew she wouldn't rest until he gave her an answer. And for once, he couldn't lie.

"We are forced to eliminate them."

Before they kill one of our own, he wanted to add. Like they'd killed his sister. But he couldn't confide this in Leila. And he shouldn't want to feel this need to explain his reasoning to her. But for some inexplicable reason, he wanted her to understand why he had to do what he had to do. And he didn't like that feeling of vulnerability it evoked in him.

16

Leila's heart was still beating out of control when Aiden pulled the car to a stop. His words rang in her ears. The determination in his voice had shocked her to the core. Even if there were things she couldn't quite believe yet, she recognized the truth in those words. *Eliminate* he'd said, when she knew he meant *kill*. Such a clinical, cold way of saying it, as if a life meant nothing to him. Maybe it didn't.

After everything he'd told her about the demons, she understood how dangerous they were, and that it was up to her to fight them should they ever find her. Knowing what a coward she was and that she would lose any fight with the demons in two seconds flat, one thing became more important than anything: they could never be allowed to find her. If that meant that she had to remain invisible until this threat had passed and they lost interest in her, then she would do exactly that. Even if it meant tethering herself to a Stealth Guardian who she couldn't trust either. A Stealth Guardian toward whom she felt an inexplicable attraction, despite the danger he represented.

"We're here," Aiden announced and pulled out his cell phone to punch something into it.

A loud humming sound made her snap her eyes to the area ahead of them. Light started to emerge as a garage door lifted in front of them. The car edged forward and slid into one of the spots lining the far wall.

"Let's go," he ordered and jumped from the car, severing their contact.

Odd, she'd still had her hand on his thigh, and it had felt almost like a natural extension of her own body. It had calmed her at the same time as it had excited her.

Quickly, she alighted from the car and went around it to Aiden's side. But he was already walking toward the open garage door. She caught up with him and grabbed his arm.

He whirled his head to her, glancing at her hand that held onto his forearm. His eyes blazed at her, making her stumble over her own feet. When he caught her, both his hands dug into her biceps. The heat in his eyes made her feel flushed despite the cool night air that touched her skin.

"What is it?" Worry colored his voice.

"I... I," she stammered, then swallowed away her fear. She wasn't too proud to beg. Anything to be safe. "Please, you have to keep me invisible."

Slowly his features softened and the grip on her arms loosened. His hands stroked down her arms, his movements deliberate and steady. A shiver ran down her spine. She knew what he did was only to calm her, but that didn't stop her from perceiving his touch as sensual, as caressing.

She closed her eyes, unable to withstand his intense gaze any longer. It only intensified his scent that wrapped around her like a protective cocoon. Or maybe it was simply what it felt like to be invisible: hot, protected, aware of everything around her. Earlier, when they'd been at Inter Pharma, she'd been in shock and unable to understand what was happening to her. Even in the car when she'd put her hand on his thigh to remain cloaked, she had concentrated more on his words than on the effect his body had on her.

But now... now all distractions were gone, pushed into the distance, and all she felt was his presence. The power that danced on his skin, the strength that oozed from his muscles, and the heat that radiated outward.

With a sigh, she lifted her lids, her gaze colliding with his.

His face was only inches from hers, his lips parted, his breath bouncing against hers. Nervously, she licked her lower lip and noticed his eyes home in on her action. Oh, God, if he tried to kiss her now, she wouldn't be able to resist him. On the contrary, she would press her body against him shamelessly, begging him to take her. It would help her forget everything she'd been through, forget the danger she was in, even if it was only for a short time.

"We have to go inside," he suddenly said and stepped back, taking her hand into his at the same time.

In a daze, she followed him out of the garage, which he closed behind them. As they rounded the corner, she looked down the street. Yellow, orange, and red neon signs flickered on nearly each building. Her eyes adjusted, reading the signs.

Her feet froze. "This is the red light district." Sign after sign advertised personal services: *girls* they read, or *massage*; she even saw one that advertised *nude girls*.

Aiden shrugged and pulled her along. "I'm aware of that."

As they walked past a slutty looking woman—clearly a hooker—Leila instinctively made a wide berth around her. The woman gave her a lascivious smile, looking her up and down.

"How about a date?"

Leila gave her a shocked stare, surprised at being propositioned.

The whore grinned as if she enjoyed her discomfort. "A threesome then, honey? Fifty bucks and I'll eat your pussy while your man fucks me from behind."

Leila's chin dropped at the open taunt. She'd never been so speechless in her entire life.

"Maybe some other time," Aiden answered and pulled her away.

Leila found her voice again. "Oh, my God! I can't believe you said that." Was he really considering such an outrageous act?

"That's what you get for staring," he chuckled at her side.

Was he suggesting she had provoked the hooker's offer? "I didn't—"

"I'm afraid you did. And that's exactly why she teased you." He paused and gave her a sideways glance.

That's when she realized something.

"Oh, no!" How could they even see her? A shot of adrenaline bolted through her body, making her heart beat into her throat. "Why am I not invisible?"

"Relax. You're still invisible to the demons. But I chose to let us be seen by humans."

"You can do that?" Her pulse steadied a little.

"Yes."

"But why? Wouldn't it be safer if nobody saw us?"

"It takes a lot of energy to cloak us both from humans and demons. I prefer to conserve mine when there's no absolute need."

Well, it appeared even an immortal had his limitations. "But what will the demons see then?"

He shrugged. "Simply a hooker talking to herself."

"Oh."

A moment later, they came to a stop in front of a three-story building. Leila looked at the neon sign in the window. *Thai Massage* it advertised.

"What are we doing here?"

"It's our safe house."

He had to be kidding.

"We're saying here for the night."

The door opened and a woman who looked like she was in her sixties appeared. No, Leila corrected herself, a *madam* appeared. Wasn't that what the owners of these kind of establishments called themselves? Because for sure, this woman was past her prime. Maybe fifteen years ago she'd still worked as a hooker, but who would want her now? Leila chastised herself for her bitchy thoughts, writing them off to her own weariness. She needed to sleep, to rest, and to forget what had happened tonight.

"Come," the woman simply said, and ushered them into the house.

Inside, it was surprisingly clean and... homey. Leila let her eyes wander as the woman led them up to the second floor past a long row of doors with numbers on them. She shuddered at the thought of what was going on behind those doors. There was no shame in admitting to herself that she'd led a somewhat sheltered life, far away from the filth and vice of human excesses.

She'd never been inside a brothel, hell, she'd never been in this part of town before, and she hoped that after tonight, she would never have to come back to this place. Her only consolation was that here the chances of meeting anybody she knew were nil. At least, she would never have to explain this to anybody.

The corridor wound around several times as if they were entering a maze, the changing Asian artwork on the walls the only indication that they weren't walking in circles. Beneath her feet, lush rugs cushioned her steps. The scent of essential oils permeated the air, almost as if she were in a spa. Clearly, the owner was taking the label of *Thai Massage* a little too literally, as if she could fool anybody about what was really going on in this establishment.

A door to her right opened, a young woman dressed in a colorful kimono-like robe slipping out. She inclined her head in greeting and smiled. Leila slowed her steps, turning her head to watch the girl as she walked in the other direction. She didn't look anything like the slutty hooker she'd seen on the street. The girl was pretty, her features clean and pleasant. Had she met her on the street, she would have never guessed what she did for a living.

A pull on her hand made her jerk forward. Aiden gave her a reprimanding look.

"Staring again?"

"I wasn't…" She didn't finish her sentence when she noticed a smirk playing around his lips. Was he actually finding her uneasiness in this place funny? She huffed and clamped her jaw shut.

Around the next corner, the woman finally stopped in front of a door. She unlocked it, then gave Aiden the key.

"Thank you, Coralee," he acknowledged.

The old woman simply nodded and shuffled past them. As the *madam* brushed her, her gaze traveled up Leila's body, then rested on her face. Was she sizing her up like fresh meat for her brothel?

Then she tossed a glance back at Aiden. "Pretty," she said to him before she disappeared down the hallway.

Once inside, he locked the door behind them. She was alone with him again.

The room was more comfortable than she'd expected. There was a sitting area, a closet, a chest of drawers with a mirror over it, and a bed. Only one. Large, but that didn't change the fact that it was only one. She eyed the sofa.

"You need to sleep," he said. "There are clothes in the bathroom that will fit you."

She looked down at their joined hands. "Will I be alright for a couple of minutes without being cloaked?"

He nodded. "It will take them more than a couple of minutes to lock onto your presence even if they are somewhere in the vicinity. Unless they have a visual on you. Then it's instant recognition. But we're inside, and the shades are drawn."

She swallowed away her fear and opened the door to the en-suite bathroom. "I'll only be a minute."

17

Aiden watched the bathroom door close behind her. He'd just missed another perfect opportunity to tell Leila the truth. Why hadn't he come clean? Was it because for tonight it wouldn't matter anyway since she had no choice but to allow him to touch her while they both slept? Because during sleep, only his touch could cloak a human. But explaining that to Leila would have invited too many questions in her inquisitive mind. And he was too tired to play twenty questions right now. And not ready to face her wrath for his earlier deception. He'd explain everything to her tomorrow.

When he heard the bathroom door open, his head snapped in its direction. Leila stepped out gingerly, her eyes downcast, half her face hidden by her long hair. But his eyes weren't focusing on that. They were already traveling up and down her body, or what he could see of it.

Why had she dressed in the most shapeless PJs she could find in that closet? He was sure Coralee kept a good selection of nightgowns and negligees in there. Yet Leila had decided on oversized flannel pajamas that hid all her curves. The thick material didn't even hint at the sensual woman underneath.

Was she trying to hide from him? Without a word, he brushed past her and headed for the bathroom. He let the door snap in behind him.

The urge to touch her had never been stronger than now. Knowing that in a few minutes she would be sleeping in his arms, made his desire for her spike. He knew he shouldn't want this, because it was wrong: she was his charge, not his lover. Besides, Leila didn't want him—no woman wanting to be seduced wore flannel pajamas.

He let his last conversation with her replay in his mind. Maybe he'd said things she didn't want to hear. Finding out that he would eliminate her should she be seduced to the demons' side probably didn't exactly endear him to her. Maybe he should have refused to answer that question or told her a lie instead.

As he got ready for bed and undressed, he felt the events of the last few hours take their toll. Exhaustion overwhelmed him, even though nights like these were the norm. He shouldn't feel tired, not the way he did right now. Maybe it was better this way: perhaps his sexual drive would be wiped out by his tiredness and stop him from doing something stupid.

Dressed only in his boxer briefs, his cock semi-erect, he walked back into the bedroom, finding only the nightlight next to the door illuminated. He dropped his clothes on one of the chairs to have them close in an emergency.

Under the covers, Leila's shape was visible, the sheets covering her up to her neck. She'd turned toward the opposite wall, and he could only assume that she was already asleep.

Aiden glanced at the clock on the bedside table. In less than an hour the sun would rise. It was best to get a few hours of sleep before deciding on the next course of action. On bare feet, he walked to the bed and lifted the covers, silently sliding under them.

He felt the warmth of her body and moved closer when he noticed her holding her breath. She wasn't asleep as he'd assumed.

With slow movements, he reached for her. "Just so you're cloaked," he whispered.

"Yes." Her husky voice was barely audible.

Snaking an arm around her waist, he drew her into the curve of his body. When her sweet backside connected with his groin, he clenched his jaw shut to prevent himself from moaning out loud.

Fuck! He'd never survive this night. It was better if he told her the truth now and didn't continue this deception.

"Leila," he started.

But her next action stopped him: she placed her hand over his, pressing it firmer against her torso. In three heartbeats, his body pumped more blood into his cock, making him as hard as he'd ever been.

"I'm scared."

"You're safe for now." He pressed a soft kiss in her hair.

Leila's breath hitched, her body tensing for a moment.

"I'm sorry, you have nothing to fear from me. I won't do anything you don't want me to do," he said hastily.

Yeah, where had he heard that before? As if he would be able to stop once he started.

Then don't start anything, his mind warned him.

"Aiden…"

Did her voice sound just a little bit aroused, or was this simply wishful thinking on his part? And was her sweet behind pressing itself closer to him?

"Leila, there's something you should know," he tried again, his guilty conscience rearing its head.

"I don't want to talk anymore," she whispered. "I just want to forget everything that's happened."

"There's no way to make you forget. I don't have those kinds of powers."

"Just for a while," she begged.

"I wish I could help you." He pressed another soft kiss on her hair, but this time she turned her head toward him.

Even in the dark, he could see her eyes study him. When her lips moved, her breath ghosted against his face. Without thinking, he moved his head closer to hers. Her lashes fluttered.

"We shouldn't," he murmured even as his lips hovered less than an inch over hers.

"But it feels so good."

Aiden slid his lips over hers, even though he knew it was wrong. Somewhere in the Stealth Guardian rule book it was written, but for some reason, the rules didn't mean anything to him at that moment.

Perhaps this was how Manus seduced his charges: with sweet words and tender caresses.

Whispering sweet nothings into her ear involved no deception, because the things he wanted to tell her felt real, good, and right.

She sighed and relaxed against him, her lips parting under his. He only gave her the softest of kisses, before he withdrew.

"Leila, do you remember what you did earlier tonight when you were in your own bed?"

A gasp escaped her, but she didn't move away from him. "Yes."

"It was beautiful watching you."

He planted kisses along the graceful column of her neck. Then he allowed his hand to move. His fingers found the waistband of her PJs and slipped underneath.

"I wanted to join in earlier. You excite me." In snail's pace, his hand traveled lower. "Let me pleasure you now. Say yes," he urged as his fingers dove lower and delved into the nest of curls guarding her sex.

"Aiden…" she stammered at the same time as her hips tilted toward his hand.

"Say yes, and I'll help you forget."

Just like he needed to forget what danger she'd escaped tonight. Only feeling her shudder in his arms would make him forget. What he wanted to confess only moments earlier was forgotten.

"Yes, forget," she repeated.

He didn't lose a second in capturing her lips and searing them with a passionate kiss. He turned her on her back and stroked his fingers against her moist cleft, nearly lifting her off the bed in the process.

"Easy, baby," he cautioned. "I'll give you what you need."

His moist finger trailed upwards and met with her engorged clit. He circled it, then stroked over it lightly.

"Oh!"

He didn't dare switch on the light. Under cover of darkness, she seemed to feel safe with him. At least his superior night vision gave him a glimpse of the aroused expression on her face without her being aware of it.

"Did you fantasize about me when you touched yourself earlier?"

Aiden swiped his thumb over her sensitive flesh and moved his finger lower to where moisture oozed from her.

"Tell me." He underscored his demand by sliding one thick finger into her tight channel.

She pushed against his hand, taking him deep. "Yes," she admitted finally. "I was thinking about you."

"Tell me more."

He heard her swallow hard as if she was embarrassed to tell him. But he knew how to coax those words from her. His thumb worked harder, painting small circles over her clit, stroking her with more pressure, increasing his tempo.

"Now, baby, tell me."

"I imagined you touching me, like this… and your mouth on me."

God, yes, he wanted that, wanted to eat her beautiful pussy and drink her nectar. "You want my mouth on your pussy?"

He thrust his finger deeper into her, fucking her in earnest now. In and out while his thumb stroked her clit without interruption.

"Yes," she cried out.

"Good, because when we're done here, when I've made you come with my fingers, I'll have you come in my mouth."

"Oh, God!"

"Was there anything else you were fantasizing about?" Would she want his cock in her? Would she want him to ride her hard until she collapsed underneath him?

Her breath hitched. "I… I want…" Harsh breathing turned her sentence into a list of single words.

"What, Leila, what do you want?" He needed to know.

"Your… your cock… inside…" Her voice died as her body tensed.

"Aiden!"

Shock made him still his movements. The voice that had called for him wasn't Leila's. And it hadn't come from within the room.

"Aiden!"

"Shit!" he hissed when he recognized Manus's voice.

Next to him, Leila scrambled away.

He reached for her. "It's okay. He's a friend."

When he switched on the light a second later, he saw that she avoided looking at him and pulled the covers up to her neck. He didn't need to be a genius to figure out that she was embarrassed.

"Are you letting me in or not?" Manus's voice came again.

He jumped from the bed and opened the door. His second instantly ran his eyes over Aiden's half-nude body, resting them on the noticeable bulge in his boxer briefs. A raised eyebrow and a smirk around Manus's lips confirmed that the state of Aiden's cock hadn't escaped his notice.

"Well, hope I'm not interrupting anything." He grinned and stepped past him to enter the bedroom.

Aiden shut the door behind him, deciding not to answer Manus's question. He noticed his second peruse the bed with Leila in it for longer than necessary.

"So, it looks like you've finally decided to cloak your charge by touching her and give your mind a rest."

"Manus, you—"

"What did he say?" Leila, sitting upright in the bed now, the covers pressed to her chest, glared at him.

Oh, shit! Manus and his big blabbermouth!

18

Leila stared at Aiden's guilty face, then moved her gaze back to the handsome stranger, who'd interrupted them.

Manus returned her look with a sheepish grin, then glanced at Aiden who snatched his pants from a chair and hastily pulled them over his thighs.

"Nothing," Manus answered.

She noticed the two men exchange a look. "You said something about Aiden cloaking me with his touch. What's wrong with it?"

"Nothing wrong with that," he murmured.

"But?" she asked, lending her voice a sharper edge to make it clear that she wouldn't accept any bullshit.

Manus pretended interest in his shoes, avoiding her question.

"I asked you: what did you mean by that?"

Lifting his head, he gave Aiden an apologetic glance. "There's no need to touch."

"What?"

"He… he could have cloaked you with his mind, but at night it's advisable to—"

"You jerk! You lied to me!" she yelled at Aiden, who stood there, guilt written all over his face. That bastard had deceived her in order to get into her pants!

"Great, Manus, that's just great," Aiden said in dry tones, giving his friend a sideways glance.

"Sorry, man. I didn't mean to… I thought she knew."

"Well, I do now!" she spat.

Aiden met her glare. "I was going to tell you, but you didn't give me a chance. I wanted to explain, but then you…"

"I what? Oh my God, are you suggesting…"

She couldn't finish her sentence, because he was right: she had asked him to touch her. She'd been the one who'd invited him. Oh God, she'd turned into a slut!

Heat suffused her cheeks. But she needed to defend herself, she couldn't let this accusation hang in the air. "You didn't…"

"Stop? No, I didn't. How could I?" he cut her off, a strange glint of regret in his eyes.

She could see it in his eyes now, he'd wanted it, wanted her. And she had wanted him, and he knew it. Embarrassment choked off her ability to speak. She'd almost had sex with a stranger she'd known only a few hours. What was happening to her? What had made her react like that?

God, they'd even engaged in sex talk, something she'd never done before. Remembering this now made her want to sink into a hole in the ground. Unfortunately no pre-dug ditch was appearing when she needed it.

"Shall I give you guys a minute?" Manus interrupted her thought process, obviously uncomfortable being in the middle of their exchange.

"No, don't bother!"

Leila jumped out of the bed and marched toward the door, wanting to get out of there, unable to face Aiden and his friend now.

"You're not going anywhere," Aiden ordered and grabbed her arm.

"You can't stop me!" She clenched her jaw together, turning her face away from him.

"You're not leaving this house."

"But I'm leaving this room, and you can't stop me from doing that."

"There's a kitchen down the hall," Manus suggested. "I'm sure Coralee has got some coffee brewing there."

She ripped her arm from his grip and stormed out of the bedroom, slamming the door behind her for good measure.

She heard the door open again a moment later, but continued walking.

"Coralee knows not to let you leave the house," Aiden called after her.

Leila ignored him and followed the corridor, trying to find the kitchen Manus had mentioned. She could do with a cup of coffee right about now, knowing that sleep wasn't to be had anyway, not when she felt all riled up.

Her eyes perused the doors she passed, ignoring those that had numbers on them. Clearly those were the rooms the prostitutes used. Turning around the corner, she reached a dead end. The three doors without numbers were closed. She perceived a faint scent of coffee and guessed that one of them had to be the kitchen, just as Manus had said.

She listened for sounds, but it was quiet. Reaching for the first door, she turned the doorknob and pushed the door inwards.

Semidarkness greeted her and froze her into place. This was clearly not the kitchen, because the dish that was being served up on the massage table in the middle of the room, was too rich for her liking.

A naked man lay on his back while a young woman dressed in nothing but a see-through caftan bent between his legs and licked whipped cream off his cock. At the same time another woman was bent over his head, her breasts, which were also covered in whipped cream, dangling over his mouth.

When the man sucked one breast into his mouth and suckled on it with much gusto, a gasp escaped her. Instantly, the two women whirled their heads in Leila's direction.

Her hands shaking, she yanked the door shut. Her cheeks burned with embarrassment, and her heart raced at the thought of what the threesome was doing.

Damn it, this wasn't a place she wanted to be at. This wasn't her life.

Behind her a door opened. She spun around, her nerves already on edge. A young woman stepped from the room, a steaming cup of coffee in her hands. She smiled briefly and walked past without saying a word.

Leila sighed with relief and walked into the room she'd exited. At least, she'd found the kitchen. Maybe she'd feel better after a cup of coffee.

The room was surprisingly homey and well-equipped. On the counter stood an oversized coffeemaker with cups lined up next to it. She poured herself one and added milk. As she sat down at the round table in the middle of the room, she noticed the TV that stood in the corner. It was switched on, but somebody had muted it.

Leila took a sip of the hot coffee and allowed it to warm her overtired limbs. She hadn't pulled an all-nighter since her residency and felt that her age was showing now. In her teens and early twenties, she'd had no problems staying up all night, but now she felt the strain physically.

As she lifted her head from the coffee cup, her gaze drifted back to the TV. A red stripe scrolled on the bottom of it. It said *Breaking News*. Then a reporter appeared in front of a building she recognized instantly: Inter Pharma.

Leila jumped from her chair and rushed to the TV, frantically searching for the button to increase the volume.

~ ~ ~

Manus rubbed the back of his neck. "That didn't go well."

"As always you have great timing," Aiden replied.

"Hey, I said I'm sorry, and I tried to explain to her that at night that's just what you need to do to get some rest, but you saw how she cut me off. Besides, how did I know you're resorting to cheap tricks to get your charge into bed? Should have simply used your charm." He gave a half-hearted grin. "Works for me."

"She wanted it."

His second lifted his arms. "Hey, hey, I'm not denying that. It was pretty obvious by the way she blushed, but you've got lots to learn about women."

As if he hadn't figured that out himself. "I don't need a lecture. I'll handle this."

How, he had no idea. They were both adults; she knew what she was getting into, and still she'd let him proceed. Wasn't she the one who had started it? Hadn't she asked him to make her forget? Nevertheless, he had to somehow get her to forgive him.

Aiden cleared his throat. "Now tell me what you've found out."

Manus flopped down on the couch and put his feet on the coffee table. "The car that nearly ran your charge over was stolen last night."

"That's not a good sign."

"I'm thinking the same thing. Somebody could have stolen it solely for the purpose of killing her with it."

While Aiden had to agree with that assessment, one thing didn't make sense. "But why would the demons want to kill her? She's in the final stages with her research. If they kill her now and the drug doesn't work, they've cut their own arm off. It would be stupid."

"Is there a chance that they already have a sample of the drug and know it's working?" Manus asked. "Maybe they don't need her anymore."

"I don't know. We'll have to ask her about that possibility. What about the fire?"

"Ah, the fire. I rode with the fire truck and played fly on the wall. Looks like they suspect arson, most likely some incendiary device. They found something in the kitchen where the fire started. Could have been a timer."

Aiden rubbed his temple. If somebody had deliberately set the house fire after failing to run her over, then he couldn't write off any of these events as a coincidence or just bad luck. Two attempts on her life in one night couldn't be explained away so easily.

"I heard a loud sound. Could have been some sort of explosion. What if something in her kitchen malfunctioned? There were plenty of electrical devices that could have shorted out and caused a fire. Or it could have been the gas stove."

"The fire chief doesn't think so. It definitely wasn't the gas stove, and that's the only appliance in her kitchen that could have produced the sound of an explosion if that's what you heard. It's still early in the investigation, but he seemed pretty convinced that it was arson, and I'm inclined to agree with him. I had a look at the kitchen. There was no electrical cable or outlet in sight where they believe the fire started: on the counter."

Aiden nodded. "We have to figure out who could have brought something into her apartment without me or her noticing. I was there before she got home. I didn't see anything suspicious."

Manus shrugged. "Then somebody must have planted something later."

"Impossible. I was in the apartment most of the night. Nobody could have gotten past me."

His friend lifted one side of his mouth. "So you were watching the door all night?"

Heat shot through his chest. Did Manus know that he'd been in Leila's bedroom, watching her pleasure herself?

"How I do my job is none of your business," he snapped.

Manus jumped up from the couch and faced him. "Really? Is that because you don't want to admit that you're just like me? That fucking a charge excites you? That Leila excites you?"

Aiden growled low and dark.

"Can't you just admit it?"

"There's nothing to admit."

"Isn't there?"

Aiden clenched his hands into fists, trying to rein in his fury. While he'd never before fucked a charge, unfortunately the rest of Manus's accusations came too close for comfort. Leila excited him, and he wanted her.

Manus took a step back, nodding. "Well, I guess we'd better talk to Leila about her drug then. Besides—" He pulled out a little box from his jacket pocket. "—I have a birthday present for her. She loves Swiss chocolate, you know."

Aiden stared at his second. "Her birthday."

"Of course, I thought you read her file."

Realization flooded his senses. How could he have missed that? It had happened right in front of his own eyes. "It's her birthday. Of course. That's it."

Then he turned toward the door.

"What are you talking about?" he heard Manus ask behind him.

"Come."

19

The first thing Aiden noticed when he entered the kitchen, followed by Manus, was that Leila's face looked like she'd seen a ghost. The second thing he noticed was that her eyes were transfixed on the TV screen.

He instantly followed her blank stare and focused in on the sound coming from the program.

"*...no signs of the missing researcher. The police have not revealed whether Dr. Cruickshank is considered a suspect in the brutal murder of her boss, however, they have called her a person of interest, since she was the only other person in the building at the time of the murder besides the security guard.*"

The newswoman suddenly glanced to the side and listened to somebody off camera. A moment later, she looked back into the camera.

"*I am just being informed that the apartment Dr. Cruickshank lives at was gutted by fire earlier tonight. Fire investigators have not announced a conclusion as to the cause, but suspect arson. Whether these two incidences are related is unclear at this point. This is Deborah Winters, WOTK News.*"

Aiden walked to the TV and switched it off. He'd expected this, however, he'd hoped to prevent Leila from seeing this.

"They think I did it," she muttered as if talking to herself.

"You don't know that."

Her head shot up, and she stared at him. "They think I killed Patten. They're looking for me."

"The press is just making assumptions. We know you didn't do it."

"*We*, yes, but how about the police? How can I go back now?"

Manus sat down next to her. "Listen, Leila, you can't think about that now. It's not important. What's important is to keep you safe. Here, happy birthday." He placed the small box of chocolates on the table in front of her. "Your favorites: dark chocolate truffles."

Did his fellow Stealth Guardian really think he could distract her with *truffles*?

Her hand reached for the box, but she only stared at it without opening it. "Thanks."

"There's something else we need to talk about," Aiden started and took a tentative step closer to the table. After their earlier confrontation he thought it wise not to approach too closely. For all he knew, she could still scratch his eyes out. And he wouldn't even blame her if she did.

When she looked back at him, he suddenly noticed the tiredness in her eyes, as if resignation had set in. "What else is there to talk about? My life is practically over. Everything I've worked for…"

"I'm sorry," Aiden replied, looking for a way to smoothly turn the conversation to what he needed to ask her. "But there are important things we need to figure out. And we need your help."

Manus patted her on her forearm, making Aiden want to hiss like a beast. "As much as I hate to agree with him, he's right. There are a few things that don't make sense."

"Like that there are demons in this world?" she mocked.

Aiden shifted from one foot to the other. "No. Unfortunately that makes perfect sense. But we don't understand why they want to kill you when they want what you have."

Leila raised her eyes and tossed him an inquisitive look.

"The Fire Department believes that the fire that broke out in your apartment was arson."

"How? You were there. Wouldn't you have seen if somebody had started a fire?"

Aiden pushed the rising memory back, not wanting to be reminded right now how she'd looked lying in her bed. "It was an incendiary device, a little bomb, most likely with a timer on it."

"Oh my God! The demons did that?"

Aiden scratched the back of his neck. "Actually, I'm not sure."

"Why not? You told me the demons are after me. And now you're saying they're not?"

Manus lifted his hand. "That's not what Aiden means. What's strange is why the demons would kill you when they don't have the formula for your drug or a sample of your drug in their hands yet. Don't you see? Why kill the goose that lays the golden egg?

You're valuable to them. They wouldn't kill you until they've gotten what they wanted."

"But then why did they kill Patten?"

"I'm not sure they were the ones who killed him," Aiden answered, drawing her gaze onto him. "Tell me something. We know that they didn't get your drug's formula because you'd already wiped the backup disk, and the data on the laptop was fried. But is there a chance that the demons could lay their hands on a sample of the actually serum?"

Leila instantly shook her head. "Impossible. The clinical trials are conducted in Inter Pharma's outpatient satellite clinic."

"What does that mean?"

"Well, normally clinical trials take place in clinics of hospitals and medical centers, but we wanted to maintain confidentiality and prevent any chance of our data leaking out. So we required the test subjects to come to our own clinic, where their doctors would administer the drug under our supervision. It was the only way to make sure that nobody else had any samples of the drug. We only gave them one dosage at a time and supervised its administration. Nobody could have taken a sample."

Her voice had taken on a calm and efficient tone, and he realized that she had slipped back into the skin she felt most comfortable in, the brilliant researcher.

"And you're sure there's no other copy of the data anywhere?" He searched her eyes.

Leila blinked, her fingers playing with her diamond studded pendant. "I'm sure."

Manus let out a long breath. "Then it doesn't make sense that the demons would have tried to kill you. They still need you, because the only way for them to get at it now is for them to force you to reproduce it from memory."

His colleague was right. Which then invited another question. "What do you know about Jonathan?" Aiden asked.

"Who?" Her eyebrows snapped together in confusion.

"Your upstairs neighbor."

Her mouth dropped open. "What does Jonathan have to do with any of this?"

"He planted the incendiary device."

"That's impossible. He would never... he's a nice guy."

Aiden shook his head. Humans could so easily be fooled by a friendly face. "He gave you a present for your birthday. The bomb must have been in there."

In disbelief, Leila moved her head from side to side. "But... but I don't believe that."

Why was she so vehemently denying the obvious? Did she have any feelings for this guy?

"He even told you not to open it before today."

"How...?" She broke off, realization flooding her intelligent eyes. "You were watching even then."

There was no need to deny it.

"It still doesn't mean it was him. I've known him for over a year. Why would he suddenly try to kill me?"

Manus drummed his fingers on the table, drawing his attention away from Leila. "Can we cut to the chase here?" When Leila looked at him, he continued, "According to the Fire Department, the fire started in the kitchen. Did you by any chance place the birthday present he gave you on the kitchen counter?"

Leila's blue eyes widened at the same time as her mouth fell open. Finally she accepted their suspicion. After a long pause, she closed her eyes, then looked back at them. "Why would he do that? He seemed so nice."

Manus shrugged. "We'll find out. Somebody must have gotten to him."

"Unless he didn't know what he was handing you," Aiden added. "He's human, I know that for sure. And if the demons didn't influence him, which I don't believe they did, somebody else could have used him, either with Jonathan's knowledge or covertly."

"And Patten? He couldn't have killed Patten, too."

Aiden contemplated the idea for a moment. "Unlikely. To get into Inter Pharma's building without being stopped by the security guard takes some skill. Somehow I doubt he's capable of this. However—" He glanced at Manus. "—he needs to be checked out. Manus, find out all you can about him: what he does, where he works, who he knows, who visited him in the last few days, who he's met with—"

"I know the drill," Manus interrupted.

"We need to find out who is behind this."

Manus rose. "I'm on it."

"And what about the police?" Leila gave him a questioning look.

"What about them?" Aiden asked.

"How are we going to tell them that I'm not involved? They have to know that I'm innocent."

He took a step toward her, cupping her shoulders with his hands. "They can't find out where you are. Nobody can. We'll arrange for our people to make it look like you died. You'll be safest then."

"Died?" she croaked. "You can't do that. My... my—"

"It's the best solution," Manus piped behind him. "I'll arrange it. We'll get a body from the morgue that fits your description."

"Don't forget the teeth," Aiden cautioned.

"Don't worry, I'll get a cast from her dentist and get our crew to work on the teeth of the body so they'll match."

"What?" Leila gasped.

Aiden looked back at her and found her staring at them in disbelief.

"Yeah, you know," Manus continued, "they'll file down the teeth, make fillings where yours are. They're experts in that. They can create a perfect match..."

"You can't just... that's not... but..." Tears brimmed in her eyes, ready to burst to the surface once more.

"Do it," Aiden commanded his friend without taking his eyes off Leila.

A panicked look suddenly crossed her face when his second headed for the door. Was she worried about being alone with him again? Or simply worried about what Manus was going to do? Whatever it was, she pushed away from him, making him drop his hold on her shoulders.

"Oh, almost forgot." Manus turned back to face him. "I brought you a less conspicuous car. I'm afraid your sports car will stick out like a sore thumb if you're trying to make a fast getaway."

Aiden nodded. He was aware of that, which meant he rarely ever got to drive his fancy ride. It barely had five thousand miles on it, and he'd owned it for two years already. He patted his jeans pockets for the key, and realized that they were empty.

"My keys are in the room." He looked at Leila. "I'll be back in a minute."

He turned and followed Manus out of the kitchen.

~ ~ ~

Leila pushed the tears back and tried to control the trembling of her hands, but the knowledge of what the two Stealth Guardians were planning made her blood freeze in her veins. They were trying to make everybody believe she was dead.

Her parents would be devastated once they found out. Despite the fact that they were both suffering from Alzheimer's, their minds were still clear enough to recognize her on their good days and know who she was. If they saw the news on TV, they would break down. She couldn't cause her parents such unnecessary pain. It would be cruel.

She had to warn them and tell them not to believe anything they heard on TV. Telling the caretaker not to let them watch TV wouldn't be enough. It was their pastime. Nothing could keep them from that box that provided them with entertainment in their monotonous lives. Besides, the newspapers would print the story too. There were too many ways they could find out the terrible news. Hell, the neighbors would stop by with condolence cards and flowers.

Leila glanced at the clock on the coffee maker and hoped it wasn't too late already. With some luck, the caregiver was just getting them up and hadn't mentioned anything to them about her disappearance yet. That alone could cause her father's heart to stutter and her mother's blood pressure to spike.

Knowing she couldn't go back to the room to get her cell phone from her bag, she glanced around the kitchen. A landline telephone was attached to the wall next to the fridge. She had to make a quick decision. Aiden would be back shortly. It was now or never.

Casting a glance over her shoulder, she took the phone off the hook and punched in the number. With one ear she listened to the ringing on the other end, with the other to any sounds coming from the hallway. Three rings, four. If nobody picked up, the answering machine would kick in any moment.

"Hello?"

Leila breathed a sigh of relief when she recognized the low voice on the other end. "Mom, it's Leila."

"Hello?" she responded.

"Mom, can you hear me? It's Leila," she repeated a fraction louder, wondering whether her mother's hearing aid was on.

"Oh, hello. Now I can hear you."

Her heart made an excited salto. Her mother sounded clear as a bell. Maybe this was one of her good days.

"It's Leila, Mom," she repeated, just for good measure.

"Good morning, Leila."

"It's so good to hear your voice. Listen, Mom, I don't have much time, but I want you to know something." She paused to make sure her mother had understood her.

"Go on, I always like to talk. Nancy is such a sourpuss some days. She rarely chats."

Well, she'd take Nancy, the caretaker, to task some other day, but now she had more important things to do.

"Mom, you're going to see stuff on TV about me. They'll say that I disappeared, or even that I died. But don't believe any of it. I'm fine. Everything's fine." Hell, who was she kidding? "I just have to go away for a few days. There are things happening at work that I can't explain right now. Do you understand that?"

"Of course, dear. You have to go away."

"Yes, Mom. But I don't want you and Dad to worry about me. I'm safe where I am. Nothing can happen to me. I just worry about you and Dad."

"There's no need to worry about us. We're fine."

It was a relief to hear her say that.

"And don't worry about Nancy. When I'm back, I'll tell her to sit down more often and chat with you, so you don't feel too lonely."

"Who feels lonely, dear?" her mother replied.

Had she not just seconds earlier complained about Nancy not chatting with her? "But, you said Nancy…"

"Nancy!" her mother suddenly called, sounding more distant as if she was holding the phone away from her mouth.

"Yes, Ellie?" Leila recognized the caretaker's voice in the background.

"There's somebody who wants to talk to you."

"No, Mom," she tried to stop her, but her mother clearly didn't hear her.

"Who is it?"

"Oh, it's the neighbor's girl. I think she's a little loopy in the head."

Oh, no! Her mother hadn't recognized her. "Mom!" she shouted into the phone.

"Nancy will call you back later."

Then there was a click in the line, and the call was disconnected. Shocked, she let the receiver slide back onto the cradle. It hadn't been one of her mother's good days. She hadn't really heard a single word Leila had told her.

She felt like screaming out her frustration. Gripping the receiver once more, she knew she had to try again. Maybe this time Nancy would pick up and she could explain everything to her. Oh, God, she hoped so.

Her hand froze on the receiver when she heard the door handle being turned.

20

Aiden hesitated before opening the kitchen door. How would Leila react to him now that their buffer, Manus, was gone? It turned out that he didn't have to worry about it. When he opened the door, she was still staring at the TV, watching the same news program. He knew enough about her to realize that it wouldn't make her feel any better, so he walked to the TV and switched it off.

"You should rest."

To his surprise, she nodded and didn't protest when he ushered her back to their room. Aiden closed the shades to make it more comfortable for Leila to sleep while the sun was shining brightly outside. She now lay curled up on the bed—fully clothed this time. It appeared she didn't want him touching her ever again.

Frustrated and feeling more than just a little bit guilty about his earlier deception, he lay stretched out on the couch, knowing his presence in the bed wasn't welcome. This fact did nothing to quell his growing desire for her. Neither did thinking about her for hours while she slept only feet away from him.

When Coralee delivered food to the room sometime well past midday, Aiden placed the tray on the coffee table and opened the shades before walking to the bed. Leila looked vulnerable with her eyes closed, her hair open and spread around her like a halo. He felt the urge to take her into his arms, to protect her and assure her that she would be safe. But he couldn't do that. Neither did she want his touch, nor would he be telling the truth if he told her she was safe. She would only be safe once he and his fellow Stealth Guardians could trick the demons into thinking that she was dead and with her all chances of recreating the drug.

Even once they'd achieved that, they would have to keep tabs on her. And she would have to assume a new identity, as if she were in the federal witness protection program. It was no different from that. But they needed her cooperation for that, which meant

Aiden had to start mending what he'd screwed up. The quicker the better.

"Leila," he called softly, but she didn't stir. He tried again, but received no response, so he gently shook her shoulder.

She reared up with a frightened look on her face and wriggled away from him. "What do you want?"

He instantly pulled back, giving her space so she wouldn't perceive him as a threat. "I want to apologize." Nervously, he ran a hand through his hair, messing it up even more than it already was. "I shouldn't have..." His voice died. Hell, he'd never learned how to apologize to anybody. This was harder than fighting two demons in a dark alley with one hand tied behind his back.

Her ocean blue eyes lowered to evade his gaze. "I don't want to talk about it."

Did he imagine it, or was a soft, rosy blush building on her cheeks? Oddly enough, it didn't appear that she was angry at him, despite her words. It look more like she was... shy. The confident, determined Dr. Cruickshank was shy when it came to intimacy? Could that be the reason why she'd reacted so vehemently when they'd been interrupted by Manus?

"I need to explain one thing. Please."

She gave an almost unperceivable nod.

"Thank you... There was one thing Manus was trying to explain to you: while a Stealth Guardian sleeps, his ability to cloak a human with his mind disappears. Only his touch is still effective. I needed to touch you if I wanted to sleep. But..." He cast her a cautious glance, noticing that she watched him closely. "...I have no excuses for touching you the way I did, other than that I'm attracted to you. I'm sorry. I should have explained it to you and just asked to take your hand while you slept."

Her eyes assessed him for a long moment. "Is that what you do with the other women you protect?"

"No!" His protest was instant. "No... It's not like that. When I need sleep, I call my second, Manus or one of the others, so he can take over while I catch a few hours of sleep."

He sought her eyes. "I don't... touch my charges when I can avoid it. But you..." He dropped his head. "I'm sorry. It was wrong of me."

When she didn't immediately answer, he motioned his head toward the coffee table. "Coralee brought us some food. You must be hungry."

She nodded and rose from the bed.

When she sat down on the couch and reached for one of the plates, he let himself sink into the armchair. At least he'd said his peace; he only hoped that eventually she would understand and forgive his transgressions.

"How long do we have to stay here?" she asked.

Aiden grabbed a plate. "Maybe two or three days. By then Manus should have initiated everything to stage your death."

He noticed a shudder going through her at his last word.

"You say that as if that happens all the time."

"It doesn't. But occasionally, we have no choice in order to get the demons off our charges' tails. They'll only give up once they think they've lost. And in your case, simply making sure that they can't get to your research isn't enough. If they get to you, they can get you to reproduce it for them." He shoved a fork full of Pad Thai into his mouth.

She shook her head. "I wouldn't do that. I'd never work for the demons." Her body tensed visibly. "Not after all that's happened to me because of them."

Aiden put his fork down and chewed, contemplating his next words. How should he explain to her that just like other humans before her, she would succumb to them? "It's not that easy to resist them when they are trying to seduce you to their side."

"I don't see why. Now that I know what they are and what their agenda is, I think they've lost that mental power over me. There isn't anything with which they could seduce me to their side." Leila thrust up her chin in a determined gesture, indicating that she was prepared to fight.

"Trust me, they'll find something even you won't be able to resist. They'll look long enough to find your weak point, find something you really want, and then promise you that you'll get it if you work for them. I've seen it before."

His last charge had succumbed. The demons only had to find the right trigger. They would find Leila's, too. Nobody could hide their deepest desires for long, least of all a human. And lately he wondered if even he as a Stealth Guardian could hide his desires any longer.

"I've not gotten to where I am right now by being weak," Leila claimed.

"I'm not suggesting that," Aiden denied, trying to remain calm. "I'm simply explaining what their modus operandi is. They are very resourceful. And they won't stop until they know that their dream of possessing this drug won't come true."

"You can't just expect me to live in hiding forever. I can't do that. My parents... my work, I have to go on."

Aiden set his nearly empty plate onto the tray. "That's exactly what you'll have to do if you want to live."

Her eyes narrowed. "But you said the demons don't want to kill me, because they want what I can give them."

He stared at her, warring with himself whether to spell it out once more: if she worked for the demons, he or one of his fellow Stealth Guardians would have to eliminate her. Yet looking into her eyes now, he realized that he wouldn't be capable of it. Would he go so far as to defend her even against his own brothers should they try to harm her?

Suddenly her eyes widened, and her mouth dropped open. "Oh, my God, you *do* mean it, don't you? You would kill me without as much as blinking."

"By the looks of it, he wouldn't enjoy it though."

At the sound of the familiar male voice in the room, Aiden snapped his gaze to the door, jumping up from his chair simultaneously.

Shit!

The tall rugged stranger who had appeared out of nowhere and now stood near the door was none other than Hamish.

"You guys have to stop doing this. There's only so much I can take," Leila snapped and slammed her plate onto the coffee table.

"Leila, get behind me, now!" Aiden ordered.

Hamish looked just as he always had: dark brown hair, parted in the middle, the longer strands hanging into this eyes. He wore a four-day stubble, and his eyebrows were slightly elevated ridges when he furrowed them as he did now.

Glaring at his old friend, Aiden pulled his ancient dagger from his boot, ready for combat.

When Leila didn't move, he repeated his order. "I said now!"

Hamish raised a hand, his stance remaining strangely relaxed. "That's not necessary."

"What the fuck, Hamish! You've got nerves showing up here." Aiden advanced on him, both relieved and angry at the same time. Relieved that his friend wasn't dead, and angry because he couldn't tell whose side he was on.

"I had no choice, but I have no time to explain now. We have to leave." Hamish nodded at Leila. "Get all your things. It's not safe here anymore."

"The hell she will." Aiden glanced at her. "You can't trust him, Leila. He went rogue. He might be working for the demons now."

With a shriek she rushed to his side. Aiden acknowledged her presence by squeezing her arm briefly.

Hamish let out an audible breath. "That's not true. And in your gut you know it. I'm not working for them. I'll explain everything, but later."

Aiden shook his head. He didn't know what to believe. Could he really trust his gut? Or Hamish's words for that matter? Conflicted, he let his eyes wander over Hamish's face, focusing on his eyes. They stared back at him as always, clear and without blinking, a soft brown. Not a hint of green. But was that proof enough?

"Explain it now. We have all the time in the world. And if I don't like your explanation, I'll acquaint you with my dagger." It was best to make his position clear immediately. He wouldn't take any bullshit.

Hamish gave a slow shake of his head. "I understand your sentiments, I do. The circumstances don't show me in a favorable light."

Aiden snorted. No, they didn't. They showed him in a crappy light. So why had he shown up here?

"But you would have done the same in my situation."

Aiden growled low and dark. "You abandoned me and my charge. Because of you, the demons got control over her. Because of you, I had to kill her."

Hamish darted a nervous look past them toward the window. Early afternoon sun shone into the room.

"I had bigger fish to fry, and once you know the whole story, you'll agree with me. Now pack up your charge and let's get out of here before they come," Hamish insisted.

Bigger fish than fighting the demons and saving his charge? Aiden had a hard time believing that claim. "We're not going anywhere with you. You can't expect me to trust you after all that's happened. The council is already on your heels, but frankly I'm glad, that I'm facing you first. We have a score to settle." Aiden pushed Leila behind him and took a step forward, arms stretched out to his sides, hips squared.

"As much as I'd like to fight this out, there isn't the time."

The barking of a dog came from outside the building.

Hamish blinked. "Shit, they brought dogs."

"The demons?" Aiden asked.

"No, it's not the demons who are after your charge, not right now anyway."

"Who is after me?" Leila asked from behind him, her voice laced with panic.

Hamish shrugged. "Honey, I wish I knew, but whoever they are, they just found you."

Aiden heard the barking of the dogs come closer. This wasn't good. He knew exactly what the arrival of dogs could mean.

"But how?" she despaired.

"Take your pick: Manus, a mole in the council, a phone call traced back to here, it doesn't matter..."

Suddenly, a loud bang came from downstairs. Instantly, excited voices echoed in the building, doors opened and closed, and hasty footsteps filled the corridors.

"Raid!" somebody screamed.

Hamish rushed to the door and opened it an inch, peering out into the hallway. "They're making it look like a police raid, but they're coming after Leila."

He looked over his shoulder. "It's up to you now, Aiden. Do you want to save your charge or not? Because if you don't come with me now, they'll be here in thirty seconds and kill her. There are too many of them to fight off."

21

Aiden realized he only had seconds to make a decision. He faced two immediate dangers: falling into the hands of the people raiding the Thai massage parlor, or being led into a trap by Hamish, the man he once called brother. Had he judged his friend too quickly? Could there really be a legitimate reason why he had disappeared and not backed him up on his last assignment?

Next to him, Leila fidgeted. "Why the dogs? Are they attack dogs?"

He took her hand and squeezed it. "No. Whoever is coming knows I can make you invisible, but the dogs will still be able to trace you, because they can smell you."

"Oh, no!"

Her panicked expression made the decision for him. They had to escape right now. Once they were out of this mess, he could deal with Hamish. And he hoped for all their sakes that his old friend had an explanation he could believe. Because he wasn't ready to lose him. They'd been through too much together.

"Where to?"

Hamish nodded. "Follow me."

Leila freed herself from his grip and rushed to the bed where she snatched her handbag and slung it diagonally across her torso. As he took her hand in his again, she nodded at him, indicating she was ready.

Aiden used his powers to assure that he and Leila were invisible to all but Hamish as they followed him out the door and into the hallway. He gave her a sign to be silent by putting a finger across his lips.

The corridor was a chaos. Half-clad masseuses and their clients scrambled toward the emergency exits. Pulling Leila with him, he ran after Hamish, every so often evading people barreling toward them, not realizing that they would run into an obstacle. It was one disadvantage of being invisible, one he dealt with gladly if it would get them out in one piece.

Looking down one corridor as he passed it, he saw men in riot gear charge through the hallways, pushing door after door open, their dogs on leashes, sniffing out every room before they moved on.

Excited barking sounded all of a sudden. How the dogs could catch Leila's scent was beyond him, unless these people, whoever they were, had managed to salvage something with her smell on it from her burnt apartment or maybe her office.

He couldn't worry about it right now as he tried to keep up with Hamish, who ran through the maze of corridors and stairs as if he knew exactly where he was going.

As they moved up another flight of stairs, Aiden grabbed Hamish's shoulder and stopped him. "There's no way out from up there," he said in a low voice.

Hamish looked over his shoulder and gave him a serious look. "You're gonna have to trust me. I'll get us out."

Aiden wished he had the same confidence in his former second that he'd once had, the knowledge that he could trust him with his life. Unfortunately, his doubts about Hamish's motives hadn't dissipated. "I wish I had more than your word on that."

"My word is still as good as ever."

Leila fidgeted next to him. "Better him than those men and their dogs," she whispered.

It had gotten quieter up on the top floor with all the staff and their clients having scrambled for the fire exits. Eventually the intruders would reach them and the dogs would close in on the three of them, whether they were cloaked or not.

Aiden nodded his agreement to Hamish who turned and headed for a narrow flight of stairs. *Roof Access*, a sign on the wall said.

As Hamish reached for the door handle, Aiden put his hand over his and stopped him.

"What guarantee do I have that there are no demons waiting for us on the roof?"

His fellow Stealth Guardian tilted his head toward the green neon sign over the door that said 'Exit'. It burned steadily.

Aiden breathed a sigh of relief. "Good. Let's go."

"What?" Leila asked behind him. "Please, what's going on?"

He turned to face her. "The aura of the demons reacts with two gases: neon and mercury, which are inside of fluorescent and neon light tubes. If they come too close, the light starts to flicker first, then it burns out."

That fact had often alerted them to the presence of demons and given them a few seconds of advance warning in times of need. Just as that same fact confirmed now that no demons were waiting for them beyond that door. And it also made another thing absolutely certain: whoever the intruders were, they weren't demons, otherwise the many neon signs in the Thai massage parlor would have flickered and burned out instantly.

But in order to be sure that the coast was truly clear, he stepped past Hamish.

"I'll be right back," he whispered to Leila and released her hand, then passed through the closed door.

Outside, bright afternoon light shone into Aiden's face. It took a fraction of a second for his eyes to adjust, but as soon as he took in the sight of the empty roof, he was satisfied and dove back inside the building.

"All clear," he assured Leila and clasped her hand.

A look of relief covered her face, and it seemed as if she squeezed his hand tighter. But maybe he was just imagining it.

Aiden turned the handle of the door and pushed, but nothing happened. It was locked. He rattled it and tossed Hamish an inquisitive look.

"Shit!" Hamish cursed under his breath.

"Did you not check the door before you decided to use it as an escape route?" Aiden hissed.

"It was open last time I was here, besides, I wouldn't need it unlocked..." He glanced at Leila.

"Aiden, can't we just go through it the way you just did?" Leila gave him a hopeful look.

"*We* can, but *you* can't."

A Stealth Guardian's power of dematerializing his body and rematerializing behind a solid object couldn't be extended to a human body.

"A human's body is too fragile to survive this. If I were to drag you through with me, your cells would never reassemble correctly on the other side. You would be..." He couldn't even say it.

And looking at Leila's face, he knew he didn't have to. She understood only too well.

He released her hand and looked at Hamish. "Tell me you brought tools."

His fellow Stealth Guardian unzipped his jacket and reached inside, pulling out an array of metal tools any thief would have been proud of. "Anything here tickle your fancy?"

Aiden snatched a thin blade from his hand, then turned to the lock. "Watch our back."

As he proceeded to pick the lock, Leila moved closer to him. "Have you ever done this before?"

"More often than you'd want to know," he lied. Sure, he'd learned how to pick a lock, but he rarely needed to use this skill. In most cases, he simply walked through a closed door, but today was different, and occasions on which he'd had to break a door open to bring a charge through had been rare lately. He was a little out of practice.

"They're coming closer," Hamish whispered.

"Almost done." Aiden twisted the blade inside the tumbler and turned until he heard a click. Instantly, he pressed the handle and pushed. The door eased open.

"Now!" Hamish ordered and pushed both him and Leila through the door.

Leila tripped, and Aiden caught her as they rushed outside, Hamish slamming the door shut behind them as loud voices and barking came from the inside.

"Shit!" Aiden cursed. The intruders were already hot on their heels.

Scanning the roof for anything to barricade the door with, his eyes fell on a two by four. He snatched it and jammed it through the door handle and the aligned iron loop next to the door. It would hold, if only for a few minutes.

"Let's go!" Hamish ordered as their would-be attackers banged on the door.

Scanning the roof once more, Aiden assessed the situation: the roof was flat, and except for a few washing lines and a satellite dish, it was empty.

When he looked back at Leila, she gave him a scared look, her shoulders pulled up, her brow furrowed. He hated to see her like this.

"Over the other roof," he called out to Hamish who looked over his shoulder, then pointed in the opposite direction, at a roof which was a floor lower than theirs.

Aiden was about to object and opt for the roof that was of the same height and would have been easier to navigate, when Hamish continued, "Trust me."

He'd done a lot of that in the last few minutes: trust his former friend who had betrayed him. Would it come back to bite him?

But something in Hamish's gaze made Aiden follow his friend's suggestion. Or maybe he simply *wanted* to believe his friend. Taking Leila's hand once more, he ran toward him. At the edge of the roof, he turned to Leila.

"We've done this before. You'll be all right."

She nodded. "Yes."

Without having to be prompted, she slung her arms around him. It felt good to feel her so close and for a moment all he wanted was to revel in her touch, but there was no time to lose. The rattling of the door a few yards behind them became more insistent. They would soon manage to open it.

Hamish jumped first, then turned and waved at Aiden to follow.

With Leila in his arms, he jumped down, landing squarely on his two feet, allowing his knees to take the impact. Instantly, he released her from his arms. They rushed after Hamish who was already rounding the makeshift structure on the neighboring roof.

As they reached the same spot, Aiden rocked to a halt. Hamish was gone.

Shit! If this was a trap—

"Aiden, here!" Hamish's voice came from next to him.

He whirled his head toward the sound and saw Hamish peek out from a window in the rickety shed. Lifting up Leila, Aiden quickly heaved her through the opening and followed.

Inside, it was dark, but his superior vision adjusted and allowed him to see the staircase leading down. Hamish was already taking it.

He felt Leila reaching for him. "I can't see anything."

"I'll be your eyes."

In the darkness, he guided her downstairs, making sure she didn't trip. When they reached the bottom, music drifted to them, together with loud cheering sounds.

Hamish pushed a door in front of them open. Dim light illuminated the corridor they found themselves in. The cheesy seventies tune, 'Stayin' Alive' from the Bee Gees, became more distinct as they advanced.

Aiden was startled when a door to his left opened, and a barely-clothed young man, wearing a costume of some sort, stepped through it. He caught a glimpse of the room behind him and raised an eyebrow. It appeared that it was a changing room of a theater, even though he wasn't aware that this part of town had any theaters.

Still cloaked, he flattened himself against the wall and motioned for Leila to do the same, so the man wouldn't bump into them. From the corner of his eye, he caught how Leila let her gaze run over the man's semi-nude body. An odd twinge of something he couldn't quite identify coursed through him: he didn't like the way she looked at this, admittedly very perfect male form. Hell, he didn't want her to even look at a fully dressed man, let alone a half-naked one.

For a moment, the fact that they were still trying to escape their enemies faded into the background. Aiden pulled Leila's hand toward his chest and dragged her against him. Her hip connected with his thigh. When she lifted her head to give him a surprised look, he noticed her breath catch. Before she could lower her lids to hide the expression in them, he tipped her chin up and forced her to acknowledge him.

Her lips parted, and her breath ghosted over his face. Without thinking, he lowered his head.

"No time to waste."

Hamish's harsh command jolted him, making him release her instantly. A faint rose blush stole over her cheeks.

"Where to?" Aiden asked, clearing his throat. He'd nearly kissed her, right here in front of Hamish. If that wasn't screwed up, then what was?

Hamish motioned his head to a door that said *Stage*. He opened it and slipped in. Aiden did likewise, pulling Leila with him.

A curtain obstructed the view, but lights flashed behind it, and music blared from large speakers all around them.

"I'm stayin' alive," the audience joined in the chorus.

"We have to get to the other side of the stage," Hamish whispered into his ear. "There's a portal over there."

Aiden wasn't sure he'd understood correctly over the noise of the music, because for sure there would be no portal in this joint. Only compounds had portals. He shrugged it off and followed as Hamish moved the curtain aside and slipped onto the stage.

As he walked past the curtain and took two steps onto the stage, Aiden felt Leila stop in her tracks. A quick glance at her confirmed that her mouth had dropped open as she stared at the performance.

There, on a stage bathed in glittering lights, five barely dressed hunks danced a seductive striptease. They looked like Chippendales, albeit a little less classy, strutting their junk like a bunch of dogs at a dog show. Their string-clad asses reflected the lights that bounced off the tacky eighties disco ball that hung from the ceiling. Nothing but tassels covered their precious jewels, shifting as the dancers moved with the music.

The audience, a few women and a lot more guys, cheered every time a tassel revealed the flesh beneath. Now, a male spectator leaned over the stage, where one performer dropped down lower, allowing the audience member to stick a twenty-dollar bill into his string. But the spectator's hand quickly drifted off course, copping a feel. The performer slapped him playfully on the hand and simply laughed, eliciting raucous laughter from the audience.

Aiden had seen enough. He pulled on Leila's hand and dragged her across the stage, evading the dancers as best he could. None too gently, he tugged on her hand, finally getting Leila to focus her attention on him and not on the semi-nude dancers.

As they reached the other side of the stage, Hamish was waiting impatiently.

"What took you so long?"

Aiden aimed an annoyed look at Leila. "Somebody was a little too fascinated with the show."

Leila huffed and eased her hand from his grip. "That is not true!"

Hamish rolled his eyes. "Sorry to cut the party short."

"Where to from here?" Aiden asked.

"There's a portal."

"What?" This time he was sure he hadn't misheard. "Here?"

Hamish nodded.

"That's not possible. There are no portals outside the compounds." Every Stealth Guardian knew that.

"Well, then be prepared for a surprise." Hamish waved him to a staircase that led down.

Reluctantly, Aiden followed, Leila by his side. Hamish had to be crazy if he thought that he'd found a portal outside of the compounds. Something was fishy. His hand slid to the dagger he'd tugged into the waistband of his pants after nearly attacking Hamish with it in the Thai massage parlor. If he needed to use it now, he wouldn't hesitate.

In the dimly lit basement that was filled with old costumes, stage furniture and boxes upon boxes, his fellow Stealth Guardian navigated them to the back of the building before turning to a barely-visible indentation in the dust covered stone wall.

Hamish laid his palm flat against the indentation that looked as if it could be simply an imperfection in the stone. However, on closer inspection, as his friend brushed the dust off it, Aiden recognized it as their secret symbol: an ancient blade.

"Oh, my God! How can there be a portal outside of the compounds?"

Aiden brushed his hands over the symbol, then pressed his palm against it. As the warmth of his skin flooded the symbol, it began to glow beneath his hand. A moment later, the wall disintegrated and a dark tunnel appeared before them.

The portal was open.

22

Leila stared at the hole in the wall. This couldn't be happening. Some sort of portal had opened up right in front of them, just by Aiden putting his hand on the wall. She instantly remembered what he'd told her earlier about portals.

"I thought only demons had portals."

It confused her. Why hadn't he told her about his?

"Stealth Guardians do too. However—" Aiden looked at Hamish. "—I thought that they didn't exist outside the compounds."

"We all thought that. I'll explain that later. Now, we'd better go."

He stepped inside the dark tunnel. Aiden reached for her hand and pulled her with him. She had no choice. Even if she'd wanted to, she couldn't have stayed where she was. Eventually the people who were following them would find her here.

"I'm claustrophobic," she admitted.

"It won't take long," Aiden promised, pulling her close to him.

A moment later, the dim light from the basement disappeared as if the door to the tunnel had been closed.

"Where to?" Aiden asked.

"Take my hand," Hamish's voice commanded.

She felt how Aiden pulled her close to him with one arm around her waist, his other hand presumably clutching Hamish's. Then the air stirred up around them as if a fierce storm was approaching.

Fear gripped her, and she began to shiver. She felt her body being lifted in the air, floating weightlessly and without direction. Both her arms went around Aiden, holding on for dear life. She was afraid of being dropped, of falling into a bottomless pit, eternal darkness around her.

"Shh," Aiden cooed, his mouth at her ear.

Then he shifted, and his lips brushed over her cheek, then slowly and carefully approached her lips. She could have moved away from him, turned her head so he couldn't kiss her, but she didn't. Instead, she allowed his lips to press against hers, his tongue to gently glide over them, to part them and sweep inside.

In the dark she felt strangely safe with him. With a sigh, she angled her head, urging him for a deeper kiss. He obliged her. When his tongue stroked against hers and his lips moved firmly over her mouth, the storm around her moved into the distance. All she felt were his firm strokes, his earthy taste, and his hard body that pressed against her, holding her firmly and securely in his arms. Forgotten was the fact that he'd lied to her about having to touch her to cloak her.

Maybe she wouldn't have reacted so strongly to that revelation, if they hadn't been caught by Manus in the middle of the act. She'd been too embarrassed to think of anything else but the humiliation that she'd felt.

But now, all that didn't matter. Aiden's kiss was as sinful as it had been before, and it made her want things beyond a kiss, beyond a mere touch, even beyond the intimate touches they'd shared at the massage parlor. Way beyond that.

"Hate to interrupt," Hamish said wryly, "but we can't stay here forever."

Leila opened her eyes, heat rushing to her cheeks once more. Did she always have to get caught doing something... something so forbidden? Because what she was doing with Aiden had to be wrong: he was there to protect her, and beyond that she knew she couldn't trust him. He'd confirmed this only a short while earlier when he'd confessed to Hamish that he'd killed his former charge.

Sobering, she avoided looking at Aiden and withdrew from his embrace. Instead, she perused her surroundings. They were in some sort of cave. Rows of oak barrels lined the vast space, each with a number and a few letters on it, marking their content.

"Where are we?" Aiden asked.

"About an hour north of San Francisco, in the wine country," Hamish answered.

"You have to explain to me how come there's a portal here when there are supposed to be none outside the compounds," Aiden demanded, his voice tight.

Hamish nodded. "I will, on the way to our safe house."

He headed for the door, unlatched it, and opened it. Then he peered outside. "All clear."

Curious, Leila followed him, feeling Aiden at her back. Outside, it was sunny and clear. She looked back at the cave and realized that it had been built into the side of the hill, thus taking advantage of the natural cool earth to keep the barrels at a constant temperature. In the distance, she saw several buildings, one that looked like a barn with big stainless steel silos, another one that probably contained the tasting room and offices.

Nobody seemed to be around.

The dirt path Hamish led them on ended at a wooden shack. Inside was an old beat-up Toyota that looked like the loser of a demolition derby. She piled in the back seat, letting Hamish and Aiden take the front. By the looks of it, they had much to talk about anyway.

As they rumbled down the hill and through the vineyard, Hamish finally addressed Aiden's earlier question.

"You're right, there shouldn't be any portals outside the compounds, so you can imagine my surprise when I found one."

"How did you find it?" Aiden instantly wanted to know.

"Well, that brings me to the bigger issue here. I have reason to believe that one of the council members is working for the demons. I can't—"

From the backseat, Leila could firmly see how Aiden jolted at the news.

"That can't be!" His head whipped sideways to glare at his friend. "If you think you can accuse somebody to lessen your own failings—"

"Those were not my failings!" Hamish shot back. "If I could have helped you I would have. But I was being pursued. Had I not disappeared when I did, I would be dead now."

~ ~ ~

Aiden pulled in a breath. What his former second was insinuating was outrageous. But often the truth was unbelievable. And he hoped Hamish was telling the truth.

"I want the whole story," he demanded. "And start with how you found Leila and me."

"Oh, you're gonna get it, but you won't like it," Hamish promised, gracing him with an ominous look.

Somehow that look was enough for Aiden to realize that whatever it was he was about to hear would uproot his entire belief in their race. "Go on."

"Well, finding you was easy. I've been shadowing you for days. I had this gut feeling that you're in danger. Figured if they tried to move me out of the way, what's stopping them from doing the same with you? I kept an eye on you from afar so I could interfere if need be."

Hamish gave him a sideways glance. "Anyway, to get to the real story, a few weeks ago, I noticed strange coincidences, demons showing up close to safe houses and other places we were hiding charges. I looked at the location logs and plotted those occurrences, cross-referencing them with who accessed the location files as these assignments were taking place. I came across an encoded access signature in each of those incidences. It leads to the council."

"That doesn't have to mean anything. The council has the right to access those files whenever they want to. That's how they can find out where we are."

"What does that mean?" Leila asked from the back seat. "Do they know where we are now?"

Aiden turned his head to her. "No. I would have to sign into the system to announce my location."

"Which you're not going to do," Hamish added quickly. "Nobody can know where we are right now. Not as long as we don't know who on the council is a traitor."

Aiden hated the thought of that. "You must be wrong. The council is above reproach."

"Don't be so naïve. They're just like us. They have desires. But that aside, as I started digging and trying to get past the encryption, I had the strange feeling of being followed. Several times. I can't be sure, but I knew something was wrong. During our last assignment, I ran into a problem."

Aiden felt his gut constrict at the thought of how that last assignment had ended.

"I received a message, which looked like it was coming from command central. It sent me to a place, which I thought was your location. It wasn't. Instead, I ended up in a trap. But whoever set it up underestimated me. They'd only sent two demons. I killed them, but I knew they wouldn't be the last ones coming for me."

Hamish gave him a sideways glance. "They didn't want me to help you keep Sarah safe. They wanted her too badly, so whoever on the council was feeding the demons information, didn't mind sacrificing one of their own for it."

In disbelief, Aiden shook his head. "Someone on the council would get a Stealth Guardian killed to help the demons? But why?"

Hamish shrugged. "I don't know. Not yet, anyway. That's why I had to disappear. The only way to be sure that I had no tracking devices on me was to leave my clothes and my cell behind me. I couldn't tell you. It would have put you in danger. You're my best friend. I couldn't do that."

Aiden nodded. He understood, and he would have done the same had he been in that situation. "Brothers?"

"Always," his best friend replied. They locked eyes for a moment, their trust restored.

"Now what?"

Hamish pulled the car to a stop in front of a small farmhouse. "Let's get inside, then we can talk more."

23

Aiden sank back into the comfortable couch as Leila excused herself to freshen up in the bathroom. Personally, he didn't want to wash her smell off him. He could still taste her kiss, one she'd had every opportunity to deny him, yet had openly participated in. However, as much as he wanted to daydream about it, there were more important things to think about.

"How did you ever find that portal?"

Hamish, who sat opposite him, popped the lid off a beer bottle and gulped down half of it before answering. "By accident. On one of those occasions when I thought I was being followed, I ended up in that strip club. I thought I'd seen somebody disappear into the basement, so I followed. But nobody was there. Instead, I found the portal. The dust was disturbed where the symbol was; that's why I even noticed it."

"So you think it was a Stealth Guardian who followed you and then disappeared through the portal?"

"Most definitely. I would have known if it was a demon. There are way too many neon signs in that club not to notice the presence of a demon."

Aiden had to agree. It would have been impossible for a demon to sneak past Hamish without destroying all the lights. But the thought that somebody on the council was aiding their enemies was still too disturbing a thought.

"Are you suspecting anybody in particular?" For a moment, he held his breath. When he met his friend's gaze, he already knew the answer.

"Nobody is above suspicion." Hamish paused. "Not even your father."

Aiden jumped up and walked to the kitchen, pulling a beer from the fridge.

"I'm sorry to be so blunt, but it could be anybody. And just because he's your father doesn't make him immune to the influences of the demons."

Aiden twisted the cap off the bottle and tossed it in the trash before turning back toward the open plan living area. "My father is a strong willed man. He would never allow the demons to influence him. Besides, he's got everything he wants. What could they possibly tempt him with?"

The only thing anyone in his family could be tempted with was to have Julia back, but even the demons couldn't resurrect the dead.

Slowly, he walked back to the couch and slouched down.

"If I knew what went on in the head of each council member, trust me, I wouldn't be sitting here wondering about it. I would be taking the asshole down. Whoever it is, he is betraying all of us. And putting us in danger," Hamish said

"What do you propose to do about it, considering you're a wanted man right now?"

Hamish grinned. "Now that's where you come in."

"Why do I get the feeling that I'm being used?"

"What are friends for? Besides, didn't I just save you and your charge's ass? And what a lovely ass it is."

Aiden glared at him. "Leave her out of this." He wasn't in the mood to discuss Leila's assets with him.

"So I wasn't mistaken then. You do have the hots for a human. You never cease to surprise me."

"It's not like that. And it's not up for discussion either."

Particularly because he didn't want to face the facts: with every minute he spent with her, the thought of having to hurt her one day sickened him more and more. He couldn't remain objective about her and treat her like he'd treated every charge before her. The indifference and emotional detachment that had served him so well in the past had deserted him on this assignment. If he wasn't careful, he'd form an attachment to her that he would have a hard time severing later.

"Can we change the subject? I believe we were talking about how to ferret out the traitor."

"Very well. Let's start with who knew you were at the safe house."

"But as we both know, the attack on the safe house wasn't staged by the demons," Aiden explained. "Ergo, this won't lead us to the traitor."

"We can't know for sure. Maybe they didn't want to kill your charge but capture her instead. I know who she is."

Aiden sucked in a quick breath. "How much do you know?"

"Most of it: that she's a talented researcher, and that her boss just got killed and she's somehow involved," Hamish admitted.

"That's only the half of it." He leaned forward. As he filled Hamish in on the details of why the demons wanted Leila, he listened to the sound of the shower down the hallway. He blocked out the thought of it, and concentrated on giving Hamish all the information he had.

When he leaned back a few minutes later, Hamish took another sip from his beer and set the empty bottle on the coffee table. "No shit!"

"Yep, that's it in a nutshell."

"So we're up against two enemies: the demons who want her drug, and since no copy of it exists anymore, they have to get her; and somebody else who wants to eliminate her before the demons get to her."

Aiden twisted the bottle in his hands. "And since the only people who know what threat she represents are sitting on the council, whoever wants to eliminate her, is also on the council."

"Two birds to catch then. One traitor, and one, let's say, misguided council member who doesn't like the fact that he was outvoted and is now taking matters into his own hands to ensure the desired outcome."

"Exactly."

Hamish rubbed the back of his neck. "There's one other person who knows what kind of danger Leila represents."

Aiden blinked. "Manus." He slammed his hand into the sofa cushion. "He was the only other person who knew where we were. He came to switch out the cars. He even brought Leila some chocolate for her birthday, which proves he's read her file from cover to cover."

"It's a possibility. But don't forget that besides Manus, the council could have checked into your location log and found where you were."

He shook his head. "No. They couldn't have known. When I claimed the safe house, the request was anonymous, and I hadn't checked my position in with central command yet."

"After being at the house for what, at least eight hours?" Hamish sent an incredulous look his way.

"I know it's against procedure, but there were circumstances that prevented me..." Ah, hell, who was he kidding? He'd forgotten to send his position to central command. He'd been too preoccupied with Leila. A great Stealth Guardian that made him.

"So that confirms it," Hamish agreed. "The only one who knew you were at the Thai massage parlor was Manus. That means he's the one who sent the dogs after you."

"Shit!" Aiden cursed.

"No!" Leila's voice came from the corridor as she stepped into the living area. "It's not Manus's fault. It's mine."

~ ~ ~

Leila collected all her courage and stared past Aiden, unable to look him in the eye right now. Yet she couldn't keep silent about this and let an innocent take the blame for what she'd done. It had bugged her ever since Hamish had shown up at the safe house and said that a phone call could have been traced back to it.

"I'm sorry, I just meant to... my parents, I didn't want them to worry when they heard the news about what happened to me. I had to tell them I was okay." She pulled the belt of the bathrobe she'd found in one of the closets tighter around her waist.

"You did what?" Aiden leapt from the couch.

"I called them from the safe house."

Aiden closed his eyes for a moment and clenched his jaw. She noticed how his hand curled into a fist as if he wanted to punch somebody, presumably her.

When he opened his eyes again, they blazed with anger. "Do you want to die? Do you? Because you're making it damn hard for me to protect you."

"But they needed to know. I couldn't—"

"You couldn't what? So you'd rather put yourself and everybody else in danger because of what? Sentiments? I'm afraid you don't have that luxury." He marched toward her, his steps slow like a tiger ready to attack.

"That's not fair!" she bit back. Maybe he had no parents to care about, but she did.

"Fair?" he yelled. "Life isn't fair! Those demons aren't fair, and neither is that Stealth Guardian who's after you to eliminate you!"

"What?" she echoed. Had she heard correctly? "The Stealth Guardians want to kill me?" Instinctively, she took several steps back and hit the wall behind her.

Aiden slammed his fist into the wall beside her head, jolting her. She'd never seen him so angry.

"Fuck, yes! Everybody is after you."

"Stop it, Aiden!" Hamish jumped up and went to his side.

Aiden ignored him. "Not only are the demons after you. Whoever tried to attack you today, or last night for that matter is one of our own. And you worry about what your parents think?"

Leila shivered, not understanding why he still blamed his colleague. "I'm sorry, but I told you it wasn't Manus's fault."

"I'm not talking about Manus!"

Hamish put a hand on Aiden's shoulder, then looked straight at her. "It appears that somebody on our governing council would rather see you dead and your research die with you than risk that you fall into the demons' hands."

Her mouth fell open and her heart pounded into her throat. "But those are the same people who sent you, aren't they?"

Both nodded.

Her voice shook, when she continued, "Then did they order you to kill me now?"

Aiden let out a breath, sounding somewhat calmer as he continued, "No. Whoever wants you dead is a rogue and is working against the council's orders."

Leila swallowed away the rising bile. She felt all power drain from her. She wasn't safe anywhere, not even with him. "So not only do I have the demons after me, your own people want me dead."

"Only one of them," Aiden answered.

"You can't know that. How many voted to eliminate me?"

"We don't know."

Hamish ran his hand through his hair. "But most likely only one of them is actually doing anything about it. And we'll find him."

"He'll use anything to get to you, I can promise you that," Aiden added.

At his words, she instantly realized where she was most vulnerable. "My parents. You have to make sure they're okay. They have to be protected. If anything happens to them..." She would never forgive herself for it.

"We don't have the manpower to protect your parents. Not when we don't know who we can trust."

"Please," she pleaded and took a step closer to Aiden, tears threatening to overwhelm her. "I need to know that they're alright. Please."

She looked at Aiden, then at Hamish, hoping that one of them would give in to her.

"Don't you have parents? Don't you know how much it hurts not to know if they are okay?"

"Okay, I'll go," Hamish relented.

Instantly Aiden slapped his palm on his friend's arm. "No, I'll go." Then he stared back at her. "I need some air."

He turned away from her, but she caught his resigned look nevertheless.

She didn't know what suddenly made her want to know, but she couldn't stop the words leaving her lips. "If you were on the council, how would you have voted?"

He hesitated, his voice shaking slightly when he finally answered, "I'm not sure about that answer anymore."

24

It took Aiden an hour to reach her parents' house. Hamish had explained to him that the portals outside the compounds worked the same way as those inside: he only had to concentrate on his destination and the portal would carry him to whatever portal was closest to his desired location. Simple as that. The reason nobody using the portals within the compounds had accidentally stumbled upon the portals that Hamish now called *lost portals*, was probably because nobody had ever tried to concentrate on a location other than the known portals. However, he was nevertheless baffled how their existence could have remained a secret for so long.

He was glad to have had an excuse to leave. The knowledge that Leila's action had put her in danger again, had sent bolts of fear through his body. And had made him act irrationally. What had happened wasn't her fault. It was his.

He should have taken better precautions and explained the ground rules to her. This could have been avoided if he'd used his brain instead of letting another part of his body inform his actions.

And maybe he wouldn't even be so pissed about this fact if he wasn't so emotionally involved. There, he'd admitted it to himself: he cared about her. When she'd pressed herself against him when they were in the portal and allowed him to kiss her, he'd thought for a moment that everything would turn out fine between them. Unfortunately he'd just pushed her away again with the way he'd yelled at her, when really, the fury he'd unleashed was aimed at himself for not protecting her sufficiently.

With a sigh, he perused his surroundings.

The house was a two-story Edwardian with a large front yard and an even larger garden in the back. Ivy grew on its façade, and the hedges around the grounds needed trimming. These were the suburbs, but the fancy ones. No doubt, the family had money.

Night had already fallen, and lights inside the home were ablaze. Aiden walked past the old station wagon that was parked

in the driveway in front of the two-car garage. Did the
Cruickshanks have visitors?

There was an easy way to find out. A familiar tingling went
through his entire body as he dematerialized and passed through
the front door, sneaking inside the cozy foyer a moment later.
Remaining invisible, he walked along the wallpapered hallway
with all the stealth he'd been taught.

The house smelled homey, the scent of freshly baked cookies
drifting into his nose. He could almost picture Leila as a little girl,
running down the stairs and toward the kitchen to collect her treat.
Odd that she appeared in much softer terms to him now, when in
the environment he'd met her first—her lab and her apartment—
none of that softness was evident. Maybe he was simply imagining
it.

A female voice came from the back of the house. He followed
it and reached an open door. Halting there, he peered into the
kitchen. It was spacious, with a large island in the middle, and a
dining nook near a large bay window.

A middle-aged woman, presumably the housekeeper, stood at
the island and cut bread into slices. At the dining nook, an elderly
couple sat, waiting silently. The woman was probably in her mid
to late sixties, and the man possibly five to ten years her senior.
Those two had to be Leila's parents. In fact, now that he entered
the kitchen to take a closer look, he recognized similarities.

Her father had the same ocean-blue eyes as his daughter, yet
they lacked the sparkle and passion he'd seen in Leila's. There
was a dull sheen over them as he stared past his wife, almost as if
he was so preoccupied with his thoughts that he didn't really see
her. Well, maybe after being married for several decades, that was
what relationships turned into, for his wife didn't look at him
either. She played with her napkin, folding it first that way, then
the other.

Somehow, the scene didn't look like the companionable
silence he'd occasionally observed with his own parents. It felt
awkward. Had they quarreled?

"The soup is coming," the housekeeper said in a cheerful
voice, the same one he'd heard from the corridor earlier. "Mmm,
you'll like it. I made you pumpkin soup today, fresh with lots of
cream, just the way you like it."

Aiden turned to the woman, surprised at her tone. She sounded as if she were talking to a child. He got out of her way and moved to the other side of the table when she carried two bowls with steaming hot soup and set them in front of the couple.

"There," she said. "How about some fresh rosemary bread with that?"

Leila's mother nodded. "And butter. Don't forget the butter. You always forget the butter."

Aiden caught how the housekeeper rolled her eyes. "I never forget the butter, Ellie. Don't you remember how I put it on extra thick this morning?"

"You didn't give me bread this morning," Ellie protested.

Her husband shook his head. "I didn't get bread this morning either."

Ellie tossed him a chiding look and waved the housekeeper closer. In a whisper, she spoke to her. "Do I always have to eat with him? Nancy, why doesn't he go home?"

Nancy sighed and sat down on the empty chair. "But, Ellie, that's George. You know George, don't you? Your husband?"

Ellie's eyes darted toward him, looking him up and down. Then she bent closer to the housekeeper once more. "I don't think that's my husband. He's old. I married a handsome young man named George."

George only grunted and started eating his soup.

Aiden watched the exchange with surprise. Something wasn't right here. Was there a chance that the demons had already gotten to Leila's parents and somehow distorted their sense of reality?

"Why don't you start your soup, Ellie, and I'll get you your meds, huh? Maybe you'll feel better afterwards."

Nancy lifted herself from the chair and went over to the kitchen counter where an array of medicine bottles and containers took up an entire corner. She took two long plastic containers, which were embossed with the days of the week and *Ellie* and *George*, and went back to the dining table.

Aiden didn't follow her. Instead, he stared at the medicine bottles and read the labels. Since he wasn't a doctor, he didn't know what any of them were for, however, he needed to find out. Something he couldn't explain compelled him to. He pulled out his smartphone, switched it on in silent mode, and entered the name of the first medication. A few second later, search results were back. He clicked on the first, read it. A knot started forming in his chest.

He entered the next one, and more results came back. Again, he read the first, and again, he couldn't believe his eyes. He perused the bottles, noticing that both Leila's parents took almost identical medication.

Shocked, Aiden stalked out of the kitchen and fled into the front of the house where he found the living room and let himself fall onto the couch.

Both Leila's parents took medication for the treatment of Alzheimer's.

Now everything suddenly made sense: the determination Leila showed in her research, the single-minded purpose that reflected in her private life or the lack thereof, her devastation when she'd found her research destroyed. She did all this for her parents. She wanted to save them.

She wasn't looking for the recognition of her peers and humanity at large to become the inventor of the first Alzheimer's drug that would halt the disease. All she wanted was to cure her parents and reverse some of the damage the disease had done to their minds.

Aiden felt shame radiate through him. He'd callously demanded that all copies of her research be destroyed, would have destroyed them himself had somebody else not beaten him to it. And all the while, her dreams destroyed, her hopes squashed, Leila had kept her true pain hidden from him.

No wonder she hated him and his kind. It was a miracle, she hadn't tried to give him any more resistance, or tried to escape a second time. Now that he knew what was really at stake for her, he wouldn't even blame her if she tried. Wouldn't he do the same? Wouldn't he try to do everything to save his parents if he had the means to do it? Would he care that by doing so, he would jeopardize the entire human race?

Could she be so selfless in the end to put humanity's needs before her own? If she could do that, if she could look beyond her own desires, all he could do was admire her for it. Because it would mean she wasn't weak. She was strong, stronger than any human or Stealth Guardian he'd ever met.

A woman he could fall on his knees for and wish for things he'd previously believed impossible.

If she ever forgave him.

25

Leila accepted the cup of tea Hamish handed her as he joined her on the couch in the living room. She had gotten dressed in jeans and T-shirt again.

Hamish leaned back in his corner and saluted her with a glass of Scotch, which he'd told her was the preferred drink among Stealth Guardians.

"Why whiskey?" she asked.

He shrugged. "I guess it's our heritage. We're descendents from an ancient tribe that lived in Scotland, or rather on an island off Scotland. It's cold up there. And the Scotch warms us."

"Aiden mentioned something like that, the Outer Hebrides, I think he said. Well, I prefer tea." At least it would keep her head clear.

Hamish smiled and took a swig. She watched as he savored the drink coating his throat. He was as tall as Aiden, but a little broader around the shoulders and the hips. His features were a little more worn, with more pronounced lines crisscrossing his face and dark shadows under his eyes as if he hadn't slept in days. As if some big worry had kept him up.

"So, what else has he told you about us?"

Leila set her mug on the coffee table. "Not much, only what your powers are; that you can cloak humans, and walk through walls. Is there more?"

He quirked an eyebrow. "That's about it."

"How many of you are there?"

"Not enough." He expelled a bitter laugh. "And at this point I'm not even sure which one of our people I can trust. It's sad to see that even among our kind there are those who put their own profit before the good of the community. And we're not immune to temptations, as you might have noticed."

She felt herself blush under his suggestive gaze, knowing only too well what he was referring to: the fact that she and Aiden had kissed passionately when Hamish had transported them to the wine country. She could only blame her fear of dark spaces for having provoked this kiss. Otherwise, she was sure she wouldn't have allowed it, not after everything that had happened between her and Aiden previously. After all, he'd lied to her—repeatedly.

And so have you.

She tried to squash the little voice in her head that reminded her that she hadn't confessed that one copy of her research still existed. Instinctively, her hand went to her pendant that still hung inconspicuously around her neck.

"So," she searched hastily for something to say, "how long have you and Aiden known each other?"

"Almost two hundred years, we grew—"

"Two hundred years?" Shock made her sit up straight. "You're two hundred years old?" He didn't look a day over thirty-five, and neither did Aiden.

A charming grin spread over Hamish's lips. "Yeah, that always gets a reaction." He winked at her. "But we're only just hitting our prime. Unfortunately, *rasen* can be a pain in the butt."

Her eyebrows snapped together in confusion. "*Rasen*? What's that?"

"Mating season. The closer we get to our 200th birthday, the more urgent the drive to find a mate becomes. It's a bit like a human woman's biological clock, only a lot more intense."

"Oh." She hadn't really wanted to talk about anything related to relationships. Maybe it was best to change the subject. "That's okay, I wasn't really asking about that."

But Hamish didn't let her off the hook. "You wanted to know more about Aiden. I'm willing to talk. You might as well take the offer. Who knows whether I'll feel this generous ever again."

She reached for the mug, feeling the need to steady her hands with something to distract from the fact that she was nervous. "I'm really not interested in talking about him. He's obviously mad at me for calling my parents. I'm sorry, but I had to. I couldn't just let them believe that—"

Hamish held up his hand. "I understand. But you're misinterpreting Aiden. He isn't mad at you. Of course, he has his reasons for reacting the way he did. But since you're not interested in finding out more, I'll just keep those to myself."

Leila glared at him. She understood exactly what he was doing: he was baiting her. As if she were that easy to manipulate.

Taking a quick sip from her tea, she told herself that she didn't care what Aiden's reasons for his outburst were. It didn't matter at all.

When she looked up, Hamish sat there in silence as if waiting for her to crack. She wouldn't. She didn't want to hear excuses for his behavior.

"You surprise me," he suddenly said.

"In what way?"

"Your self-control."

When she gave him a confused look, he continued, "Most women would jump at the chance of getting the inside scoop on a guy they're into, but you—"

"I'm not *into* him!" she snapped.

"Well, my bad."

She huffed and hugged her arms around her torso.

"We grew up together. We've been best friends since we broke out of our crib for the first time at age two. If anybody knows him, I do."

"Fine! Go ahead, tell me what you want to tell me and get it over with. Obviously, he told you to pacify me and make excuses for his behavior." But she would take it all with a grain of salt.

"Aiden? He would rip my head off if he found out about it. He's a very private man. He never even tells me anything, but I know what he feels. He can't hide things from me."

She had to agree with him on that statement: Aiden didn't tell her much either. Rather, he liked to omit things, important ones. And he didn't explain why he made certain decisions either. At least if she knew why certain things had to happen, she could try to come to grips with them. The scientist in her could accept that. But there had to be compelling reasons. Irrational behavior she could not excuse.

Leila settled back into her corner of the couch, and tucked her legs beneath her.

"He has a soft heart," Hamish started, making her scoff instantly.

He gave her a chiding look. "Which he hides well. His sister and he were very close. Twins. They did everything together, so it was only natural that when Aiden decided to get into the trenches and train for the most dangerous jobs to fight the demons, Julia was right there with him. She was fearless."

She shuddered, knowing she herself would be too much of a coward to do the same.

"And of course, when we were young, we all thought we were invincible. I was the same; we all thought we could overcome any obstacle, defeat any enemy, save any human." He paused. "We couldn't."

Leila noticed the pain that was suddenly evident in his eyes. "What happened?"

He continued as if he hadn't even heard her question. "Aiden didn't hate humans. In fact, he was rather curious about them. He liked watching them go about their lives, oblivious to the dangers around them, and he felt proud to be there to protect them. Every time he saved a human from the clutches of the demons, you could see the pride and satisfaction in his eyes. He loved what he was doing. Julia did, too. They were cut from the same cloth: fierce, loyal, and so proud of their achievements. And convinced they could do no wrong."

He sighed, and Leila held her breath, sensing that something did go wrong after all.

"Aiden had never killed a human before. He'd never had to. And he believed strongly that everyone could be saved, that even if the demons got close to them, he could still pull them back and turn them onto the right path." Hamish let out a bitter laugh.

"How wrong he was. How wrong we all were. But of course we didn't listen to our elders, we didn't listen to experience. Because we were young and invincible, remember?"

"Like we all are when we're young," Leila murmured. She had thought the same when she'd started out her career and hoped to conquer the world only to be brought down to reality when her parents had been diagnosed with Alzheimer's.

"Yes, just like humans. But it was worse, because we knew we were immortal. Well, as immortal as you can get: there is only one sort of weapon that can kill us, but we were too full of ourselves to believe it would ever affect us. We'd trained to fight the demons; we fought them on a regular basis; we were good. But we weren't perfect."

"Nobody can ever be perfect."

Hamish looked at her then, his eyes brimming with the pain from his past. "No, but we sure as hell tried. And failed. We all paid the price in the end. Aiden and Julia were on a mission, but things went south. They were protecting a brilliant young physicist, ambitious and driven. He was on the verge of a breakthrough that would have pushed Stephen Hawking's work into the background. But as it is often with people who want to succeed, no price is too high."

His words sunk deep into her, and she felt how they resonated with her. Would it be the same for her? Would she be willing to pay any price just to succeed and reach her goal? And what would she give up for it? Her soul?

"The demons took control of him, but Aiden thought he could still save him, even though it was too late for him. He already belonged to them. In the fight that resulted, the human, controlled by the demons, drove a blade forged in the Dark Days into Julia. In blind rage, Aiden massacred him. I've never seen so much blood and gore in my entire life. But Julia, it was too late for her. She died in Aiden's arms."

Leila gasped, tears threatening to burst from her eyes. "Oh my God." Her heart bled for him.

"To this day, he blames himself. And he despises humans for their weakness, for their lack of strength in resisting the demons. He still protects them, but…"

"But what?" She nudged forward, eager to hear more.

"When he had to kill his charge last week, I can only imagine that the memories of what happened to Julia came flooding back to him. I haven't seen him so agitated since her death. He won't hesitate again to kill a human if he believes the demons have taken hold."

She nodded numbly. "How can he even be around me? He must see all the parallels between me and Julia's murderer. He must think that I will succumb too."

Hamish gave a soft smile. "And yet, he seeks to be near you." He hesitated. "Maybe you can help him restore his faith in humankind. Perhaps if he sees that not every human is weak, he will finally realize that what happened was a terrible tragedy, but it doesn't mean every human poses the same danger."

"But how can I do that? Did I mention that I'm a coward? I felt claustrophobic in that portal you took us through. I was shaking like a leaf. I'm not strong," she protested. She shied away from any kind of danger.

"You're stronger than you think."

"But Aiden… he's so angry with me now. Because I called my parents." How could he forgive her when she'd reacted like one of the weak humans he despised?

"He's not angry. He's scared because he thinks he's failed to protect you."

"I wish I could believe that." She sighed and paused for a moment. "Uh… may I ask you something?"

"Sure."

"You said he despises humans for their weakness." She searched his eyes for confirmation and found it. "He told me he doesn't touch his charges… that he never…" She broke off. Maybe she shouldn't go down that road. "Forget it."

"Leila, I've seen the way he looks at you," Hamish helped.

Heat shot up her cheeks as she made another attempt to get her question out. "Does he ever get involved with humans?"

"A few days ago I would have said 'no', but today, seeing him with you, I have to revise my answer."

"But… what does he want from me?"

"Why don't you ask him that yourself?"

The sound of footsteps coming from the entrance door made her look up. Aiden stood at the door to the living room, his eyes trained on her. Their gazes locked, and the world around her faded into the background. All she saw was the man and his heart, vulnerable, bare, and without protection. She understood now what he needed.

26

They'd been talking about him, but Aiden had only heard the last couple of sentences. But at present he didn't even care what Hamish had been saying behind his back, because all he could do was stare at Leila and lose himself in the depth of her ocean blue eyes. Eyes she didn't avert, but with which she looked at him with equal intensity.

"Why don't I go to the village for some food?" Hamish's words barely registered, nor did the fact that his friend brushed past him and left the house.

All of a sudden Aiden stood in front of her, pulled her from the couch, cupping her shoulders.

"Your parents are safe."

He saw the relief that went through her, then continued, "Why didn't you tell me?"

"Tell you what?" she echoed, her lips parting in the most inviting way he'd ever seen. A sheen of moisture covered them, making him want to swipe his tongue over it and lick it off her.

"That both your parents suffer from Alzheimer's."

Her eyes widened as if she'd been caught. As if she hadn't wanted him to know, when she could have used that information to elicit his sympathy.

"I... I didn't want..."

He shook his head. "I'm sorry. I understand now what all this means to you, what the loss of your research means." He lifted his hand from her shoulder and stroked his knuckles over her cheek. "I'm so sorry."

She sucked in a breath, releasing a quiet sigh, but if she had wanted to respond, he didn't give her a chance. Instead, he slanted his lips over her mouth and kissed her. Gently first, softly, without any pressure, giving her occasion to withdraw should she choose to. But she didn't pull back from him. Under his lips, her mouth opened, offering surrender. He didn't hesitate to claim what she presented to him so openly.

His tongue swept inside the sweet caverns of her mouth, exploring and conquering. Without haste, he stroked against her tongue, tasting her essence, pressing more firmly against her, at the same time as he dragged her against his body. A body that had been hot and wanting from the instant he'd entered the house and smelled her scent.

When her arms came around him, one sliding to his lower back, the other hand running through his hair, he intensified his kiss, turning it more demanding, more urgent by the second. Cupping the back of her head, he held her to him so she couldn't escape, not that he thought that it was necessary, but he loved to cradle her like this, to hold her captive in his embrace.

Leila was soft and yielding in his arms, molding herself to him as if she were made for him. As if it didn't matter that only hours earlier they had quarreled. That thought sobered him.

He ripped his lips from her. "You asked me how I would have voted if I were on the council. I know the answer now: to protect you. And I would have tried to convince all the others to vote the same way. I didn't mean all those things I said to you. I would never hurt you." Then his mouth was back, ravishing her once more like a savage, unable to hold back any longer.

Her fresh scent wrapped around him, the clean smell of soap and body lotion. It made him aware that he hadn't showered since he'd started shadowing her.

"I should shower," he whispered against her, pulling her upper lip between his and nibbling on it.

"No, don't stop, please," she insisted and slid her hand down to his ass, suddenly pressing him closer. She moaned into his mouth. "Oh, God, you're hard. I want you. Now. No waiting."

"No waiting," he repeated, unable to stop a grin from forming on his lips. But he felt filthy, and he didn't want to subject her to this. Their first time would be perfect, he'd make sure of it.

Without another word, he lifted her up and carried her toward the bathroom, pushing the door open with his foot. When she realized where he was taking her, she separated her lips from his.

"But I don't want to wait."

The way she pouted made him even harder. The zipper of his pants pressed painfully into his aroused flesh.

"You won't have to, baby. Shower with me, and I promise you, you won't consider it a wait."

As he set her back on her feet and shut the door behind them, she already reached for his shirt, pulling it over his head.

He smiled at her. "Now you."

A faint blush rose to her cheeks as he pulled the T-shirt from her jeans. When he lifted it and exposed the creamy flesh underneath, he was reminded instantly that she wasn't wearing a bra. When they'd escaped the fire in her apartment there hadn't been time for her to put one on.

"You're beautiful," he murmured in encouragement as he freed her from the T-shirt and feasted his eyes on her gorgeous breasts. His hands instantly moved in to feel her flesh, encountering a perfect combination of softness and firmness. Round, the size of grapefruits, they fit perfectly in his hands, her pert nipples brushing against his palms as he cupped them.

"When I saw you that night in your bed, I wanted to touch you so badly," he confessed.

Her lids lowered halfway, trying to hide the desire in her eyes, but he saw it nevertheless. "Did you watch the entire time?"

Aiden lowered his head and captured one nipple between his lips, licking it slowly, then releasing it. "Yes, I watched every second of it. And I wished all the while that those were my hands touching you." When he kissed her other nipple, she moaned, tossing her head back and arching into his mouth.

Leila's fingers slid over his torso, leaving trails of fire as hot as lava in their wake. He was burning up and would combust into a raging fireball if he didn't make love to her soon.

"Undress me," he ordered as he unsnapped the button of her jeans and pulled her zipper down.

She followed his command and did the same to him, but when she lowered the zipper, her hand brushed his hard flesh, and the contact sent a flame of lust through his entire body.

He closed his eyes and hissed out a breath of air. "Fuck, baby!"

"Like that?" she purred.

He gazed at her. When had she suddenly turned into a temptress? "Exactly like that."

He helped her shimmy out of her pants and drop them to the floor. She wore no panties—there had been no time to search for any in her burning apartment. As he tossed off his shoes, Leila pushed his pants past his hips, her hands catching in his boxer briefs, pulling them down as well. Cool air hit his cock as it jutted out, hard and heavy, curving upwards in its rigidity.

When he was naked in front of her, he drew her back into his embrace, his shaft pressing against her stomach.

Not wanting to waste another minute, he lifted her into the shower with him and turned on the water. At first it ran cold, but he was glad for it, his body so overheated, he welcomed the cooling effect the water had on him.

He reached for the liquid soap and lathered his hand when she stopped him.

"Let me do that."

He could have never imagined how exciting it would be to be touched by a woman's soapy hands as they stroked over his torso, lathering his skin in thick foam, her hands gliding smoothly over him. When her fingers caught on his nipples, he let out a low moan. He hadn't realized that they would be as sensitive as he imagined hers to be. But before he could concentrate on that sensation, her hands moved south.

"Oh, God, Leila!" he ground out.

~ ~ ~

His moaned words gave her courage to proceed as she dipped her hands into the dark nest of curls that surrounded his erection. She'd never seen a man so well endowed. And the thought of feeling this, him, inside her soon, made her toss all her inhibitions in the wind.

His body was perfect: his torso sculpted with hard muscles, a scar here and there, but otherwise as beautiful as a marble statue. And lower, where her soap-covered hands now roamed, male perfection greeted her. His shaft stood upright in the midst of his dark hair, and below, his balls had pulled tight. She ran one hand along the veined flesh, feeling its soft skin, covering the iron-hard rod beneath.

Aiden leaned backwards against the tile wall. "Leila, you don't have to…"

His voice died when she wrapped her hand around him and slipped down all the way to the base. The thought that this powerful warrior, this immortal, turned to putty in her hands, excited her. It made her feel strong and powerful herself, as if she were feeding off his power.

With slow strokes she continued to wash him, her other hand reaching for the sac below. As she cradled it in her palm, she felt a shudder go through him.

His voice hoarse, he commanded, "You have to stop, Leila."

"I don't want to." Touching him gave her more pleasure than touching any other man ever had.

A firm grip around her wrist arrested her movement and prevented her from sliding down his length once more.

"I believe I promised you'd enjoy the shower, but you're not giving me a chance," he said as he bent his head to her neck and planted kisses alongside it. "I want to pleasure you."

He turned them to the side, allowing the water to run between them, sluicing the soap from his body and rinsing him clean. Suddenly she found herself pressed against the tile wall with his mouth on her breasts, his hands encircling her wrists, holding them to her sides.

His firm grip tantalized her senses. She knew she couldn't escape him now if she wanted to. Did he realize that? "What are you doing?"

He looked up from under dark lashes, rivulets of water running from his hair over his face and down his body. "Making sure you let me pleasure you. I've waited long enough, don't you think?"

She recognized his playful tone and responded likewise. "And I, haven't I waited long enough?"

He grinned and shook his head. "I saw you first. I was hard for you long before tonight. Now I get to take what I need."

At his possessive words, a moan dislodged from her chest.

His gaze grew even more intense as he ground his hips into her. "Yes, baby, I get to enjoy your pleasure now."

Then he dropped to his knees, bringing his head level with her sex, confirming the meaning of his words. As he raised her leg and draped it over his shoulder, so he could move into her center, he looked back up at her.

"I'm sorry to be so selfish," he said, "but I need this from you now."

Selfish? He called himself selfish? But she couldn't continue her train of thought, because a second later, his mouth was on her, his tongue taking a long lick over her sensitive flesh. Reality disappeared, blurred. As if she were in a dream, the lover at her feet swept her away with the sensual onslaught of his tongue, the soft press of his mouth, and the urging touch of his fingers as they parted her flesh and explored her.

Her pulse raced, trying to catch up with her breathing, which had gone the way of galloping horses without her even noticing. Had she not already been wet from the shower, she would have broken out in sweat, because the flames of white hot heat Aiden sent through her were bringing her to the point of incineration.

She panted, giving her body the oxygen it needed. Yet it wasn't enough. His touch was more than she could handle. The texture of his tongue licking over her engorged clit had an explosive effect on her. Every time he connected with that little bundle of flesh, shudders went through her body, her womb clenched, reveling in the sweet torture he delivered so masterfully.

Pressing herself closer to the wall at her back, she tried to maintain her balance, a task becoming more impossible by the second. She steadied herself with one hand on his shoulder, the other combing through his hair, but still her body trembled.

"Aiden," she panted.

As if wanting to respond to her, one finger teased at the entrance to her core, and a moment later, he plunged inside. Her muscles convulsed around him, eager to keep him there. When he moved, she felt like howling, but then he was back, driving deeper into her. His tongue continued to lick her clit, harder and faster now, and in the same rhythm his finger thrust in and out of her.

His muffled groans bounced against her aroused flesh, only intensifying the sensations he unleashed on her, until it was all too much. With a violent shudder, her body exploded into a symphony of crashing waves rushing over the edge of a giant waterfall. Warmth spread through her entire body as Aiden stilled and pressed gentle kisses onto her trembling flesh.

Feeling like she was floating on a cloud of cotton wool, she barely noticed how he lifted her out of the shower and wrapped her in a large bath towel, drying her inch by inch. She dropped her face into the crook of his neck and wrapped her arms around him.

"Aiden," was all she could murmur before he lifted her into his strong arms and carried her out of the bathroom.

27

Aiden carried Leila into one of the bedrooms and laid her on the Queen-sized bed. While he normally preferred a King-sized bed, he didn't mind this time at all: he was planning on staying very close to her all night, and truth be told, a Full-size would have sufficed.

Tasting her essence and feeling her body give in to a shattering orgasm, had made him even hotter than before. He'd thought watching her touch herself that night had been scorching hot, but being the one to give her that pleasure was even better.

He covered her with his body, bracing himself on his arms and legs to keep his full weight off her. As he brushed a strand of damp hair from her cheek, she lifted her lashes and looked at him.

"Aiden, that was... wonderful."

Her eyes glowed and he couldn't stop gazing into their depth.

"I love tasting you," he admitted and slanted his lips over hers.

As he pressed gently, her lips parted and her tongue snaked out to meet his. He took the invitation and delved into her, pouring all his desires into this kiss. Beneath him, her legs spread farther, making him slide perfectly into her midst, his cock already poised at her wet pussy.

When he nudged forward, her hands pushed against his shoulders and her lips separated from him.

"Condom," she whispered.

He shook his head. "Immortals carry no disease."

"But I'm not on the pill."

Oddly enough, the fact that she wasn't using birth control pleased him, even though it didn't matter: only once bonded to a human could a Stealth Guardian father children. In the meantime his sperm remained sterile.

"You won't get pregnant." As soon as he said it, a twinge of regret surged through him. Why did he suddenly wish that his seed would leave something lasting in her, when he'd never had this wish before? This could be nothing more than a fling, an affair that would last no longer than his assignment. To think of it as more was only inviting trouble. Yet at the same time, something in him revolted against the notion of leaving her.

"Are you sure?"

"I'm sure, Leila."

Gazing into the deep blue of her eyes, he nudged forward, his cock parting her outer lips, her moist heat coating his bulbous head. He clenched his jaw at the tightness of her muscles and slid farther inside.

His heart rate accelerated and all the air left his lungs. Then he felt her legs wrap around his hips, her heels digging into his backside. Knowing he couldn't hold off any longer, he plunged inside—into pure heaven.

Like a silken glove, she wrapped around him, her interior muscles velvety soft, yet gripping him firmly, her juices making him slide into her as if into liquid heat. His whole body burned from the intensity of the contact with Leila, his pulse beating violently under his skin. As blood raced through his veins, he moved inside her, withdrew, then thrust back in. First slowly, then with more determination.

Underneath him, she responded to his movements, arching her back, undulating her hips to urge him closer and deeper. As if, like him, she couldn't get enough of this new connection. And it felt like a connection, not just mindless copulating, but a connection of two bodies that seemed perfect for each other. His previous one-night-stands had been frantic fucks without much involvement, simply rides toward completion. This was different. His gaze locked with hers, he looked into her and recognized the desire and passion that burned there, the need for more waiting in the wings. He was unable to tear himself away from the sight and continued to revel in her inner beauty—beauty he could see shining beneath her pretty shell.

The strength he saw there was what made this all the more exciting. For the first time, he shared intimacies with a human whose strength he admired, whose determination he understood. And as her body took him inside her, trusting him not to hurt her, he felt the walls he'd build around himself crumble. As they did, he felt his entire body begin to shimmer in a silvery fog. It engulfed Leila with him.

The moment she seemed to notice this change in him, her eyes widened. "What's happening?" she asked, gasping.

He brushed his lips against her mouth. "I'm making love to you the Stealth Guardian way." Something he'd never done before, never felt safe enough with anybody before. "Hold on, baby."

Allowing his energy to flow freely, the fog intensified, whirling around them like a storm. The room seemed to disappear and only their bodies remained, floating. Sparks of energy lit around them as he continued driving into her, his strokes hard and deep, increasing in speed and intensity as the fog grew thicker.

Sealing her lips with a kiss and intertwining his tongue with hers, he held her tightly, his cock pounding into her soft flesh harder than any human woman could take. Yet he wouldn't hurt her, because as he made love to her, he shared his energy and strength with her, let her feel the essence of his power so she could taste ultimate ecstasy.

The pressure in his balls built and intensified to a point where he could hold back no longer. As his orgasm claimed him, his seed shot through his cock and into her body. With it, a spear of energy surged into her, the Stealth Guardian's *virta*, making her body shimmer in a golden light. In the same instant, she screamed out her release, her muscles contracting around him.

Slowly, they floated back down, the fog around them vanishing, and the room reappearing.

He looked down at her and into her stunned eyes.

"Oh, my God!" she whispered, then looked at her arms, inspecting them. "I'm glowing." She stared at him, a thousand questions reflecting in her eyes.

"Yes, and you'll glow for a few hours like that."

"What did you do to me?" There was no accusation in her voice, only curiosity.

"When a Stealth Guardian makes love the ancient way, his energy flows into his partner. It will stay there for hours after lovemaking."

"Why?"

"Because of this." He grinned and shifted, pulling his cock back and then plunging back inside. A gasp was her answer as her eyelids fluttered and shudders went through her sensitive body.

"As long as you glow, the slightest touch by me will give you another orgasm. A Stealth Guardian takes care of his woman."

"I'll never survive this," she said in disbelief.

He laughed out loud and threw his head back. "You will, Leila, because while you glow you're nearly as strong as I am." He paused and winked mischievously. "And nearly as insatiable."

"So there is an ulterior motive to this glowing trick. You want to make sure your women don't get tired of sex."

"Well, I did mention earlier that I was selfish, did I not?"

She smiled back at him and licked her lips, her pink tongue so enticing that he felt more blood rush to his cock. "What happens when you make a woman glow who's already insatiable to begin with?"

His heart made a somersault at her seductive remark. "It makes for a very, very wild night. Without sleep, without rest, and without regret."

Leila batted her eyelashes at him and slid her hand behind his head, pulling him to her. "Then let's see if I'm really almost as strong as you."

Before he knew what she was planning to do, she'd flipped him on his back and was on top of him.

He smirked. "Maybe I should have thought twice about making you glow."

Slowly she began to ride him, moving up and down on his shaft, her muscles squeezing him harder now than before, an effect of the power he'd poured into her.

"Or maybe not," he conceded and pulled her head to him for a kiss. "Ride me, my beautiful Leila."

~ ~ ~

Leila felt amazing, free, powerful, and above all fearless. All of a sudden, all her fear had dissipated, dissolved into nothing, into meaningless thoughts that had no place in her body now—a body that felt reenergized and elevated, lifted from its ordinary life to something so different, she had a hard time putting it into words.

When Aiden had come inside of her and her entire body had all of a sudden started to glow, she'd felt an instant surge of power inside her, making her feel as if she could run a marathon and win it. But that wasn't even the most amazing thing about it. More importantly, she'd suddenly seen a tiny glimpse of his soul, of the vulnerable man inside. It had been so fleeting that she'd dismissed it as impossible. Yet when he'd explained to her that he'd shared his power with her, she'd realized that he must have shared more—even more than he thought he had.

That knowledge wiped out her mistrust in him. And at the same time, it brought forward the guilt about what she was still hiding from him. Even now, as she was on top of him, impaled on his rock-hard cock, the pendant that contained the last copy of her research data hung around her neck. It felt as if it burned there against her flesh, urging her to tell him the truth. To confess.

But at the same time she remembered what he'd said to her earlier, that all her data must be destroyed. For the sake of her parents, she couldn't let it happen. She had to hold onto the hope that maybe soon he'd understand, that maybe after a night in each other's arms they would grow closer. Then she could ask him to reconsider, to help her find a way to keep her research alive.

Tomorrow, she promised herself, *tomorrow I'll tell him.*

Tonight was meant for lovemaking and nothing else. Her body was primed for it, her own desire for him, coupled with his power inside her, making for an intoxicating cocktail of sensations. Sensations she couldn't and wouldn't deny herself now. The lust raging in her was too strong to hold back.

"How do you want it?" she whispered against his lips.

"Surprise me."

Then his hands went to her hips, gripping them. With one forceful move, he slammed her down onto him, driving his cock into her to the hilt, sending another wave of ecstasy through her body.

"And do it soon, or I'll take over," he warned between clenched teeth. "Because every time you come while I'm connected to you, you drive me to the edge."

Taking his hands by the wrists, she pried them off her hips and pinned them next to his head, leaning over him, her breasts dangling close to his face. Slowly, she gyrated her hips, letting his cock slide in and out.

"If you want to come, then you'll have to do something for it." She lowered her lids to indicate her breasts.

"Nothing easier than that," he agreed and lifted his head, wrapping his lips around one nipple.

As he sucked it into his mouth and licked his tongue over it, waves of pleasure rocked through her body once more. Of their own volition, her hips started to move in a rhythm as old as time, and she rode him the way the waves dictated to her. As in an African mating dance, she let her body take over, move in synch with his, giving and taking all at once.

She heard moans fill the room, his and her own, and listened to the sounds of flesh slapping together. The scent of sex permeated the air around them, and the dim bedside lamp created a tableau of light and shadows that danced on their skin.

Beneath her, Aiden sucked greedily at her breasts, licked and tortured her nipples that had long ago turned into hard points so sensitive a light breeze could ignite them. Inside her, an inferno was raging that felt hotter than the fires of hell could possibly be.

And all the while, she rode his marble-hard shaft, bringing him to the edge of his release again and again. With each of her orgasms, he screamed out in pure passion, and thrust deeper into her.

"Now," he urged, his body bathed in sweat. "Give me everything."

Instinct that could only come from Aiden's power made her place her hand over his heart as she threw her head back and only concentrated on him and how much she wanted to feel his release.

A sudden warmth flooded her, and she felt it run down her shoulder to her arm, into her elbow and lower still.

Before it could reach her fingertips and connect with his skin, she felt her hand ripped from his chest. She snapped her head toward Aiden, noticing a shocked expression on his face.

A second later, she felt him explode inside her, harder than the first time.

She collapsed onto him and felt his arms wrap around her as his body trembled from the aftershocks of his orgasm.

"How did you know?" he asked, his voice hoarse.

But before she could form a word, darkness claimed her.

28

Aiden watched the coffee drip into the pot and ran a shaky hand through his tousled hair recalling the events of the previous night. He'd never had a more satisfying sexual encounter than what he'd experienced with Leila, however that wasn't the focus of his thoughts right now. Rather, he couldn't get out of his head how she could have known about the Stealth Guardians' bonding ritual. Only Stealth Guardians and their chosen mates were aware of how it worked, that by collecting all the *virta* that he'd poured into her and channeling it back to his heart, she would bond with him. It had never even been written down in their history books. As a matter of protection, it had been left out. Should their history books ever fall into the wrong hands, at least this secret would remain safe.

Because it was a secret that could kill a Stealth Guardian. It could have killed him last night, had he not stopped her in time. A bonding ritual performed between two lovers who didn't share true love, was fatal for both of them.

It had nearly happened to Hamish the year before. He'd been in love with a human. And she had confessed her undying love to him. But it had all been a lie. The demons had influenced her, making her believe that she truly loved Hamish when in fact, she didn't. When Hamish had found out shortly before their bonding ritual, he'd been devastated. Aiden had tried to console his friend by reminding him that had he gone through with it he would have died, yet Hamish had only given him an empty stare, professing he would rather be dead than live without her.

Ever since then, Hamish had stayed away from women, and to Aiden's knowledge hadn't touched one since. He'd lost the woman he'd believed to be his mate, and nobody could help him over the grief.

Nor could anybody explain how the demons had instigated the entire deception and how they could possibly know about the mating ritual and what it would do to a Stealth Guardian if he mated with someone who didn't truly love him.

Just as Leila couldn't be aware of it. He'd never even mentioned anything about the Stealth Guardians' mating habits to her. And why should he? She was his charge, not his girlfriend. Girlfriend? Gods, he sounded like a human.

The night with Leila had clearly shaken him. What had gotten into him to make love to her the Stealth Guardian way, sharing *virta* with her? He'd never done that. It was reserved for their mates only and not meant to be shared with casual flings. Maybe *rasen* was getting to him. Damn hormones! They didn't make it easy for him to think straight.

Aiden reached for the coffee pot and poured himself a mug. He sat down at the kitchen table when Hamish entered, also dressed only in a pair of jeans.

"Morning," he greeted his friend and motioned to the coffee pot. "Just made coffee."

"Great. I need it." Hamish walked to the counter and poured himself a cup before joining him at the kitchen table. "I've had a busy night."

Aiden raised an inquiring eyebrow. "I thought you were just going out for some food."

His friend shook his head and grinned. "I didn't really want to hang around here; figured you didn't need my company."

"We had things to talk about," Aiden admitted and looked away.

Hamish didn't call him on his blatant lie. Instead, he took a sip of his coffee before giving him a serious look. "Anyway, I went back East last night to see if I could find out anything else about who's after Leila, apart from the demons of course."

"Where did you go?"

"I snuck into the compound to see what our boys know."

"You didn't—"

Hamish held up his hand. "Of course not. They didn't even know I was there. But just FYI, Manus is major pissed at you, because you haven't called in. The names he's calling you, frankly, not even I want to repeat those."

"He can suck it up." Pissing off Manus was just a bonus he'd take any day. However, wouldn't Manus's annoyance prove something else? "Are you sure he wasn't just playing being pissed?"

"Oh, I'm sure. He was fuming, and you know how he can't keep a lid on it when he's ticked off."

"For once I'm glad that Manus has such a short fuse. That means that he's definitely not involved in ratting out our safe house. It had to have been that phone call being traced back to the parlor."

"Agreed. Just as well, because I think we need some help. There are things we can't do from here. It would be good if we could bring Manus back in and have him do some investigating for us."

Aiden contemplated Hamish's words and nodded. "Let's do that."

"Excellent. Because there's something odd that's come up."

"Odd? Since when are the things we deal with not odd?"

His friend shrugged. "I stopped by the police last night, rifled through their files about the murder of the Inter Pharma CEO."

Aiden looked up from his coffee mug. "What about it?"

"Turns out the majority shareholder of the company disappeared a few nights earlier."

He listened up. "You think the two events are connected?"

"Too much of a coincidence for my liking."

"I agree," Aiden said. "Do they have any leads?"

"Nothing. All I know is that this shareholder, Zoltan, apparently had a meeting with the CEO a few days before Patten's death. And now he's nowhere to be found."

"Zoltan?" Leila's voice interrupted.

Aiden shifted his gaze and watched as she walked into the kitchen, dressed in jeans and a T-shirt, her pretty pendant around her neck. Her body still glowed golden. When their eyes connected, she quickly looked away and tried to cover her exposed arms by wrapping them around her waist, but there was no hiding what had happened. Her face showed the same glow. It should have worn off by now, but it seemed that sharing his power with her had been more intense than even he had realized. Almost as if he hadn't been able to control himself.

Next to him, Hamish gasped, his mouth dropping open. "She glows." His friend pinned him with a questioning look.

Without him saying anything else, Aiden knew what he was thinking. That he had gone too far. That he'd shared something with a charge that was reserved only for the most serious of relationships.

Leila's embarrassment was evident. Beneath her golden glow, a red blush tried to burst through. It made for a most intoxicating view. Instantly, Aiden felt himself get hard. The knowledge that as long as she was still glowing, he could trigger an orgasm in her with a simple touch, made him almost salivate.

As she walked toward them, he ran his eyes over her, remembering every inch of her delectable body, every curve, every indentation. And every moan and sigh that had crossed her luscious lips last night. Every wanton movement, every sinful touch.

"Did I hear you say that Mr. Zoltan disappeared?" she asked, addressing Hamish.

His friend gave her a curious look. "Do you know him?"

"No, but I know he wanted to see my research."

Aiden pulled the chair next to him back, surprised at this revelation. "Tell us everything you know about him. It could be important."

She walked to the counter to pour herself a cup of coffee. "I've never met him, but I don't like him." She sat down on the chair, making sure not to get too close to him. Clearly, she didn't want to risk being touched by him and have an orgasm in front of Hamish.

"How come?" Hamish asked.

"He came to see Patten and demanded that I show him my research. He wanted to *look over my shoulder*. I told Patten it wasn't right. But he went on about this man being a major shareholder and having every right." She took a quick sip of her coffee. Then she looked back at him. "That's when I erased that external hard drive with my data on it. I knew Patten could get into the safe and take it out."

"Good instincts," Hamish praised.

Aiden looked at her with admiration. With her decisive action, she'd prevented her data from falling into the wrong hands.

"I think he was a demon," she added.

"Why do you think that?" He felt the urge to touch her shaking hand but refrained from it.

"Patten was waffling on about his lights burning out just when Mr. Zoltan arrived. He was quite embarrassed about it. When we escaped the massage parlor, you told me that fluorescent and neon lights would flicker and then burn out if demons were close by. Well, the overhead lights in Patten's office were fluorescent."

Aiden exchanged a quick look with Hamish.

"That confirms it. The demons got to Patten," Hamish stated.

Aiden raised his hand in objection. "No, they didn't. They may have been there earlier, but the night we found Patten's body, the lights were working." He looked back at Leila. "I'm assuming Patten had the lights in his office repaired before his death?"

"Yes, of course. He would have had facilities management there the next morning to change out the fluorescent tubes."

Then she suddenly straightened her back as if remembering something. She stared at him. "Remember my lab and office? All fluorescent lights were working the night I found the safe open."

Aiden nodded, admiring her perceptive mind. "Then the person who killed Patten and tried to steal the data was not a demon. He or she had to be human."

"Or a Stealth Guardian," Hamish added.

The thought hadn't escaped Aiden. How else would the murderer have gotten past security? "Is there any other way into the building at night, other than getting past the security guard? Think, Leila, could a human have gotten in there without the security guard noticing?"

She bit her lips, contemplating his questions. "I don't know. Max does his rounds, but the door would have been locked."

"Another employee with access maybe?" Hamish suggested.

Leila shook her head. "No. Our access cards are restricted to daytime access only. After nine p.m., they won't unlock any doors. Max would have been the only one to grant access."

Aiden had expected the answer, but didn't like it. It made a betrayal by a Stealth Guardian much more likely. Yet, he had to face the facts. Hamish had warned him.

"Okay, then we've got two things to do: find Zoltan. He's obviously been given information about Leila and was there to keep an eye on her; he'll lead us to the traitor on the council," Aiden announced.

"And the second thing?" Hamish asked.

"Find the person on the council who tried to kill Leila and who initiated the raid on the massage parlor."

"But how?" Leila interrupted.

"Manus will help us with that. He's already investigating Jonathan, and by now he knows of the raid on the parlor, so he is probably looking into how that could have happened. We'll need to let him know to check your parents' phone records and see if there's a trace on their line. With Pearce's IT skills, we should be able to follow the trace back and have it lead us to whoever planted it."

"Looks like the council will soon have two vacancies," Hamish predicted.

And Aiden hoped that neither vacancy would be the position of Primus. "I'm afraid you're right."

As he rose to grab his phone from the counter to call Manus, the flickering of the light underneath the hanging cabinets caught his eye.

"Shit!"

"Demons!" Hamish called out in warning just as the entrance door burst open and three men charged in.

~ ~ ~

Leila froze in shock while the intruders advanced. Hamish and Aiden instantly reared up from their chairs and attacked, moving faster than she'd ever seen anybody move. Out of nowhere, they'd pulled weapons and now threw themselves onto the three demons.

She stumbled from her chair and backed away, trying to stay out of the melee, fear cutting off her windpipe. All she could do was stare at the fight.

The demons looked entirely human, just as Aiden had told her. There was no outward sign that would have indicated that she was facing an otherworldly being. Except... did their eyes sparkle in an unusually bright green? She stared at one of them, who at present engaged Aiden, when the intruder suddenly glared at her.

He let go of Aiden who continued to fight his second opponent, and rushed toward her.

In panic, she screamed, her hands frantically searching the kitchen counter for any weapon. There was nothing to grab.

"Leila!" Aiden shouted, but a quick glance told her that both he and Hamish needed all their strength to fight off the two demons, exchanging blow after blow.

He couldn't get past the demon he was battling to help her. She was on her own.

The massive demon who suddenly towered over her wore fatigues and an olive colored T-shirt, green liquid oozing from several gashes on his arms and chest. But the injuries didn't seem to be severe, because he lashed a nasty grin at her.

"Gotcha!"

His voice made her shiver as it slid through her like a sharp knife.

Then his hand shot out to grab her. She evaded him by sliding sideways along the kitchen counter, surprising herself with her speed and agility. When he went after her and reached for her, she punched him, and felt a force in her body that seemed foreign to her. Was this an aftereffect of Aiden having poured his power into her?

"Come to Zoltan," the demon hissed.

Oh, God, so it was he! How had he found them here? She backed away, ending up in the corner, the coffee pot at her back, and no escape route open to her.

Zoltan was on her a second later.

Behind him, she heard the grunts of the men and the clashing of daggers, but she couldn't see them anymore, Zoltan's massive frame blocking her view.

When he was a few feet away from her and approaching, she swung around and grabbed the coffee pot, hitting his head with it. The pot broke and the hot liquid spilled. It covered most of his face, but also her own hand, and despite the heat, she barely felt it. Neither, apparently, did Zoltan.

However, he looked pissed now.

"Let's see what else is inside that pretty little head." He reached for her neck, choking her.

She croaked, her hands flailing, trying to find another weapon, but there was none.

His head came closer, his teeth flashing, his green eyes more luminous now, like a traffic light. For the first time she noticed the handsomeness of his features, so unlike what a demon should look like. A straight nose, a square jaw, an even complexion. Full lips and straight, white teeth completed the picture that seemed to somehow keep her captivated. As if he were reeling her in, pulling her closer to him. Showing her that he wasn't an ugly beast. All of a sudden, she felt his thoughts invading her mind.

Give it to me, give me what I want, she heard him urge her. *I'll give you everything you've ever dreamed of. Your parents, they will love you again.*

Oh God, he knew her deepest wish! And he was tempting her with it. He was trying to seduce her!

Leila fought against him, trying to expel him from her mind. She couldn't succumb, no, she couldn't allow it. Aiden trusted her to be strong. What he'd given her last night proved that. She couldn't disappoint him.

With the last of her breath, she raised her knee and kicked Zoltan in the nuts.

He cursed violently, then behind him shouts rang out.

"Take that to hell!" Aiden cried triumphantly as a body made a loud thump on the floor.

Zoltan's hand slid from her neck and caught in her necklace. The chain broke, tangling itself up in Zoltan's fingers as he turned and tossed a glance over his shoulder.

Leila saw Aiden charging toward them, but before he reached them, Zoltan jumped out of the way and vaulted himself through the kitchen window as if he were a Chinese gymnast.

Horrified she touched her naked throat.

"Leila, are you all right?" Aiden pulled her into his arms, but she pushed against him instantly, cutting off the waves of pleasure that started pouring through her at his touch.

Behind him, Hamish appeared, a bloody gash on his chest, but otherwise unharmed.

"My necklace... Zoltan got my necklace," she stammered. Her data, the last copy of her data was in the possession of the demon now. Devastation coiled her stomach into knots.

"Don't worry about it. Demons love shiny objects to trade. It can be replaced," Hamish calmed her.

She shook her head and lifted her eyes, tears brimming at their rim. "No. It can't be. It can't..."

"Leila, my sweet, please, you're in shock." Aiden lifted his hand to reach for her hair but she shrank back.

With fear in her heart, she shifted her gaze to him. "There's a USB drive inside it."

Aiden's eyes widened, his body visibly tightening.

"It contains a copy of my research data. The last copy," she confessed.

He didn't say a single word, only stared at her, disbelief spreading in his eyes as realization sank in.

"They don't know what's in it. Nobody knows. It's hard to open if you don't know how," she stammered.

Aiden clenched his jaw, and a low hiss escaped him as he stared at her, disappointment in his gaze. "I trusted you."

29

After burning the two demon bodies, they packed up and left the house, driving back to the portal. Aiden could barely look at Leila. He'd never been so disappointed in another person before. She'd lied to him all this time, all the while knowing what could happen. She'd deliberately kept the existence of the last copy of her research data hidden from him. Gods, she'd lied to his face. He'd been such a fool to trust her, to even admire her for the strength she'd shown when he'd thought she'd lost everything.

And to think that he'd made love to her and poured his power into her, his heart, his very soul. And she'd taken it all and tossed it to the dogs. As if it meant nothing to her.

He glanced at her as they entered the wine cellar. Her glow had dissipated. It was probably the one thing that had saved her and made her hold Zoltan off as long as she had. The demon Aiden had fought against had been stronger than others he'd encountered previously, and it had taken him longer to kill him than he'd expected. Hamish had had as much difficulty, and hadn't been able to help Leila either.

But somehow Aiden could find no satisfaction in his latest kill, nor in the fact that Leila had fought so valiantly. Any other time he would have admired her for it. All he could focus on right now was that she'd betrayed him. He finally understood now how Hamish must have felt when he'd found out that his lover had deceived him about her feelings. How his heart must have shattered into a million pieces at the knowledge that he'd opened himself up to someone who didn't deserve his trust.

As they stood in the portal now, he didn't reach for Leila's hand, but instead let Hamish guide her through the journey. He felt her shiver and recognized that her claustrophobia was encroaching on her again, but he couldn't find it in him to pull her into his embrace. Too much fury and anger coursed through his cells, too much pain settled in his heart.

Transporting through the portal took mere seconds. As they stepped out of it, Aiden smelled the familiar smells of home. Without waiting for Hamish or Leila, he headed for the door and charged upstairs, leaving the basement behind. Their footsteps followed him, but he didn't turn. From now on, she was simply a charge. He should have never wished for more. It was a mistake to allow his emotions to get the better of him. All it had led to was pain. The sooner this assignment was over, the better.

When he barreled into the kitchen, he instantly spotted Manus and Enya, who sat at the kitchen counter, eating. His second dropped his sandwich when he saw him and slid off the barstool. Enya had her mouth full and swallowed quickly.

"Where the fuck have you been?" Manus glared at him. "Did it occur to you that we might all be looking for you?"

"There was a raid—"

"I know there was a fucking raid. Why do you think I was leaving you messages? And you couldn't even be bothered to send word back that you're fine. Fucking asshole!"

Aiden hadn't seen any messages on his cell. "What are you talking about? You never left a message!"

Enya's eyes widened. "Hamish?" She jumped off her chair and ran toward the door. "Hamish!"

Aiden turned to see how Enya flew right into Hamish's outstretched arms. "Hey little one."

"I'm not little," she protested and squeezed him before pulling back from his embrace.

Her expression instantly changed when she saw Leila, who stood a few steps back, clearly uncomfortable.

"What the fuck?" Enya hissed, tossing glares between Aiden and Hamish. "You brought a human here?"

"Are you fucking nuts?" Manus added. "Your charge, you brought your charge to the compound? Have you lost it?"

"Believe me, we had no choice," Aiden replied. He knew this would happen. Still, he didn't like the hostile looks with which both Stealth Guardians sized Leila up. The urge to protect her welled up in him out of nowhere. Nobody had the right to hurt her.

"There's always a choice." Enya scowled at him. "You've compromised us all."

"But first things first," Manus said calmly and pointed at Hamish. "What happened to you? No offense, but some of us here assumed you'd gone over to the dark side. Some even set the council on you."

Hamish grinned and cast a sideways glance at Aiden, who could but cringe. He should have had more faith in his best friend.

"So I heard. Sorry to disappoint you guys, but you'll have to continue putting up with me. I ain't going nowhere, particularly not to the dark side; never quite liked that look."

"Then why did you disappear?" Enya asked, her eyebrows snapping together, her lips pursing.

Hamish ruffled her hair, earning himself an impatient grunt from her. He'd always treated her like a younger sister, and she normally played along; but apparently she was at the end of her nerves, and told him so. "Hamish!"

"Well, it's a long story, and it's got a lot to do with why we're all here. And why we had to bring Aiden's charge."

"I'm listening," Manus announced and crossed his arms over his chest.

"There's a traitor on the council, working for the demons."

Both of their fellow Stealth Guardians gasped.

Aiden held up his hand. He wasn't finished with the bad news yet. "And the demons now have the blueprint for the drug."

"You're fucking shitting me!" Manus stared at them in disbelief.

Enya's protest followed. "That can't be true! Tell us that's not true!"

Aiden interrupted. "It's true, but before we tell that story twice, where is everybody?"

"Pearce is in the command room, Logan is in his quarters. Sean and Jay are out on assignment."

"I'll get Pearce and Logan," Enya offered. As she walked to the door, Leila took a step toward her.

"Excuse me, could you please show me the bathroom?"

Enya scowled, but then relented. "Come with me. And you'd better not be going anywhere else but the bathroom, or I'm on you like a bee on honey." To underscore her threat, she put her hand on the handle of her dagger.

Leila nodded quickly and followed her out of the room. Aiden watched her disappear, then looked back at Manus.

"You said you left messages. I didn't get any."

"That's not possible," Manus protested. "Just admit that you didn't want to let me know where you were, because you were too busy shacking up with your charge."

Aiden gritted his teeth. "I got no fucking message from you."

Manus narrowed his eyes. "If that's true then we'd better have Pearce look at your cell phone. Because I swear I left you three messages in the last twenty-four hours."

He knew his friend wasn't lying. Which could only mean one thing. "Somebody must have tampered with my phone."

Hamish tossed him a look. "Do you think that's how the demons found us in Sonoma, via your phone?"

"It was switched off the entire time. And I'd already disabled the GPS tracking device before we even went to the Thai massage parlor."

"Somebody could have reactivated it," Hamish guessed.

"Let's ask Pearce," Manus suggested.

The door opened. "Let's ask Pearce what?" the man in question answered. He motioned his head toward Hamish. "Good to see you back in one piece."

"Good to be back."

"So what do you guys need to know?"

Aiden pulled out his cell phone. "Manus says he left me three messages. I never got them. Which makes me think somebody did something to my phone. Can you check it out?"

Pearce accepted the phone. "Can you be a little bit more specific what you're looking for?"

"We were attacked by demons this morning. There was no way they could have traced us to our safe place. My cell phone was off, and my GPS was disabled. Is there any way somebody could have reactivated it?"

"Hmm, let me comb through all the software you've got on it and see whether anything shakes."

"How long?"

"A few hours, at most."

"Thanks." Aiden let out a relieved breath. They would need a few hours anyway to formulate a plan and get everybody on board.

"Oh, and while you're at it, can you see who might have put a tap on Leila's parents phone line? She called her parents from the Thai parlor, and we believe that's why they set the dogs on us."

"Ah shit, after all we told her?" Manus cursed.

Aiden felt the inexplicable urge to defend her. It was his own fault as much as it was hers. But his anger over her lies won out. He ignored his friend and patted Pearce on the shoulder. "Can you do it?"

"Piece of cake."

"Thanks, man."

A moment later, the door opened and Enya and Logan entered.

Hamish cleared his throat. "Well, since we're all here, let's get you guys up to date."

~ ~ ~

Zoltan pressed the cell phone to his ear and looked around him before answering. He already knew who was calling him—very few had this number.

"Yes?"

"Did you get it?" the Stealth Guardian's voice came through the line.

He felt fury rise up through his stomach. His last mission had been a bust. And he knew exactly who to blame.

"You neglected to tell me he had help. Because of your useless information I lost two men." Two men who were entirely expendable, and he would have not batted an eyelid about the loss had he come away with his prize.

"Aiden defeated you?"

"Did you the fuck not listen to what I said?" he barked into the phone, angry for having to deal with such an imbecile. "There was a second Stealth Guardian helping him. And the human was strong, she had *virta* in her. You didn't mention that either."

"I didn't know, I swear," the man stammered.

Zoltan could fairly sense the fear in him, and it only fed his anger more. He let out a growl, not caring that he sounded like a wild beast. It was best for the Stealth Guardian to know how displeased he was.

"I want results, not excuses," he hissed. "Now, you go back and get me information I can work with. Do you understand?"

"Yes. I'll make sure of it. And once you have what you want, you'll hold up your end of the bargain?"

Zoltan kept his chuckle to himself, listening to the nervous breaths of the man on the other line.

"We had an agreement."

"Yes, we agreed," Zoltan confirmed. Didn't mean he had to keep his word. Not to a conniving Stealth Guardian who sold out his own race to gain power and world domination.

The Stealth Guardian continued, "I will reward you well for it later when I'm your leader. When we've overthrown the Great One together and I have taken the throne of the Demons of Fear. You'll be my right hand then. Together we'll wield real power. With me at the helm, this world will finally see what it means to be ruled by a powerful leader. They will bow down before me."

"As you say, this world will have a new leader soon."

But it wouldn't be a Stealth Guardian. And Zoltan would make sure of *that*.

30

It took almost an hour for Hamish and Aiden to convey everything they knew to their fellow Stealth Guardians and to answer their many questions.

"So what now?" Manus asked.

"Our highest priority is finding Zoltan and getting the pendant back. It's well disguised as an ordinary necklace. I myself never suspected otherwise. And Leila said it's not easy to open and figure out what's inside, so he might not even know yet what he has in his hands," Aiden announced, hoping he was right. "Pearce, you know what to do. Whoever tapped Leila's parents' phone must have set the dogs on us at the Thai massage parlor; and if somebody tampered with my phone, it should lead us to the traitor on the council. The traitor is our first priority. He'll lead us to Zoltan."

Pearce rose and walked to the door. "Let me get on that right away."

"And you're sure we're looking for two different people?" Enya nudged forward on her seat.

Hamish answered in Aiden's stead. "Yes. It makes no sense for the demons to want her dead, and clearly somebody has been making attempts on her life—"

"Which reminds me," Aiden interrupted, turning to Manus. "Did you find anything out about the neighbor who delivered the bomb?"

"Jonathan? Well, I'm afraid he's a dead end. I had a word with him, if you know what I mean. He almost peed in his pants." Manus let out a bitter chuckle. "Turns out, some woman approached him and asked him to give the present to Leila."

"Excuse me?" Enya asked. "What kind of dufus wouldn't see through that thin veil?"

Manus shrugged. "Apparently, Jonathan is susceptible to sob stories. She told him that she was an old friend of Leila's, and that they'd fallen out over some guy. And that she wanted to make up, but Leila would never take the present if she knew it was from her. Yada, yada, yada. The guy ate it up like Banana Cream Pie."

"Idiot!" Aiden cursed. "Could he at least describe her?"

"Average height, average built—"

"—average looking." Aiden knew the drill. It could have been anybody, probably just a human who'd been hired by a Stealth Guardian. There were plenty of them in their service. "So that's not going to lead us to the guilty party. Anything else?"

"I'm still working on getting the right body to stage Leila's death," Manus answered.

"Hold off on that for now," he instructed, an idea forming in his head. "Once Pearce has got some data for us, we'll regroup. And I believe I don't have to say this, but nobody outside these four walls can know that Hamish and I are back. Is that clear?"

"We're not daft!" Enya rolled her eyes.

Then Aiden suddenly looked around the room. Shit, having concentrated on getting his friends up to speed had made him forget one thing. "Where the hell is Leila?"

Enya rose. "I think she threw up in the bathroom. Came out white like a sheet. So I put her in your quarters to lie down."

Aiden shot up from his armchair. "You what?"

"I locked her in—"

Without listening to the rest, he charged toward the door and rushed into the corridor.

~ ~ ~

Leila dried her face with a towel that smelled like Aiden. It didn't make her feel any better. At least her bout of nausea had passed: the terrifying attack by the demons and then the claustrophobic journey through the portal had caused that. The first time she'd used the portal, she hadn't felt sick, but then again, Aiden had kissed her when he'd realized how frightening the prospect of hurtling through dark space was for her.

This time, however, he'd shunned her. She couldn't even blame him. Everything he'd said was true: she'd lied to him, she'd kept the existence of the data hidden from him. But he didn't really understand why she'd done it. He could never understand it: he wasn't the one about to lose his parents. She would be all alone now. It would take her years to reconstruct the blueprint for the drug from memory. By then, her parents would be too far gone for her drug to be of any use.

She left the bathroom and walked back into the bedroom. There was no doubt about who this suite of rooms belonged to. Not only was Aiden's masculine scent imprinted on the bed she'd briefly rested on, but there were pictures of him and his family. And a shrine of sorts, a special place over the fireplace, where the picture of a beautiful dark haired woman was framed. Dried white lilies surrounded the frame. She didn't have to be a brain surgeon to figure out who this was. Clearly, he'd worshipped Julia and reminded himself daily of her death. Almost as if he wanted to keep the pain alive.

Her hand reached toward the picture, compelled to stroke the woman's beautiful features, so much like Aiden, yet so much softer, mischief in her eyes, and a smile on her face.

"You shouldn't be in here."

Startled, Leila spun on her heels and faced Aiden. She hadn't heard a door opening, but then again, he probably never used a door.

"Enya brought me—"

"She had no right!" Aiden glared at her, his eyes shifting to Julia's picture behind her.

"I didn't mean to invade your privacy. I'll go then." She took a couple of steps, but he blocked her exit by stepping into her path, his body only a foot away from hers.

"And where do you think you're going?"

"Out of your way until you've calmed down."

"Calmed down?" He narrowed his eyes and drew closer. "I'm calm, I'm very calm right now."

Leila swallowed the lump in her throat. She might as well face the music now. There was no need to drag this out any longer. "Go ahead then. Tell me what you think of me: tell me how much you hate me for what I've done! I've got nothing more to lose. I'll never get my parents back! Are you happy now?"

Aiden grabbed her shoulders. Instinctively, she took a couple of steps back, but he didn't let go. Instead he pressed her against the nearest wall. "Happy? I wish I'd never met you! I wish I'd never known what it feels like to be betrayed like this."

"What did you expect me to do?" she yelled back. "Hand over the last copy of my data so you could destroy it? So you could squash all my dreams of saving my parents? Of preserving my family? You of all people should understand that I couldn't do that. You know what it's like to lose someone."

His head snapped to Julia's picture over the mantle, then back to her. "Hamish!" he cursed. "He had no right to tell you!"

"I'm glad he did."

"Julia is not up for discussion here. I won't let a human—"

"So that's what this is about: you hate me because I'm human, because I'm not as strong as she was."

He pressed her harder against the wall, his fingers digging painfully into her flesh.

"I told you to keep Julia out of this. This is about you deceiving me."

She was beyond fear now. Whatever he did to her, it didn't matter anymore, but she wouldn't go down without a fight. "Do you think she'd be happy knowing what you're doing to yourself? How you keep blaming yourself day after day?"

A flash of pain sparked in his eyes, but a second later, he had himself under control again.

"You don't know anything about me!"

Leila shook her head, remembering the glimpse of his soul she'd seen the night they'd made love. She understood him better than he thought. "I wish I didn't. You know why? Because then I could just walk away and not care. But you've shown me too much of yourself. I can't pretend not to feel your pain. I can't pretend not to want to help you."

"Help me?" He stared at her with incredulity. "You're the one who's in need of help, not I! I'm not the one the demons are after, I'm not the one who's got a price on her head. And you want to help me? Get real, Dr. Cruickshank!"

"I'm so sorry," she whispered, unable to yell any longer. "I wish I could make it all undone, Julia's death, your hatred for humans, us meeting..." She closed her eyes. Would she really want to wipe any memories of her time with Aiden from her mind if she could? It took only a second for her heart to find the answer. "No. I take that back. Us meeting, I wouldn't undo that."

When she opened her eyes, she collided with his heated gaze.

"God damn it!" he cursed and sank his lips onto hers.

She felt his anger in the way he kissed her, rough, hard, as if he wanted to punish her for what she'd said.

His hands let go of her shoulders, then went down to her jeans. He dug them into the waistband, but instead of simply opening the button and lowering the zipper, he tore at the fabric and shredded it like it was paper, making her aware that he could tear her body just as easily if he wished.

She gasped into his mouth, both shocked and excited at the same time. Cool air wafted against her naked skin before his hot hand was between her legs, sliding over her sex, just as he ripped his mouth from hers.

"I'll tell you how you can help me. By spreading your legs for me."

His eyes still held some of the anger in them that she'd seen there earlier, but now they were glazed with lust and desire, and she knew instinctively that he wouldn't hurt her.

Without giving it a second thought, she unbuttoned his pants, lowered the zipper and pushed his jeans down to his thighs. Before she could do any more, he lifted her, spreading her legs wide.

Without a word, he plunged into her, his cock harder than ever.

~ ~ ~

As he thrust into her wet heat, Aiden knew what he needed now was to show her that he couldn't be played with. He had to make it clear to her that she would be punished if she ever hurt him again.

When he looked at her face, he saw how she'd leaned her head back against the wall, her lips parted, her eyes half closed.

"More," Leila panted.

She showed no sign of distress despite his rough handling of her. On the contrary. Her legs wrapped around his waist, urging him on to fuck her harder, to go deeper, to take more of her.

Unable to resist, he took her lips again, this time with more passion and less anger. Gods, she tasted good—so good he couldn't imagine ever giving this up, ever giving her up. Despite everything, despite the fact that she was human, she'd held her own when confronted with his fury. She hadn't backed down, just as she didn't flinch now as he drove even harder into her.

"I need you," he mumbled against her lips before he delved his tongue back into her, thrusting it in the same rhythm as his cock.

He wasn't lying this time: he needed her. She gave him the strength not only to face the demons that were after her, but his own personal demons, the ones that had been haunting him since Julia's death.

Breathing hard, Aiden released her lips and trailed hot kisses along her neck.

"I want you, Aiden, I want you so much," she let out, and it sounded like a sob.

He looked back into her eyes and saw a multitude of emotions brimming there. "You have me, baby," he whispered back and gently captured her lips, stroking his tongue over them.

When she sighed contentedly, his entire body filled with a newfound sense of strength. His balls tightened at the same moment, and he felt his orgasm overwhelm him. Unable to hold it back, he brought his hand between them and rubbed against her clit as he drove into her one last time. As his knees nearly buckled, waves of pleasure crashing over him, he wasn't sure where his orgasm ended and hers began.

Breathing hard, his heart racing, he leaned his forehead against hers. "No more lies. I need the truth now."

He felt her nod. "I didn't mean to hurt you."

"Tell me why you did it. Tell me why you betrayed me after all we shared."

"I love my parents, I love them so much. Like you loved Julia." She sought his eyes, and it seemed as though she looked deep into him, where he couldn't hide anymore.

"Julia was my twin. She was part of me. When I lost her, it felt like losing a part of myself."

Leila pressed her hand against his heart. "I can't even begin to imagine what you've been through. I never had a sister. I never had anybody but my parents. I feel responsible for them. It's my duty to save them, to bring them back. When I met you... when you told me what was at stake..."

"You didn't believe me then, did you?"

She shook her head, regret evident in her face. "No. I didn't. I doubted your words. But the more I saw, the more that happened... I started doubting myself, my own convictions. When you said you would destroy my research, I saw my dream slip away."

Somehow, he understood her. "Not every dream will come true."

"I know that now. I realized that the night at the farmhouse. I wanted to tell you then, but I was afraid of how you'd react. I wanted that one night with you, even if you would never touch me again after that. Just that one time, I wanted to do something selfish, something that was only for me, without having to think of my duty to my parents."

She raised her lids and looked at him, open, vulnerable. She wasn't hiding anything from him anymore.

And he was just as bare in front of her.

"What will you do now?" Leila asked.

He pulled his head back and smiled at her, letting a long look trail down her semi-nude body. "For starters, I'll have to lend you a bathrobe."

Then he released her. A minute later he wrapped her into an oversized bathrobe. But he wasn't ready to sever his contact with her, so he lifted her into his arms and sat down on the couch, keeping her in his lap.

His hand tunneled under the robe, caressing her warm thighs.

"I wanted to tell you about the pendant this morning at the house, but I never got a chance." Her fingers stroked over his parted lips.

"Even though you knew I wanted to destroy the data?"

"I hoped to convince you not to, but I know now that I was wrong."

"How so?"

"Zoltan. When he attacked, I felt his thoughts in my head. He was trying to seduce me to his side, to give him what he wanted. He'll never give up. And sooner or later he'll find me."

"I'll make sure he won't."

"I know that."

He gave her a surprised look. "How come you trust me now?"

"When you made love to me last night, I felt you."

His heartbeat accelerated. "You felt me?"

"Yes, I saw a glimpse of your soul."

Had he really opened himself up this much without realizing? "That's impossible."

Leila brushed her lips against his in a feather light kiss. "I felt you. I felt something so good and pure inside you, it made me feel so terrible about lying to you."

Aiden slid his hand into her hair, cupping her nape, his thumb stroking her neck. "And I was taking advantage of you when we first met. But as much as I want to regret it, I can't. If the fire hadn't broken out in your apartment, I would have been in your bed, my mouth on your pussy. Believe me when I tell you that I've never touched any of my charges, but with you, it was different from the very start. When I saw you the first time, all I could think of was touching you when I knew I should stay away from you."

"Because you might one day have to kill me?"

He flinched. How could he ever do that now when losing her would tear his heart out?

"You told me more than once," she insisted, her gaze steady and without accusation, as if she'd accepted her fate.

"I can't kill you. I know I said it. I know it's expected of me should you ever…" He couldn't even say the words.

"…if the demons get to me," she finished his sentence.

"I can't, Leila."

"But you'll have to. Promise me that if they get me, you'll kill me."

"NO!" He kissed her hard. "How can I hurt you after this? After last night? I've never shared *virta* with anybody."

"*Virta*?" she asked.

"My power, my energy. I've never felt so complete in my life. I can't let you go. Don't you know that?"

She planted soft kisses on his cheek, then his eyes. "But the demons… if they get me, I won't be the same…"

"I won't let them get you. Never. You hear me? Never." He felt his heart pound.

A serious expression spread in her eyes. "You can't always protect me. I have a life I have to return to eventually."

"Your life is with me." The words simply burst from him before he knew what he was saying.

"With you? You're an immortal, Aiden. Have you forgotten that? Our lives are so different."

An impatient knock at the door stopped him from answering.

"Aiden!" came Pearce's insistent voice.

His friend had shitty timing. "Give me a moment!" he called out.

Releasing Leila, he gave her a tender kiss on her lips. "We'll talk about it later." He caressed her cheek with his knuckles. "Why don't you take a shower while I talk to Pearce? I'll arrange new jeans for you later."

She nodded.

"I promise you, everything will work out for the best." His decision was made. It had been made for him the moment he'd first seen her. He understood that now. He'd never had a chance against the forces that had brought them together. And he was glad for it. He would fight it no longer.

As Leila walked into the bathroom and shut the door behind her, he called out, "Come in, Pearce!"

A second later, he watched his fellow Stealth Guardian pass through the door and appear in his room. Pearce surveyed the room briefly, his eyes catching on something behind Aiden.

"Is your guest all right?" he asked.

"Why shouldn't she be?"

Pearce motioned his head to a spot on the floor. Aiden turned and realized what he was looking at: Leila's shredded jeans.

"She's perfectly fine," he insisted and turned his gaze back to his visitor, unable to even feel embarrassed about what he'd done.

"Good, good. Anyway, I wouldn't have disturbed you, but I have a couple pieces of news."

Aiden listened intently. "Don't make me pull it out of your nose."

"About Zoltan. The news just came through that the body of a Mr. Zoltan has been found. He's been dead for days. The news station showed his picture, but Hamish said it's not the demon who attacked you at the farmhouse."

Aiden rubbed the back of his neck, contemplating the news. "He must have killed the real Zoltan and then taken his identity to infiltrate Inter Pharma."

"I agree. Wouldn't be a first that a demon is impersonating a real person to get what he wanted. Anyway, unfortunately that's not gonna get us any closer to him."

"You're right. Anything about my phone?"

"Yep. Somebody uploaded a little program that made it possible to operate your GPS remotely, switching it on and off whenever they wanted."

"Shit! How?"

"I'll spare you the technical details, but the only way to have done that would be to physically have had possession of your phone. I've deactivated it now." Pearce scratched his head.

Aiden furrowed his brows. "But who could have gotten hold of my phone?"

"Exactly. The only time you leave it lying around, is here in the compound."

"You mean someone here could have done that?" He shook off the thought. No, that couldn't be. If that was the case, he and Leila weren't safe here.

"I mean, unless you've left it somewhere else for somebody to access it, but I can't see how a council member—"

"That's it. I know how they did it." Why hadn't he thought of that earlier?

"How?"

He ignored the question. There wasn't the time now, because he'd just figured out how to trap the traitor on the council. "Can you replicate the software and upload it to other cell phones?"

"Sure, but aren't you gonna tell me whose phones?"

"I'll tell you when we get there."

"Get where?"

"My father's place."

31

After presenting his plan to Hamish and the others, Aiden felt confident that they could ferret out the traitor and in turn find Zoltan and the pendant.

"And when you get the pendant back, what then?" Leila asked, now dressed in clothes Enya had lent her.

He brushed his knuckles over her cheek. "We'll cross that bridge when we get to it." Then he pressed a quick kiss on her lips, not caring whether his friends were watching or not. They would get used to it. "Trust me, baby."

She gave a quick nod. "I do."

"I'll be back in a few hours."

Flanked by Pearce, he made his way down to the basement.

"What's your plan?"

Aiden gave his friend a sideways glance. "I just told you my plan. Weren't you listening?"

Pearce made a dismissive hand movement. "Not about the traitor, about your charge."

He couldn't answer that, not because he didn't know the answer, but because the person to hear it first should be Leila. When he was back, he would talk to her about it. And he hoped she felt the same way. "There's nothing to tell."

"That surprises me, considering you shared *virta* with her."

Aiden spun his head toward him and let out a frustrated breath. "Can nobody in this joint keep a secret anymore?"

His friend made a comical face. "Must have surprised the hell out of Hamish, otherwise he wouldn't have mentioned it. So what's up with that?"

"As I said, there's nothing to tell." *Yet.*

Next time he and Leila made love, it would be like the first time again. But he hadn't told her that it would always be like that between them from now on. And at the thought of that, his chest puffed up with pride, knowing what it would do to her, do to both of them. Even now as he stepped into the portal, Pearce by his side, he felt a thrill shoot through his loins and could barely wait to have her back in his arms. He was in for the long haul with Leila, and that knowledge scared the shit out of him.

He was glad to have to concentrate on their destination and pushed all thoughts about Leila out of his mind.

Moments later, they arrived.

The place looked the same as it had in the nearly two hundred years he'd known it, and from what his father and the elders of their species said, nothing had changed in over a thousand years. The Outer Hebrides were still as untouched by civilization as always. The incessant fog hung eerily over this particular island, the one no human had set foot on in a millennium.

The portal they stepped out of was out in the open and looked like a much smaller version of Stonehenge. Surrounded by dense brush and shrouded in fog, it was nearly undetectable, unless you knew what you were looking for.

Following the small path that led downhill, he soaked in the familiar smells of home. Only his parents and a few other families still lived here. Most of the others of their species had opted to live closer to civilization. He was grateful for the island's remoteness now. Talking to his father without being seen by any other council members was paramount.

"I haven't been here in years," Pearce murmured next to him, rubbing his arms to ward off the fog. "It's freezing here."

"Getting soft in your old age?"

"Easy for you to say. You've just risen from between the thighs of a warm woman. No wonder you're not cold."

"Zip it, Pearce, or I'm going to have to polish your nose. I'm entitled to some privacy, so stay out of this."

His friend grumbled, but didn't say anything else.

In the distance, a mansion came into view. As they approached, he saw light shining from the windows, and smoke rising from the chimney. His feet moved faster as he crossed the remaining distance.

Without opening the massive oak door with its cast iron handles, he passed through it, Pearce on his heels.

"Mother? Father?"

A few moments passed in silence. Then from upstairs, he heard hurried footsteps.

"Aiden?" his mother's voice called down from the top of the stairs.

"Yes, Mother."

"Oh dear," he heard her murmur before she came running down the stairs, dressed only in a long bathrobe, covering her from neck to toe, her long hair open and slightly disheveled. But even the long robe couldn't cover what she seemed to want to hide from him as she reached the foot of the stairs: she was glowing golden.

"Aiden, it's so good to see you." She hugged him enthusiastically, sparing him having to look at her in embarrassment. No son wanted to know that his parents had just had sex.

"You should have let us know you were visiting," his father said as he walked down the stairs, dressed in jogging pants and nothing else.

Releasing his mother and stepping back, he nodded at his father, acknowledging the slight reprimand. Ever since he'd moved out from home to reside in one of the compounds, his parents had viewed their home as their private little love nest. He should have thought of that. His father was still virile despite his age and would remain so for his entire life. Strangely enough, despite the embarrassing looks now being exchanged between all four of them, the thought that a couple could still keep their sex life exciting and—by the looks of it—very satisfying after such a long time, made him yearn for Leila. Could he have something like this with her?

"We're sorry to intrude," Pearce apologized, clearing his throat as he avoided looking at Aiden's mother.

"We wouldn't have come unannounced if it weren't urgent." Aiden looked at his father, who replied with a sheepish smile.

"Well, luckily you didn't get here any earlier than you did."

"Barclay!" his wife admonished, a blush staining her cheeks underneath the golden sheen.

He winked at his wife before looking back at Aiden and Pearce. "Come, how about some whiskey in front of the fireplace?"

"We'll need that," Aiden agreed.

They followed his father and mother as they walked into the living room, a great room with vaulted ceilings, exposed stone

walls, and a massive fireplace, which could accommodate a spit to
roast an entire pig.

Once they were all sitting down, whiskey glasses in hand, his
father gave him an expectant look. "Considering that you're
supposed to be on assignment right now, I'm assuming your visit
isn't entirely personal."

Aiden straightened, turning the glass in his hand. "My charge
is being protected at the compound right now, so I—"

His father shot up. "At the compound? What on earth has
gotten into you? It's against our rules! You'd better have a damn
good explanation for that!"

"I do. Actually more than one."

"Well, don't make me wait for it."

"Sit down, Father, this will take a while."

When he took his seat again, Aiden nipped from his glass.
"There were several attempts on Leila's life, and we have reason
to believe that a council member who wasn't happy with the
outcome of the vote, is behind it."

Both his mother and father gasped at the accusation.

"They would never!" his father said in outrage.

"They would, and they did. But that's not the worst of it.
There's more. We have a traitor on the council. A traitor who's
feeding information to the demons."

His father's face went white in shock. He exchanged a
surprised look with his wife.

"Tell me everything."

Aiden nodded, filling his father and mother in about what had
transpired up till now. With every word, his father's expression
grew grimmer. By the end, both of his parents sat there, looking
shell-shocked.

"No wonder Hamish disappeared. The boy has good instincts.
Always knew it." His father nodded as if talking to himself. Then
he stared back at him and Pearce. "I'm assuming you have a plan."

"I need to know how the council voted on Leila's case."

"The votes are secret. You know I can't tell you," his father
objected, outrage coloring his voice.

"I'm afraid you'll need to break some rules this time. We have
no lead on who on the council is responsible. We have to narrow
down the field. Whoever voted to eliminate Leila is a suspect in

the attempts on her life. And somebody who voted to protect her, must work—"

"—for the demons," Pearce concluded.

"Explain your reasoning," his father requested.

"The first is easy: the person voting to eliminate Leila wanted to make sure neither she nor her research falls into the demons' hands. He or she tried to steal the research data, killed Leila's boss and wiped the data off her laptop in the process. That same person is responsible for sending the dogs on us at our safe house." Aiden knew his reasoning was solid.

"And the traitor? Why would he have to be someone voting to protect her?"

"Because Leila's drug is only in its final stages. She's still needed to refine it. It is in the interest of the demons to keep her alive if they don't want to end up with a drug that might in the end not work. They had to keep her alive."

"And you think somebody on the council was responsible for sending this Zoltan and his thugs after you in Sonoma?"

Aiden nodded. "Yes. By that time they'd realized that all known copies of the data were destroyed, and now they had no choice but to snatch Leila if they wanted the drug. Nobody knew we were there. Only Hamish, Leila and I."

"And you trust Hamish," his father asked.

Was his father doubting his friend? "Implicitly. He helped us escape the safe house, and he was the one finding the lost portals."

"Good. You should trust your gut more often."

"So, will you help us?"

His parents exchanged looks. Then his mother gave him a soft smile. "Of course, he'll help you."

"Then who voted to protect her?"

Anxiously, Aiden leaned forward. One of the names he'd receive was the traitor who worked for the demons.

"I did," his father confessed. "But then, you knew that already. Besides me, there were Cinead, Riona, Finlay, and Norton. The others voted to eliminate her."

"Thank you."

"How are you going to trap the guilty party?"

"I need you to call an emergency council meeting."

"What do you want me to put on the agenda, son?"

"You need to tell the council members where Leila and I are hiding."

Stunned, his father stared at him. "You want to turn yourself and your charge into bait?"

"There's no other way."

32

Barclay watched as the last council member finally took his seat in the chamber before he let the gavel drop onto the table to ask for silence. He knew he would have to go slowly in order to give Pearce and Aiden sufficient time to upload the tracking software to all council members' cell phones. Beyond the closed doors of the council chambers, the two of them were already working on the cell phones, Barclay having made sure that the council assistant would be called away from his post at the door so the two could work unobserved.

The knowledge that he had violated the rules of the council by giving away how the members had voted made him feel uneasy; but, as his son had insisted, it was the only way.

He glanced at Cinead, his gut clenching at the thought that he could be a traitor. The Scotsman was his oldest friend, his opinions valued by all, his character beyond reproach. As he looked into the round, the thought of any of the others turning out to be a traitor didn't suit him any better. All members of the council were honorable men and women, chosen because they were just leaders.

Yet, Barclay trusted his son, although something about him had been different when he'd visited. He appeared less angry than usual, despite the seriousness of the issues at hand. Almost as if something or someone had a calming influence on him.

"I've called this special meeting to update you on the case of Dr. Cruickshank."

Murmurs went through the room. It was rather unusual to discuss individual cases once a vote had been taken and the charge assigned to a Stealth Guardian. He would have to be careful not to raise any suspicion as to his true agenda: to set a trap for the traitor.

"There have been some setbacks. I'm afraid after an attack on their safe house, Aiden and his charge had to flee."

"Are they unharmed?" Riona asked.

"For now, yes. However, I am surprised at Aiden's decision of how to go forward."

Cinead raised an eyebrow. "Your own son's? Weren't you the one to convince us that he was up for the job?"

Barclay bowed his head. "I don't always agree with his ideas. However, there might be some merit to his decision. He's taken her back to their last hiding place, figuring it will be where the demons won't look for him again." Cautiously, he glanced around, searching for tell tale signs in the eyes of his fellow council members. Would somebody take the bait?

"That is against protocol," Geoffrey piped. "Once a safe house is compromised, it will never be used again."

Barclay raised his hand to pacify his old friend. "I understand, however, Aiden has gone to radio silence, and since he selected his last safe house anonymously, I have no way of contacting him. We're in the dark."

"What about Manus, his second?" Finlay asked. "He would know where the safe house is."

"I'm afraid I've already checked into this avenue. Aiden cut off contact with Manus before claiming the safe house. Manus never knew where Aiden had taken her," Barclay lied.

"That's highly irregular," Finlay said. "Are you sure your son hasn't gone rogue like his friend Hamish? What if he's kidnapped his charge and is now using her as a pawn?"

Barclay felt anger about Finlay's accusation boil up in him. "My son is doing what's best for all of us."

"Primus, your son is putting us in danger," Deirdre snapped. "Without his second and any support from us, how does he expect to defeat any demons when they attack?"

"They won't find him. By using his previous hiding place, he's outsmarting them. They'll never go back to where they've already found him earlier."

Wade rose from his seat. "I agree with Deirdre. I think Aiden should be pulled off this assignment. We can't risk his erratic behavior endangering us all."

Barclay glared at Wade. "Aiden will remain on this assignment. I might not always see eye to eye with my son, but he is a capable Stealth Guardian and can protect his charge without our help."

"You're making a huge mistake." Deirdre rose and glared at him. "Have you forgotten what can happen when our guardians don't comply with rules?"

"What are you implying?" Barclay ground out. "Are you questioning Aiden's abilities?"

"What if I am?" She thrust her chin up in open challenge. "Has he not cost us dearly once before?"

Barclay gasped, shocked about what she was hinting at. "You'd better let the past remain where it belongs, Deirdre."

"You know as well as I do that I can't do that. I was Julia's godmother, I loved her like a daughter. I—"

Barclay shot from his seat. "No further! I'm warning you!"

"You shouldn't be warning me, you should be warning your son. He's putting us all in danger. He's being irrational just as he was then," Deirdre continued from between clenched teeth.

"My son is a fine guardian—"

"Yet you have no influence over him," Finlay suddenly interjected, "just like you can't control anything else, not even as Primus. Sad, really, to hold such a powerful position in our society, yet to be so powerless."

Barclay shifted his attention to the council member. "Is there something else you have to add on the powers of this council? Or are you quite done?"

"Since you're asking," Finlay gritted, "yes, there's more. All we do is sit, debate, and vote. But we take no decisive action. We let the guardians dance on our noses. You can't even control your son. How do you expect to lead our race?"

The words surprised him. He'd never realized that Finlay harbored so much discontent.

"Maybe you would like to become Primus instead."

Finlay scoffed. "I hold no such ambition."

"Anybody else who doesn't like the way the council operates?" He glared into the round.

Murmurs rippled through the chamber.

~ ~ ~

Aiden stood watching over Pearce's shoulder as his friend looked at the different colored dots that moved on the digital map on the monitor in the command room.

"Everything set up?"

Pearce nodded. "I'm locked onto them. It's time to move. I'll send you word as soon as anybody is on the move." He pointed at the dots. "Looks like the council meeting is just breaking up."

"Are Enya and Logan in place?"

"Yes, they're waiting. Time for you, Hamish, and Manus to go."

A door opened behind them. Aiden turned to see Leila slip in, followed by Hamish. When he saw her, he felt his body fill with warmth. She smiled at him and walked toward him. Without hesitation, he put his arm around her and pulled her to his side.

"You're back," she whispered.

He pressed a chaste kiss to her forehead. "Not for long. We need to leave now. Pearce is the only one to stay. He'll protect you while I'm gone."

"Can't I come with you?"

"No. You're safest here. I want you nowhere near the demons."

She pressed herself closely to him, and her gesture of trust strengthened him. Everything would be all right. He knew it in his gut.

"Let's go!" Hamish ordered.

With a last glance at Leila, he followed Hamish out the door. Outside the portal, Manus was already waiting for them, weapons in hand.

The three of them would go to the old farmhouse where they'd been attacked by the demons earlier—but this time, they'd be lying in wait for them.

Pearce would record the council members' movements and alert them to their positions.

33

Leila shivered and wrapped her arms around her torso while she watched Pearce at the console.

He cast a look over his shoulder. "Sorry, it has to be cold in here because of the computers. Why don't you get yourself a jacket from Aiden's room?"

"I think I'll do that." She walked toward the door when she heard Pearce's chair scrape along the floor.

"But come right back. I've promised Aiden I'd watch out for you."

She hesitated, wondering whether to ask the question that was bothering her. Curiosity won out. "When I arrived here, Enya said I shouldn't be here. But isn't this the safest place to hide your charges from the demons?"

She turned halfway and noticed how he watched her. "It is. But no humans are allowed here, because they can betray us to the demons. And if they ever find the location of our portals, they can destroy us. It was foolish for Aiden to have brought you here, I won't deny that…"

Leila sensed a hesitation in him. "There's a 'but,' isn't there?"

"There's always a 'but.' The rest of us here at the compound discussed this while you were in his quarters with him. We know that Aiden will hesitate to kill you should you be influenced by the demons, but let me make it perfectly clear to you: the rest of us won't."

Her breath hitched at the unveiled threat. It shouldn't surprise her, however, she had not sensed any hostility from Pearce before.

"Don't get me wrong, we all want Aiden to be happy and you seem like a nice enough woman, but if you betray our race, there's only one course of action."

She nodded, her vocal cords freezing. She might be a coward, but she wouldn't betray Aiden again. After the trust he'd shown her, she knew she'd rather die than do anything to hurt him. "I understand, but I won't betray any of you."

"Good."

Pearce turned back to his console, and Leila exited the room. As she walked through the silent hallways that were adorned with strange symbols and artwork, she suppressed the sense of foreboding that crept up her spine. She was worried about Aiden. What if this time Zoltan came back with more than just two other demons to finish them off? Already, the first time they'd attacked, they had been so strong that Hamish and Aiden had barely been able to defeat them.

Biting her fingernails, she entered Aiden's rooms. In his closet she found a bomber jacket. She slipped into it and inhaled. A faint smell of Aiden hung in the air, helping calm her nerves. When she closed the closet, her eyes fell onto her handbag, which lay on the dresser where she'd left it hours earlier. It was all she possessed now. Even the clothes on her body weren't hers.

Enya had lent her a pair of jeans with plenty of metal buttons and clasps on it that weren't really to her taste. But, she figured, beggars couldn't be choosers. At least she was glad that Enya's clothing size was identical to hers, so the jeans fit like a second skin. She'd been surprised that the female Stealth Guardian had lent her anything at all, considering the hostility with which she'd been treated by her. While the men in the compound had been polite enough, Enya had not made it a secret that she wanted her gone.

Leila opened her handbag and peered inside. She realized immediately that her cell phone was missing. Her wallet was there, together with a pair of sunglasses, a notebook, and her can of mace. She reached for it, remembering the evening she'd met Aiden and how he'd told her at the Irish bar that anybody who knew what he was doing could easily wrestle the can out of her grip. He'd proven that he could. She sighed. So much had happened since then. The things she'd been afraid of then had blended into the distance and become insignificant. There were greater dangers in this world than a few muggers who wanted her money.

And she'd thought that she could never date a policeman or a military guy because of the danger they faced every day. Funny, how she now considered these choices to be safer than losing her heart to a Stealth Guardian who battled demons on a daily basis. And she was in danger of losing her heart to Aiden, even though she knew there could be no future for them. He was an immortal. She wasn't. End of story.

Leila shoved the can of mace into her jacket pocket, not really knowing why. Stupidly enough, it made her feel safer in Aiden's absence, even though she knew that the can could never defeat a demon. She'd felt Zoltan's strength, and had she not at the time had Aiden's power in her, he would have overwhelmed her.

She shuddered at the recollection of Zoltan's face so close to hers, of his green eyes boring into her, his hands on her throat, and his thoughts in her head. Instinctively, her hand went to her neck, rubbing it, trying to wipe away the gruesome memory.

Not wanting to remain alone any longer, she made for the exit and rushed back along the corridor. As she turned a corner, she spotted the door to the command room. It was ajar.

Then everything went dark.

"Fuck!" she heard Pearce curse.

Fear gave her wings, propelling her toward the room. "Pearce!" she screamed.

"Power failure. Leila! Get in here, now!"

She ran, then stumbled, her hands flailing, gripping something.

~ ~ ~

Enya peered through the drapes, watching the street below where the hookers plied their trade. Behind her in the dark room, Logan slouched in one of the comfy chairs, his long legs resting on the coffee table.

"Anything?" he asked, bored.

"All clear so far. Not that I think that our suspect will arrive uncloaked." She turned to him. "I could have bet that by now one of the council members would be on the move. Are you sure your cell phone has reception?"

He glanced at the phone in his hands, then waved it at her. "Yep. Still no message from Pearce."

It bothered her. Her instincts were never wrong. And she knew that Aiden's plan was solid. The council member who had tried to kill Leila would assume that their last hiding place was the Thai massage parlor—unaware of the farmhouse in California—and therefore return to it to finish Leila off.

Turning away from the window, she crouched down and stroked the head of the dog who lay next to Logan's chair. The German shepherd looked up at her. "Good dog," she murmured.

The room was shrouded in darkness. On the nightstand next to the bed lay Leila's cell phone. Enya had taken it from her bag, figuring if their suspect had a way of tracing it, it would be best to bring it to the massage parlor. Pearce had pronounced the phone clear of any bugs, but she'd brought it nevertheless and even switched it on.

"What do you think of her?" Logan suddenly asked.

"Of whom?"

"The human, of course. Don't tell me you haven't formed an opinion about her yet."

In the dark, she noticed how one side of Logan's mouth curled up in a mocking grin.

"What do *you* care?"

"Just asking. Does it bother you that you're not the only female at the compound anymore?" he needled her.

"She won't be staying." She was a mere interloper, a human. She didn't belong there.

"Are you so sure about that?"

"I know Aiden. Do you really think he can be with a human after what happened to his sister?" Aiden wasn't the forgiving sort. He could hold a grudge longer than anybody she knew.

"His little friend doesn't seem to think so," Logan chuckled.

"His little what?" Then she suddenly realized what he meant. "Oh, you're so gross, Logan!"

"Nothing gross about sex." He seemed to enjoy her discomfort.

But she wouldn't give him the satisfaction of backing down now. "Just because he's stuck his dick in her, doesn't mean he's keeping her. I know how you guys work. Or why do you think I have no intention of ever spreading my legs for any of you?" There, he could chew on that.

"Spoken like a truly unsatisfied woman."

"Am not!" Enya snapped.

"Trust me, you *so* need to get laid."

"Oh, please, as if everything can be—"

The soft growling of the dog interrupted her. The animal got onto its feet, its ears standing up, its snout trained in the direction of the door.

Jumping up, Logan stared down at his phone, then shook his head 'no,' indicating that he hadn't received any message from Pearce.

Enya held her breath and cloaked herself, noticing Logan doing the same. She waited, watching the dog. It was trained to keep quiet, but his body language indicated that somebody had just entered the room.

The soft rustling of a dress or a coat disturbed the silence.

"Attack!" Enya ordered the dog.

A loud shriek came from the intruder as the dog's teeth dug into the invisible person, who fell to the floor in a reverberating thump. In the same instant, Enya launched herself onto the intruder, uncloaking herself in mid-movement. Logan simultaneously appeared to her left.

Her hand connected with an arm. She grabbed it and wrenched it. Enya could see that the dog was still tugging at something, digging its teeth deeper into the suspect.

Another scream filled the room.

"Uncloak yourself, or I'll have the dog bite your fucking leg off."

An instant later, a figure dressed in a long cloak, a hood over the head, showed itself.

"Tell the dog to stop," she yelped. A woman's voice!

Logan grabbed the woman and pulled her up.

"Rex, release." The dog let go of the woman's leg. "Good dog," Enya praised and patted its head.

"And who have we here?" Logan asked calmly.

Enya snatched the hood and pulled it off the woman's face. Blond curls tumbled down.

"Deirdre!" She knew the headstrong council member. She'd looked up to her. "How disappointing."

Deirdre knew she was caught. Her facial expression said as much. "It had to be done. The council was foolish to let her live."

"They voted," Logan said. "It's not for you to change the outcome."

"I tried to do what's best for our society."

Enya shook her head. "You can't change the rules just because they don't suit you."

"Don't think you're any better than I! If you were privy to the information the council got, you would have done the same," Deirdre hissed.

"Everyone on the council had the same information you did; you were outvoted," Enya replied.

"Let's go. I'm sure the council is interested in knowing who's been going against their orders," Logan remarked. Then he grinned. "I think the council might soon have a vacancy to fill."

Deirdre stared at them with wide eyes. "They can't do that!"

Enya bent closer to her, moving her mouth to the woman's ear. "They can, and they will. Hope you'll enjoy your lead prison."

She took a step when her foot hit something on the floor. She bent down and picked it up. It was a cell phone. "Yours?" she asked Deirdre curiously.

"Yes."

She exchanged a quick look with Logan. "If she had her phone with her, why didn't Pearce warn us?"

"Call him. Now." Logan's voice sounded tense.

Enya dialed the compound's number and let it ring. There was no reply. Panicked, she disconnected.

"His cell," Logan urged.

She speed dialed Pearce's cell phone, but after three rings it went to his voicemail. She pressed the disconnect button.

Her pulse raced. "We have to get to the compound."

"We have to deliver Deirdre to the council first. Call Aiden," Logan ordered and for once, Enya didn't mind his commanding tone.

34

Leila couldn't see the face of the man who was holding a dagger to her throat, his other arm holding her in a vice-like grip. The cold blade pressing against her skin was disincentive enough to turning her head.

"Now listen very carefully, or I'll carve up your pretty neck," he hissed into her ear.

Her vocal cords clamped down, and she didn't dare nod; however, her attacker seemed to take her silence as an agreement.

"Good. Into the command room, now. Move."

He pushed against her back, making her move forward with tentative steps, always aware of the knife that remained at her throat as he held her arms behind her back with his free hand.

"Leila? Where are you?" Pearce's voice came from the dark room.

Her captor catapulted them inside, just as lights flickered above and suddenly illuminated the room.

"Finally, the backup generator kicked in," Pearce acknowledged with relief in his voice and swiveled with his chair.

His expression turned to horror when he spotted her.

"Fuck!" Pearce cursed.

"Couldn't have said it any better," the men behind her drawled.

"Council member Finlay," Pearce greeted him with an icy voice, his eyes darting about the room as if looking for something.

Would he help her? Would he be able to defeat her attacker?

"So it's you."

"Indeed," Finlay acknowledged. "But you green boys thought I was stupid and would fall for your little tricks. I've been around longer than you, and you think you could put a simple trace on my cell?"

"You found it then." Pearce seemed calm now.

Was he not going to do anything to help her? Leila gave him a pleading look, but he concentrated on Finlay instead.

"Of course I did. That's why my cell phone is still at the council building."

Pearce tipped up his chin. "What do you want?"

"Isn't that obvious?" He laughed, the cold sound making her shiver despite the jacket she wore. "I want Dr. Cruickshank."

"To kill her?"

"To trade her. But enough of it. We don't have much time. Your friends will call in soon and realize you're not answering. And I want to be far away from here by then."

"You'll never get away with it. The council will hear of this."

Finlay chuckled. "The council? I don't give a fuck about the council! They have no power."

Pearce's mouth dropped open. "They'll know it's you."

"So what? They can't stop me now. Neither can you. The real power is with the demons."

"How can you betray us like that? They're evil."

"Evil? That's just a matter of perception. You think you're so much better than the demons? We all have our agendas. And the Stealth Guardians' doesn't suit me anymore. They're stifling my ambitions."

He tugged on Leila's arms, pulling her backward.

Pearce took a step forward.

"No farther!" Finlay warned. "Or I'll kill her."

As if to prove his intent, he pressed the knife harder to her skin. She gasped.

"You won't kill her. The demons want her," Pearce guessed. "A corpse won't do them any good."

Finlay grunted. "A little cut won't kill her, but I'm sure it'll hurt." He moved his mouth to her ear. "Won't it, dear?"

"I'll never help the demons," she professed. She would never betray Aiden like that. She'd promised him that.

"Oh, trust me. You will. They have ways of making you submit."

As he slowly moved the knife downward, fear and pain collided. She felt a burning sensation, then liquid trickling down her skin. He'd cut her.

"No!" she begged.

"Stop!" Pearce ordered.

"Well, then we're all in agreement, aren't we?"

Finlay's nonchalant tone seemed to infuriate Pearce.

"No, we're not in agreement, council member. You're a traitor, and you *will* pay for this."

Her attacker simply laughed at Pearce's warning. "Get real."

Clearly scrambling to buy more time, Pearce made another attempt at engaging Finlay. "What are the demons promising? What is it that you don't already have as a council member?"

"Power."

Leila couldn't see Finlay's eyes, but she imagined how they lit up now.

"Yes, power. Real power. The council has no true power. All they do is talk and vote and discuss everything ad nauseam. I'm sick of nobody ever taking real action. We could have taken over the world long ago, made the humans work for us instead of the other way around. What are we? Servants? Why should we devote our lives to this ungrateful race?"

Leila swallowed hard, almost choking on the lump in her throat. She felt the hatred rolling off him in waves, the frustration that must have built up over years if not centuries. And now she was at his mercy.

"Why me?" she whispered, careful not to move her neck to avoid being cut again.

He pulled on her arms, making her bend her head back.

"Because you're the key to world domination. When I deliver you, I'll become their leader. Nobody will be more powerful than I!"

An ice-cold shudder ran down her spine, chilling her to the core. He was crazy. Consumed by delusions of grandeur.

"Finlay, don't do this," Pearce warned.

"We've wasted enough time," he suddenly said and motioned toward Pearce. "It's the lead cell for you."

Pearce's eyes flashed in panic.

A chuckle was Finlay's response. "You didn't think I'd leave you here so you could alert your friends, did you now?" Then he moved the knife in an unmistakable gesture. "Now, lead, or I'll carve her up."

"What's a lead cell?" Leila asked.

"Shall I explain it to her, or would you?" Finlay answered.

Pearce gave her a resigned look. "It's a room lined with lead. If a Stealth Guardian is locked up there, it drains all his powers, making it impossible for him to walk through walls or make himself invisible. If left there for too long, the loss of power is irreversible."

Her breath hitched. People were being hurt because of her. She couldn't allow this.

"Don't do it, Pearce. Let him kill me."

"So heroic all of a sudden?" Finlay hissed at her ear. "And here I had you pegged for a coward. Or maybe you're just bluffing. I know a thing or two about that. Trust me, once you're in the demons' hands, you won't be that brave anymore. Once you stare death in the face, you—"

Finlay's voice died as Pearce unexpectedly charged him. In the same instant, Leila felt Finlay push her away from him with such force that she lost her balance and slammed against the wall. As she scrambled to get up, pain radiating up her side, Pearce and Finlay were already engaged in a fight. An uneven one, she realized with horror, because Pearce had no weapon.

Yet that didn't seem to stop the younger Stealth Guardian from fighting as ferociously as if he were armed to the teeth. With cunning Karate kicks and blows, he kept Finlay's dagger at bay. But the traitor was strong and agile. Evading yet another kick, he whirled sideways, managing to slice Pearce's bicep open with his dagger.

Leila witnessed as blood gushed from the wound, but Pearce didn't even stop for a split-second and launched another blow at his opponent. Angry grunts and groans accompanied every blow and kick, every punch and strike.

She wanted to run and get help, but the two fought too closely to the door, making her escape impossible. Her heart beat frantically as she had no choice but to watch the fight.

All of a sudden, Pearce seemed to gain the upper hand, knocking Finlay off his feet with a vicious kick. But even lying on the floor, Finlay didn't give up. As Pearce moved in to finish him off, the council member's dagger hand lashed out with lightning speed.

Pearce's scream filled the room.

Confused, Leila watched as he fought to keep his balance, but lost the struggle and fell to the floor. When his hands went to his foot, she finally saw what had happened: Finlay had sliced through Pearce's Achilles tendon. Blood gushed from the wound.

Triumphantly, Finlay jumped up.

"Bad move, boy. Hope you'll enjoy your lead cell."

Leila shivered and cast the wounded Stealth Guardian a sad look. Now another person was hurt because of her. "I'm so sorry," she whispered.

Pearce motioned his head toward Finlay, his face a mask of pain. "It's not your fault, it's his."

A tear loosened from her eye and rolled down her cheek. "Tell Aiden, I'll never betray him. Please."

Finlay let out an evil laugh. "Oh, you will betray him. Trust me on that."

The hatred that fumed in his eyes chilled her to the bones.

35

"Pearce is not responding." Aiden felt his heart stop when he heard Enya's words coming through the phone.

"What do you mean?"

"We tried the compound and his cell. He's not replying. And he never warned us about Deirde's approach. Something is wrong."

Aiden cast a quick glance at Hamish and Manus, whose concerned looks told him that they'd overheard Enya's words.

"We're heading there right now." He pressed the disconnect button and shoved the phone back in his pocket.

"There could be all kinds of reasons why he's not picking up," Hamish tried to calm him, but it didn't help.

"Yes, and I don't like any of those reasons. I have to make sure Leila is safe." She was his first priority. Nothing else mattered, not even the fact that leaving the house in Sonoma now meant they would have to set another trap for the traitor later.

"We can't just leave here. This is our best chance to catch the demons," Hamish protested.

Aiden sought his friend's gaze. "Would you think the same if this were the woman you once loved?"

Hamish's eyes flared. Aiden noticed the cords in his neck bulge, betraying the struggle raging inside him. Seconds passed until his friend finally nodded. "Fine, you win."

They headed out the door into the warm September night and rushed to the car. The ride to the portal stretched for too long—long enough for Aiden's mind to conjure up one terrible scenario after another of what could have happened at the compound.

He should have never left her there. It was a mistake. She would have been safer with him.

His heart racing, Aiden charged toward the portal the moment the car came to a standstill. His friends ran after him. The instant he stood in the portal, he concentrated on the compound's location and transported, not even waiting for his fellow Stealth Guardians. They would be only seconds behind him.

When he exited the portal at the compound, he barreled up the stairs and ran down the long corridor to the command center. The door was wide open, the lights were on, but the chair in front of the console was empty, as was the entire room.

"Leila! Pearce!" he called out.

Behind him, footsteps approached. He turned, only to face Hamish and Manus. At the same time his eyes fell on a spot on the floor where something had splattered. His heart stopped.

"Oh, God, no!" He took a shaky breath, inhaling the metallic scent of blood. His heart clenched painfully. What had happened? Was this Leila's blood? Where was Leila? He should have never left her side.

"Shit!" Hamish cursed. "There must have been a fight."

Manus darted his head out the room, then turned back. "There's a trail leading down the corridor."

"We have to find them," Aiden pressed out and rushed out of the room, following the trail of blood that looked as if somebody had been dragged. He tried not to think the worst, and instead continued running until the trail ended—in front of the lead cell.

Each compound had a cell in order to lock up Stealth Guardians who'd infringed on their laws. Theirs had never been used before.

Aiden unlocked the heavy door and jerked it open. "Leila! Pearce!" He peered into the darkness.

"Aiden, here," came Pearce's voice.

"Pearce!" Aiden rushed into the cell and found Pearce cowering on the ground. "Where is she? Where is Leila?"

"I'm sorry, Aiden. He had a knife to her throat. I tried to fight him, but I was unarmed." Pearce pointed toward his leg. "He cut my Achilles tendon."

Aiden felt the air leave his lungs, virtually choking him. "No!" He stared at Pearce's injury, knowing his friend had done what he could, but without the ability to move on his feet, he couldn't have done any more.

Manus and Hamish entered behind him and helped their friend up.

"Finlay is the traitor. He took her."

"Did he hurt her?" The thought of Leila in pain made bile shoot up from his gut.

"He didn't," Pearce alleviated his concern.

Aiden took a deep breath, trying to regain his wits. He had to get her back, somehow. And he could only do that if he could think clearly, something that seemed impossible right now.

"What happened?"

Pearce let out a long breath. "Finlay somehow caught onto us. He knew we had a trace on his phone. He left it at the council building, so I didn't know he was on the move. He transported in and cut the power. By the time the backup generator kicked in, he'd already gotten to Leila and threatened her."

"That explains why Logan and Enya didn't get a warning about Deirdre showing up at the massage parlor," Hamish interjected as he and Manus helped Pearce out of the cell.

Aiden slammed the door shut behind them.

Pearce glanced at Hamish. "Deirdre? Shit, I would have never thought she'd go that far. So she was the one trying to kill Leila?"

Hamish nodded.

"We'll deal with Deirdre later," Aiden acknowledged impatiently. She would be punished—and severely, if he had a say in it. But what was more important now was to find Leila. "What does Finlay want with her?"

Pearce's look turned to stone. "Trade her to the demons. He's crazy, Aiden." He shook his head as if he couldn't believe it himself. "He thinks the demons will crown him as their leader if he brings them this prize. He wants the power."

"I won't allow it. We'll get her back!" Aiden felt his anger rise. Nobody would take Leila away from him. He'd get her back even if he had to follow the demons into their lair and rip her from their claws. "She's mine!"

Three pairs of eyes stared at him.

"Well," Manus said deadpan, "that clears that up. I would extend my congratulations, but considering the bride is absent, I'll postpone that."

Aiden lashed a furious glare at Manus for his flippant remark.

Manus immediately lifted his free arm in a show of surrender. "No harm meant. We'd better get to work on finding your mate."

Manus's last word sank deep into Aiden's chest. Even though he'd never used it when thinking about Leila, he knew it was the truth nevertheless. Nothing had ever felt so right. There was no denying that *rasen* had finally caught up with him and delivered the only woman who could ever be his. Now all he had to do was get her back.

He nodded. "We have to figure out where Finlay took her."

Pearce motioned toward the stairs, his arms around Manus's and Hamish's shoulders for support. "Let's go to the command center. Your father can get us access to his file to see where he owns property, who he knows, where he goes. If somebody can bring me his cell phone, I might be able to trace where he's been before. Maybe we can find his meeting place with the demons that way."

As Aiden made a motion to follow his friends who assisted Pearce in negotiating the stairs, he heard a sound coming from the corridor leading to the portal.

He turned and saw Logan and Enya come toward them. He waited for them.

"We dropped off Deirdre with the council guards and came as fast as we could," Logan announced.

Aiden gave both a grave look. "Leila is gone. Finlay took her; he's the traitor."

"Shit!" Logan exclaimed.

"Well, let's go trace them and ambush him," Enya said and headed for the stairs.

Aiden felt the hopelessness of the situation crash over him once more. "We have no way of tracing Finlay. He's left his cell behind."

To his surprise, Enya grinned.

"What the—?"

"Just as well that I lent her my jeans then."

Confusion roiled through him, but before he could voice it, Enya put a hand on his forearm.

"No offense, but I didn't trust her, so I put a tracker into one of the metal buttons on the jeans. If she's still wearing them, we'll find her."

He didn't believe his ears at first, but when the words sank in, he couldn't help but hug his compound mate until she pushed against him, wanting to be released.

"You can let me go now!"

He let go of her and took a steadying breath. "I don't know how to thank you."

Enya grumbled under her breath. "It's not by groping me, that's for sure. Try that again, and you'll find my dagger in your gut."

At any other time, Aiden would have started a fight with Enya about what was considered a friendly hug and what constituted a grope, but at this moment he couldn't care less. His thoughts were with Leila, the only woman he wanted to touch for the rest of his life.

36

The sun had already set when Finlay had kidnapped her from the compound, but after hurtling through the portal and emerging at the other end, Leila saw the glow of late afternoon sun. It had to mean that they were somewhere on the West Coast. The portal behind them was hidden in a hillside, heavy brush disguising its location. Looking down the hill, Leila noticed the trees surrounding them: mostly pine trees, mixed with other varietals she didn't recognize. She inhaled, taking in the dry air. While it was still warm, it wasn't humid, another indication that her captor had transported her to the West Coast rather than the South or East. California, if she had to guess.

"Let's go, no time for sightseeing," Finlay ordered gruffly and clamped his hand harder around her upper arm.

"Where are we going?"

"Meeting your new master," he snarled and tugged on her arm, dragging her down a dirt path.

"Please, why are you doing this?"

"You would never understand! Humans are so small-minded when it comes to the important things in life. Your brain can't comprehend the grand things I'm planning for this world."

Leila snorted. "Grand? You're planning to destroy humanity. There's nothing grand about that."

He tugged at her arm, yanking her toward him. "You have no idea what I'm planning. This will be a brave new world with an order that gets things done, not your stupid little democracies that fight among each other. Your idiotic political parties that can't agree on anything. No! My new order will make things right."

"You mean tyranny."

"Call it what you will, but only a strong ruler with absolute power can make a difference. You're just too brainwashed to see that."

"It will never work," she spat.

He slapped the back of his hand over her cheek, whipping her head to the side.

"Enough. You're just a human. I told you you wouldn't understand."

Then he turned and dragged her with him.

As they hiked down the mountain and through the forest that surrounded it, Leila couldn't help but think about the mistakes she'd made. Had she not lied to Aiden about the data in the pendant, this might never have happened. He would have had no reason to go after the demons to get it back and would have been at the compound to protect her instead.

But there was no use crying over spilled milk. The damage was done; now all she could do was put an end to it. No help was coming. By the time Aiden even noticed her disappearance, she would already be in the clutches of the demons. How long would she be able to fight against their mental influence? Or would they torture her physically this time to get what they wanted? Would they hurt her so much that she would give away the secret in the pendant only so they would stop?

She shuddered at the thought. She had promised Aiden and herself that she wouldn't betray him, but could she actually keep this promise? Was she strong enough?

The longer they walked through the woods, the grimmer her mood turned. She had to face the facts: she was a coward when it came to physical and mental pain, and the demons would apply both to get what they wanted from her. She would crack. It was only a matter of time.

A silent sob worked itself up from her gut into her throat. She clamped her mouth shut so it couldn't escape. She had to be brave.

The hike through the forest took over an hour. When they cleared it, they reached what looked like a deserted parking lot, if she could trust her eyes. The sun had set during their march, and it was now pitch black. Out in the countryside were no street lights, and only the stars provided the tiniest of illumination on the moonless night.

Undeterred, Finlay pushed her forward where a hut of some sort stood out against the darkness. A faint light on its outside illuminated a board. As her captor dragged her past it, she quickly tried to read the notice. All she could catch was *Mercer Caverns* and a list of times and prices. Frantically, she searched her memory. Somewhere she'd heard that name before. She knew she'd never been here before, but at the same time the name sounded familiar.

But she had no time to think about it further, her feet so tired by now that she stumbled more than walked as Finlay led her past what seemed like an entrance, then wedged himself between two bushes and pulled her with him. Branches swiped her, getting caught in her jacket. She heard a ripping sound as he pulled her into the thick without stopping. Then one branch grazed her face, making her cry out, its ends catching in her hair, tangling it. She jolted backward.

"Don't stop!" he ordered and dragged her with him.

She felt strands of her hair being ripped from her scalp, driving tears into her eyes. But she didn't dare cry out again.

A moment later, what sounded like an old rickety wooden door was opened, and she was shoved inside. Behind her, Finlay bolted it. A strong musty smell greeted her, and the residual warmth that had held off the cold of the night while they were outside had disappeared. It was noticeably colder in here, almost as if she'd stepped into a refrigerator. Before her was a dark void—no light penetrated.

When she heard some shuffling and then a match being lit, she turned and watched Finlay light a torch. As the flame grew, it illuminated the dark space ahead. Had she come here under other circumstances, she would have stood there in utter admiration and awe, but as it was, her surroundings only added to her uneasiness.

In front of her was a staircase that led down into the cavern, but the light reached far enough for her to see what was ahead: beautiful formations of stalactites and stalagmites, reflecting back to her in a multitude of colors and shapes, glistening as even now they produced more layers over their magnificent forms. She'd seen a TV program about these caverns once. That's why the name had been so familiar. She remembered it well now, because she'd been so fascinated with this small wonder, how nature had been able to create such beautiful caves.

"Walk!" Finlay ordered.

There was only one way, and she knew from the TV program that there was no exit down there. She tried to recall the layout of the caverns and seemed to remember that there were three shafts going down. It appeared that Finlay had decided not to take the cave entrance the tourists frequented, but an older side entrance that was now defunct. Eventually, two of the shafts would meet deep underground. Not that this would help her at all. While she couldn't escape back up where she'd come from, the chances of escaping up the second shaft once she reached it were equally unrealistic. Finlay was a Stealth Guardian, and after seeing Hamish and Aiden fight, she knew how fast their kind was. Their speed was preternatural. She would never be able to outrun him. Or the demons.

As the stairs ended and turned into smoothly carved out walkways, they passed formation after formation, each more beautiful than the last. As the path widened, the cave split, and they entered the branch on the right. The light from Finlay's torch reflected on the walls and painted dancing shadows on it, creating different colors.

"That way," he demanded and pointed his hand toward another dark path beyond the cave. It felt like a tunnel when she stepped into it, and her claustrophobia surfaced at the notion that this place could collapse while she was in it. Her heartbeat accelerated, and her breath became irregular. Her palms coated themselves with dampness, and her knees began to shake.

"I can't," she whispered.

"Go!" he barked from behind her, his hand nudging her forward, not at all gently.

She had no choice but to continue. Her hands guiding her along the wall, she walked forward, one foot in front of the other, while she tried to breathe normally, hoping to chase away the fear that gripped her. It seemed to take an eternity until she finally cleared the tunnel and stepped into another branch of the cave. She stopped, hoping to rest now, but Finlay pushed on, leading her farther down the branch.

Would this never end?

They reached a massive gymnasium-size room, the ceiling at least two stories high. From above, stalactites descended in various shapes, sizes and colors, and below, from an abyss in the center of the cave, stalagmites pointed upwards like spikes as sharp as swords. Instinctively, she pulled back from the edge. If someone fell down there, the spikes would impale them like a pig on a spit.

"Sit!"

Leila turned to Finlay and saw him pointing to a spot next to a rounded formation. Hesitantly, she went there and followed his order. She watched him walk to an indentation in one of the cave walls and dipped his torch into it. As soon as it touched the little hole, the flame traveled outwards to both its sides, running a ring around the entire cave. Looking more closely, she saw the ridge that was carved into the stone and ran the entire circumference of the huge room. She guessed that it was filled with oil or some other flammable liquid.

The place was suddenly bathed in subdued light.

"What happens now?"

Finlay looked at her, his eyes suddenly shimmering in a low green light. "We're waiting for the demons to arrive."

She could only assume that lighting the fire had alerted the demons to their presence.

37

The signal from Leila's tracker had led them to Northern California, a tourist destination named Mercer Caverns, a collection of caves that ran deep underground, filled with rock formations created by nature over millions of years, thanks to the mineral-rich rocks and underground flowing water.

Under cover of darkness, Aiden directed his colleagues toward the main entrance, examining the locking mechanism. It was untouched.

"He must have taken Leila in another way," he said to nobody in particular.

Behind him, Hamish grunted. "Doesn't matter. Once we have her, we'll figure out which way to get her out. If need be, Logan can always break the door open later."

"Right," Logan confirmed.

Aiden turned back to them. In addition to Logan and Hamish, Manus and Enya were with them. Pearce had had to stay at the compound, unable to move. Besides, he had to give them a constant update of Leila's position in case she was moved again. In the meantime Pearce had also alerted Aiden's father who was on his way. Jay, one of their other compound mates, had been pulled off his assignment and was going to meet up with Barclay, then join Aiden and the others at Mercer Caverns to provide more manpower.

"Let's go," Aiden ordered.

"We should wait for the others," Enya cautioned. "You don't know how many demons Finlay is meeting with. We might be outnumbered."

"We can't risk waiting any longer. The demons can show any moment if they haven't already. And if they take her to the underworld, not even the tracker will help us." Aiden would never allow this. He was so close to getting her back, there was no way he'd let this opportunity slip through his fingers just because they might be unevenly matched against the demons.

"Fine," Hamish agreed.

"Then let's move."

One after one, they passed through the entrance and moved into the dark interior. Aiden smelled the damp air, the mustiness, as his eyes adjusted to the darkness. Not paying the natural beauty of the caverns any attention as he moved downward into the belly of the earth, he kept his senses sharp and alert, ready to cloak himself from everybody's eyes, even the Stealth Guardians' behind him, should they encounter any demons or the traitor.

His hand tested for his weapons, making sure they still were where he'd stashed them: one dagger in each boot, two at his belt, and a sword in his right hand.

The descent was a long and winding one. As soon as they reached the first branch of the cave, they scanned their surroundings. It was empty. Slowly, they moved forward along the carved-out path that led them through the labyrinth. Nobody spoke, knowing their voices would echo and give them away.

Aiden felt his heart beat faster with every step. He didn't like the silence. What if it meant they were already too late? He tried to banish the frightening thought from his mind. No, he would save her. She was here somewhere.

A hand on his shoulder stopped his progress. Then he felt Hamish's mouth at his ear and saw his hand stretching past him.

"There. Light."

Aiden nodded and edged forward toward the next cavern, holding his hand up to his friends to indicate they should wait for him. Then he reached for his power and cloaked himself.

In his invisible state, he approached and reached the edge of the walkway as it opened up to a large room. It was much bigger than the one before and illuminated by a ring of fire burning along the wall. His eyes instantly homed in on the two figures near one wall. Leila was sitting propped against a stone formation, while Finlay stood a few feet from her, scanning his surroundings, clearly waiting for somebody: the demons.

Aiden let his eyes run over Leila's body. As she lifted her head now, he noticed a red bruise on one side of her neck. His hands clenched into fists, wanting to beat Finlay to a pulp for having harmed her. But he refrained from following his urge. Satisfied that Leila was otherwise uninjured, he rushed back in silence.

He uncloaked himself when he reached his friends. They huddled around him.

"Finlay is there with Leila. Both are at the right wall, two o'clock. We'll go in cloaked. Surround them. It's a circular room. Enya, Manus, use the pathway on the left, make a loop; Logan stay at the entrance to block him from escaping. Hamish, you and I take the path to the right. Once I'm close enough to touch Leila I'll give you a signal, we'll uncloak, then attack Finlay."

"No," Hamish whispered back.

Aiden gave him a sharp look.

"We need to wait for the demons. If you attack now, the demons might smell a rat and not show," Hamish continued.

"I don't care!" Aiden bit back below his breath. They could always get the demons later. His first priority was getting Leila to safety.

"Think about it, Aiden. They're coming for her. It's our best chance of them coming close enough so we can snatch them. They're our ticket into the underworld. We'll get one of them and we can get in and find the pendant."

Aiden contemplated Hamish's idea. He'd thought the same at first, but seeing Leila sitting there in the damp cave, he couldn't help but wish for this to be over fast.

"Hamish is right," Logan said quietly. "We'll never have such a great opportunity again."

Aiden closed his eyes for a moment. Could he take this risk? Did he have a right to use Leila as bait to get to the demons? His heart screamed 'no' in the loudest of voices, but logic dictated otherwise. He knew this was the best chance they would ever have to catch the demons unawares.

Slowly, reluctantly, he nodded. "But we'll still go in cloaked now and wait with them."

"Agreed."

"Positions?" Enya asked.

"Station yourselves in a circle close to the cavern walls. Logan at 6 o'clock, Enya at 9, Manus at 11, Hamish at 12. I'll be at 4 o'clock. It's the closest we can get to Finlay and Leila, otherwise Finlay might sense us despite our cloaked state. Nobody attacks until they hear my command. Understood?"

All nodded, then lined up on the walkway, a safe distance between them.

"Cloak now," he ordered and his friends disappeared in front of his eyes.

The wait seemed to stretch forever even though Aiden's watch indicated that only a few minutes had passed before he finally heard a sound. He watched as Finlay's ears perked up, too.

Relieved that the wait was over, Aiden gripped his sword tighter and scanned the room for the spot where the demons would appear.

Without warning, a shockwave pushed him back, knocking him against a limestone formation. Black fog rose before him, blocking his direct line of sight of Leila.

Shit! He realized instantly that the demons had thrown up a vortex right in front of him, and he was caught at the back of it, cut off from reaching Leila. Panic roared through him. He couldn't step through the demons' portal, knowing that it could hurtle him into the underworld instead. While that was the ultimate plan to get Leila's research data back, he would only do so once she was safe.

Frantic, he squeezed past the edges of the vortex, trying desperately not to connect with it as he slid along the wall. His hand slipped on the damp stone he was grasping, and his body jolted forward. His arm and shoulder dove into the black fog, the iciness shocking him to the core.

An array of voices assaulted him. Yet it wasn't his ears that perceived them, but his mind: he heard the demons' thoughts as they stepped through the portal on the other side.

...some good killing tonight.

...new leader, my ass...

And then he heard the thoughts that could only come from one demon. *Finlay is a fool to think the Great One is going to make him our leader. I'm their next leader. Once I bring him the scientist, he'll make me his heir.*

Zoltan's thoughts, no doubt. And it confirmed another thing: Finlay would not get the power he craved.

With all his strength, Aiden pulled from the vortex. He'd had no idea that a connection with it would make him privy to the thoughts of the demons. But as much as this was great news, he had to wonder whether this could backfire. Had they heard his thoughts, too?

As he cleared the vortex and reached the position where Logan was supposed to be at, he could finally grasp the entire situation: several demons had stepped out of the vortex and now crowded around Leila and Finlay. He counted nine, maybe ten, recognizing Zoltan easily from the back. He was slightly taller than the others, bulkier, and his entire form oozed power and domination. And clearly, he'd gotten smart, surrounding himself with a small army this time and not only with two demons as he'd done on the previous occasion they'd met.

The demons' voices now echoed through the cavern, bouncing off the walls, the sound magnifying.

"We meet again," Zoltan said calmly.

"I brought her to you like you asked," Finlay said.

"That you have." Zoltan made a movement toward his followers. "My associates will give you what is due to you."

Chuckles went through the assembled demons. Aiden felt the tiny hairs on his arms stand up in dread. He knew what Zoltan's words meant, but Finlay still smiled. What a fool, indeed.

"Let's go," Zoltan ordered and grabbed Leila's arm.

In horror, Aiden watched as he dragged her toward the vortex, while she tried to dig her heels into the ground.

"Wait!" Finlay called. "Haven't you forgotten something?"

Zoltan turned to face the traitor. "Forgotten? Oh, right!" Then he laughed. "Deal with him!" he ordered a demon next to him and turned.

Aiden couldn't stall any longer. He could only hope that his colleagues had been able to approach the demons in stealth and were close enough to attack before Zoltan had a chance to get away.

"Uncloak now!" he screamed, his voice filling the cavern.

Zoltan's head snapped to him, just as Aiden uncloaked himself.

Yet Aiden didn't look at the demon's furious green eyes, instead his gaze fixed on the diamond-studded pendant that hung around his neck.

38

Within a split second of Aiden's voice filling the cave, a voice Leila was more than thrilled to hear, pandemonium broke out. The demons around her swarmed out, rushing toward the Stealth Guardians who materialized out of nowhere. Swords clashed and daggers went flying. Angry shouts and grunts echoed in the cavern, making it sound like a whole army had descended on them.

Yet, Leila couldn't concentrate on the fight raging around her. All she could think of now was how to get the pendant back that hung around Zoltan's neck. With the demons around him being otherwise engaged, she finally had a chance, if only a slim one.

She had never thought he would wear it, but maybe Hamish had been right after all: demons liked shiny thing, and the piece of jewelry was more than just shiny, it was brilliant. The moment she'd seen Zoltan emerge from the vortex, she had noticed it. Her mind had started churning, trying to devise a plan of how to snatch her data back and destroy it before he dragged her into hell with him. Now the chance presented itself.

Frantically, her eyes darted around the cave, trying to assess the Stealth Guardians' chances of defeating the demons. The Stealth Guardians were outnumbered, some of them having to fight not one opponent, but two. Yet their agility seemed to aid them in their fight, as did their other skills.

Leila watched as Hamish suddenly vanished, then reappeared behind a demon a second later, the clueless vile creature searching for him in panic, before Hamish's sword severed his head. Green blood spurted onto the Stealth Guardian and the rock formations around him. His friends employed the same methods to deal with their opponents, turning invisible whenever they were in a bind, then reappearing an instant later at a different spot.

Enya fought just as bravely as her male colleagues. Her long blond hair was braided tightly around her head so the strands wouldn't get in the way as she swung her sword like a samurai and spun her body as gracefully as a dancer, yet as fast and furious as a ninja. Leila had never seen a woman fight like that. She seemed fearless in the face of the demons, her hand swinging the sword with precision and cunning and with more strength than her lithe body should have been capable of.

With a triumphant growl, Enya hit the demon's arm. He howled in response, but Enya didn't stop in her movement even as he jumped onto her. She didn't flinch when he aimed his dagger at her. In mid-movement, he halted, then dropped his gaze downwards. Leila followed his eyes and saw that Enya had driven a dagger into his gut. With a satisfied grin, she now yanked the dagger higher, slitting open her opponent as if she was an experienced butcher and the demon simply a dead bull.

Zoltan saw the same scene, noticing how more and more of his demons were being slaughtered, despite the fact that they outnumbered the Stealth Guardians. Clearly, their ability to turn invisible and then reappear where the demons didn't suspect them, helped them greatly.

Yet, instead of helping his fellow demons, Zoltan didn't move, nor did he release her arm. His fingers still dug painfully into her flesh, almost like the claws of a beast, his strength undeniable.

"Let's go," he grunted and yanked her toward the vortex.

It appeared he was prepared to let his followers die without lifting a finger as long as he got away with what he wanted: her.

"You have to take me with you!" Finlay whined behind them. "You promised me!"

Zoltan spun his head back to the traitor. "I promised you nothing! Do you really think we want a leader who's willing to betray his own race? Those are not qualities we value."

Finlay took a few hesitant steps toward them. "But you have to help me. I did this for your kind. So you could be stronger. You owe me." His eyes darted nervously toward the Stealth Guardians who seemed to gain the upper hand now. "You have to help me. They'll kill me if they get to me."

"Help you?" Zoltan asked, tilting his head.

Leila watched as his expression changed, a faint smile playing around his lips, making him look more human. But the coldness in his eyes betrayed his friendly smile.

"I'll help you. I'll make sure they won't kill you…"

A relieved expression spread on Finlay's face as he took another step closer. But a moment later, Zoltan pulled his dagger and flicked his wrist, aiming the blade at the traitor. It hit him between the eyes.

"...by killing you first," he finished his sentence.

Leila felt his grip on her arm easing in the same instance as the shock of the cold-blooded murder charged through her body. It gave her the courage she needed. If she didn't act now, he would pull her into the vortex.

As Zoltan watched Finlay's dead body tumble to the ground, Leila shoved her hand into her jacket pocket and pulled out her can of mace. She pointed it at her captor and pressed the button, releasing the stinging vapor. He let out a roar, but his hand on her arm loosened and she pulled free. While his hands went to his face to cover his eyes, painful screams issuing from his throat, she reached for the pendant and ripped it from his neck.

He reached for her, one hand hitting against her shoulder. But she held onto the pendant, even as Zoltan blindly swung his fists in her direction.

"Aiden!" she yelled and whirled her head toward the fighting Stealth Guardians.

She caught Aiden's gaze as he fought a demon in the middle of the cavern.

"The pendant!" she yelled and tossed it in his direction, watching how he drove his dagger into the demon, then tossed him to the side, lunging for the pendant.

In the same instant, Zoltan, seemingly having regained some of his lost vision, snatched her wrist. She witnessed how his gaze darted to Aiden who at that moment caught the pendant in his hand, then tucked it safely into his pants pocket.

Realization spread on the demon's face. "The drug. It was in there?" He lashed her with an angry glare.

"You'll never get it!" she bit back, relief that the blueprint was out of Zoltan's hands flooding her.

"I still have you!" he hissed.

"No you don't!" Aiden's voice sounded furious.

Leila's heart beat into her throat as she witnessed Aiden jump toward Zoltan, sword in hand. Zoltan instantly released her and tossed her from him with such ferocity that she lost her balance, fell and slid to the edge of the vortex, coming to a halt only inches from the churning fog and air.

She scrambled to get away from its pulling force, her hands searching for anything to grab onto as her feet were pulled into the darkness. She saw Aiden stare at her situation in horror, but at that moment Zoltan engaged him with a weapon he'd pulled from behind his back.

They exchanged blows, the sound of the clashing blades bouncing off the walls. Zoltan was taller than Aiden, more bulky. He appeared stronger and more massive, yet Aiden fought with fire and determination. Suddenly, Aiden's form flickered briefly and he disappeared only to reappear to Zoltan's left a split second later. However, the demon seemed to have anticipated his move and had already turned to fend off the next blow.

Leila took her eyes off the fight, struggling to find a hold on the slippery limestone. Her hand found a ridge and gripped it. Steadily, she pulled, nudging her body an inch farther out of the gaping hole. It gave her enough leverage to move her other hand toward the same ridge. She found purchase with her second hand. But the pull of the vortex increased, making her unable to move. All she could do was keep her position, her legs in the vortex up to her knees, her body stretched out flat on her stomach.

When a shout of pain echoed through the cave, she snapped up her head and saw how Aiden's hand reared toward his shoulder, covering a large gash.

"Got 'em!" she heard Hamish shout an instant later, making her whirl her head in his direction.

Hamish had just defeated his opponent and was free to engage another one.

"Hamish! Help Aiden!" she yelled and caught his attention.

His head snapped in her direction, and he rushed toward Aiden and Zoltan. The demon noticed him approaching instantly, his eyes quickly assessing the fight in the cave. Only three other demons were still alive, and they would be dead soon, too, considering how well the Stealth Guardians fought.

Clearly realizing the hopelessness of the situation, Zoltan dealt another blow at Aiden, then disengaged and lunged for the portal. In midflight, he reached for her ankle, trying to pull her with him.

Oh God, no, he'd get her after all!

Panic seared through her, and she closed her eyes, her damp hands cramping over the ridge, her fingers loosening.

Come with me. I'll give you everything you desire, she heard his voice in her mind. *Your parents. I'll give you back your parents. Isn't that what you desire most?*

A sob escaped her.

"NOOOO!"

Aiden's scream was followed by several hands gripping her arms, pulling her. She felt as if she were being stretched on a rack, her body being torn in two opposite directions. Then suddenly, she was catapulted forward, the pull from the vortex ceasing from one moment to the next, the grip on her ankle gone.

Breathing hard, she opened her eyes.

Aiden drew her into his arms. Hamish next to him let out a sigh of relief.

"Oh, baby, I thought I'd lost you."

She didn't get a chance to answer, because Aiden's lips were on hers an instant later. His kiss was brief, but searing. When he released her lips, he turned his head back to the fighting. She followed his gaze and saw how Hamish jumped back into the melee, relieving Manus's opponent of his head.

Then the two charged toward Enya and Logan, making short work of the two demons they were fighting. With the last demon dead, quiet settled over the cave.

"You came for me," she whispered to Aiden.

He gazed into her eyes. "I would have gone to the underworld to get you back." He pressed her against him.

As she looked over his shoulder, she suddenly saw two men she didn't know enter the cave. She stiffened.

"What did we miss?" the elder of the two asked.

Aiden released her and turned. "A pretty good fight."

"Ah, that sucks," the younger one commented.

The older man smiled, and Leila instantly saw the similarity between him and Aiden.

"Well, knowing your mother, I'm sure she's glad I missed it. Even though—" He looked at the dead bodies of the demons. "—I wouldn't have minded a bit of demon killing myself."

Aiden nodded. "Don't worry, father, there are more where they came from. We haven't seen the last of them."

Leila shivered. "Zoltan will come back, won't he?"

He brushed a strand of hair from her cheek. "And I'll always be with you to protect you."

39

No human had ever set foot into the council chambers, yet at this emergency meeting of the Council of Nine, where only seven members sat at their designated seats, Leila was present, standing by Aiden's side as he held her hand in his.

"What are they going to do?" she whispered to him.

He turned his head, giving her a reassuring smile, drinking in her scent at the same time. They hadn't been apart for more than a few minutes since the confrontation with the demons in the cave, and he wanted nothing more than to be alone with her and shut the rest of the world out.

"Everything will be all right."

He heard the gavel drop and straightened, bringing his attention back to the council. To his other side, Hamish stood relaxed. They exchanged a quick look.

"The Council of Nine is convened," his father said and stood. "Today's business brings great sadness to all of us. Our brother Finlay succumbed to the demons' pull and paid the ultimate price. It was foolish of him to turn away from us and give into temptation that destroyed him."

He looked into the round before continuing, "We all have to fight temptation, but our collective strength will help us not to succumb. May *virta* be with all of us."

"Aye," Cinead answered.

Primus nodded. "Cinead asked earlier to make a request. Please speak."

The Scotsman rose, casting a long look at the council members, then training his eyes on Hamish. "I am pleased to learn that Hamish has returned and was indeed instrumental in ferreting out the traitor. I believe such initiative should be rewarded. Finlay's seat on the council is vacant. I propose to offer it to Hamish. We need men like him."

Aiden felt his friend stir next to him, but before Hamish could say anything, another council member spoke up.

"I second the nomination," Wade said.

"A vote then," Primus requested.

"Uh, Primus." Hamish took a step forward, approaching the u-shaped table.

"Yes?"

"I'm honored by the nomination and your trust in me, however, with all due respect, I cannot accept a position on the council."

Gasps went through the assembled. To be offered a seat on the council, particularly for one as young as Hamish, was the greatest honor that could be bestowed upon a Stealth Guardian. To turn it down was nearly blasphemous.

Hamish raised a hand. "May I make my reasoning clear?"

Primus nodded. "Very well."

"The demons are out there, getting stronger by the day. From what Aiden could gather about Zoltan, he's a rising star in the demon world. He'll be their next leader, and I think he's smarter than all of them. It's a new guard. He will try to fight us with not only brawn, but brain. And while I understand the need for the council to make decisions and rule our race, I know my place is as a guardian out there in the field. It's where I can have the most impact. I'd much rather be out there, fighting side by side with my brothers than sit on the council. No offense."

Aiden felt Hamish's words fill him with joy. He had suspected that the council would offer his friend a seat. His father had hinted at it when Aiden had spoken to him shortly before the meeting. He was glad that Hamish wasn't inclined to accept the offer. He knew that his friend would serve their race better by staying where he was: at the compound, fighting demons and protecting humans.

"Is your mind made up?" Cinead asked.

Hamish nodded.

"I am sorry to hear that, Hamish, however, at your age I wanted exactly the same. I can't blame you for your choice."

"Thank you." He bowed and moved back to stand next to Aiden.

"The council accepts your decision," Primus said, then motioned to the two council guards standing near the door. "Bring in the prisoner."

When Deirdre was led in a moment later, murmurs went through the council chambers. Aiden instinctively squeezed

Leila's hand tighter. This Stealth Guardian had tried to kill her. Not only once, but several times. If it were up to him, he'd hand out the harshest punishment.

Aiden watched her as she passed by them to stand in front of the council. Her head turned slightly, gracing him with a quick glance. There was nothing in her eyes that indicated that she regretted her actions.

"You've been brought before us to take responsibility for your deeds. You're accused of acting against the council's express wishes. What do you have to say in your defense?" Primus addressed her.

Deirdre lifted her chin, every inch of her still the council member that wielded power. "I did what was right for our community."

"We voted otherwise," Primus disagreed.

"Because you couldn't see what was right in front of you." She turned to point her finger at Leila. "She was endangering us and the entire human race. She had to be stopped. You were wrong to protect her. The demons are still after her, are they not? What makes you think they won't get her after all? I still say we eliminate her."

Aiden felt anger surge, his chest moving as he expelled an angry breath. Next to him, Leila put a hand on his arm, calming him. When he looked at her, she shook her head silently, indicating he should not interfere in the interrogation.

"You had no right to make this decision on your own. You had your vote, just like the rest of us did. We can't simply take matters into our own hands when we don't like how the council decides."

Deirdre's look softened. "Primus, I did this so we wouldn't lose our own once more. I did it to keep us all safe, just as I would have given anything to keep Julia safe. Can't you see that? I don't hate this human, but the danger she represents should she ever fall into the hands of the demons, is too great. How many of our children will die because of it?"

Primus locked eyes with her for a moment, and Aiden saw the war that raged within his father. It was true, Deirdre had loved Julia like the daughter she never had, and had been devastated by her death. But did that give her the right to unilaterally condemn another human to death? Odd, Aiden had once thought so too, but he understood now that he couldn't blame one human for the deeds of another.

Primus gave a slow nod. "We'll see to it that it doesn't happen. However, sadly, that is not one of your concerns anymore. You have broken our laws. Therefore, my suggestion to the council is to incarcerate you in a lead cell for the period of one year and one day, upon which you'll be released into the human world never to return to us. Council, how do you vote?"

Deirdre gasped. "You can't do that! My powers... you can't do that to me!"

Aiden heard the desperation in Deirdre's voice and felt how Leila drew closer, whispering in his ear. "What does she mean? A year isn't very long for attempted murder."

"It's not the length of time, but what the lead cell will do to her."

He heard the council members one by one giving their votes on the punishment.

Leila gave him a questioning look, so he continued his explanation. "A year in a lead cell will mean that all of Deirdre's powers will have been drained from her body. The change will be permanent. She won't ever be able to make herself invisible anymore; she won't walk through walls again; and her preternatural strength, her superior senses will have vanished never to return. She will be human, not Stealth Guardian."

It was a harsh punishment, one nobody wanted to issue. Losing one of their own in a time when every Stealth Guardian was needed desperately was painful.

"No!"

Aiden jolted at suddenly hearing Leila call out her disagreement to the council. He pulled on her hand, trying to hold her back, but she twisted away from him and approached the table.

"Please, don't do this to her."

His father's eyebrows rose in utter surprise.

"You have no right to interrupt council proceedings," Geoffrey reprimanded.

Primus raised his hand. "Let her speak." He gave Leila an expectant look. "I'm curious why you should want to defend her, Dr. Cruickshank. After all, it was you she tried to kill."

"I understand, but I can also see her side. I've made a lot of mistakes, because I didn't trust Aiden at first. I lied to him about the existence of another copy of my research data. It could have very easily ended with me in the hands of the demons. And then, in hindsight, wouldn't you have rather seen Deirdre succeed?" She paused for a moment, then turned her head to look back at Aiden.

"Even you wanted me dead at some point."

Her statement sliced through his heart. "No, I—"

"Please don't deny it. I don't blame you." She turned back to the council. "I don't blame any of you for what happened. Everybody did what they thought was best. I don't want to be the reason why you'll lose another one of your race. Wasn't Finlay's death enough? I'm not interested in revenge."

With every word Leila spoke, Aiden's heart expanded for her. She had so much generosity in herself, and she handed it out with grace. He admired her for the strength she showed, because it took strength to overcome one's own sentiments about an issue and make a decision that benefited all. In many ways she reminded him of Julia, and in other ways she was so different from her. And he loved her for both.

"It still leaves the fact that she acted against the council's orders," Primus conceded.

Leila gave a quick nod. "I understand, and I don't want to interfere with your laws, but surely there is a less harsh punishment you could decide on, one that would not destroy her powers."

"You mean a slap on the wrist?"

"Something like that. Maybe a different location, another project, community service so to speak."

"Very well." Primus motioned her to return to Aiden's side. "Council, a word." He stood and the others did likewise, huddling around him, talking in hushed voices.

As Leila returned to him, Aiden pressed a quick kiss on her cheek, hoping none of the council members saw him. "I'm proud of you."

"It's the right thing to do. When Zoltan comes back, you'll need every Stealth Guardian you've got."

He caught Hamish's look. "Leila is right. And Zoltan will be back. I've never seen anybody so determined. You said yourself that he'll be a new leader, stronger, smarter, and more lethal. We'll have to be prepared."

Aiden couldn't agree more. "He won't give up."

"The council has come to a decision," his father's voice suddenly sounded in the chamber.

Aiden clasped Leila's hand, then focused his attention back on the proceedings.

"Deirdre, your punishment will be two-fold: you will be staging Dr. Cruikshank's death in a way so the demons will believe it to be real. I leave the details up to you."

Leila pulled in a quick breath, making Aiden slide his arm around her waist, steadying her. This measure was necessary; otherwise the demons would never stop looking for her.

"Your seat on the council is permanently lost to you. Do you accept your punishment?"

Deirdre nodded. "Yes, Primus. Thank you, you won't regret it."

Before she turned toward the door, Primus continued, "And make sure the demons buy it. If they don't, don't bother ever coming back."

"You can rely on me. I swear it by the memory of your daughter."

A moment later, she left the chambers, her head held high.

"One more thing then." His father looked at him and Leila. "The data. We will destroy it now." He lifted the pendant and showed it to everybody in the room.

"Allow me," Leila said and walked toward him. When she reached him, he handed her the piece of jewelry.

Aiden approached, watching how Leila's nimble fingers opened the diamond-crusted pendant and removed a USB drive from its interior.

"May I keep the pendant?" she asked, lifting her eyes to face Primus.

"You may."

Aiden reached for the USB drive. "I'll destroy it for you."

She smiled at him. "No, I'll have to do it myself. You see, it's time to let go of my dream. I'm the only one who can do that."

He felt his heart clench at the obvious pain in her voice. "You're strong," he whispered.

When she looked up, his father pointed at the large flat stone boulder to one side of the chamber. On it lay a hammer. "There."

The council members rose to follow her as she laid the electronic device containing her data onto the flat surface. Aiden noticed how her hand shook slightly when she took the hammer, closing her palm around it.

"I'm proud of you," he murmured, locking eyes with her for a moment.

Then she slammed the hammer down on the USB drive, once, twice, three times, until it had shattered into a hundred little pieces, a solitary tear escaping from her eye and running down her cheek. As the tiny particles scattered on the boulder, Aiden caught her look and saw the sadness in her eyes as she watched her dreams vanish.

When the council dispersed, Aiden felt his father's hand on his shoulder and turned to him.

"There's still one issue that remains. The council has left it up to me how to handle it," his father said ominously. "Excuse us for a moment," he said to Leila and led him a few steps away.

"And that would be?"

"You brought a human to your compound. As you know that's against the rules."

Aiden's heartbeat kicked up. "You know I had no choice. It was the only safe place."

His father patted his shoulder. "I understand that, but that doesn't change the rules. There's only one set of circumstances under which a human would ever be allowed at a compound. And the council has asked me to inquire about your intentions regarding this particular circumstance."

Aiden felt certainty about his intentions fill his heart. "Tell the council that the answer is yes."

His father pulled him into a hug. "I'm very happy to hear that, son. Very happy."

40

After nearly a week at the compound during which Aiden had rarely left her side, it was finally time for Leila to step outside her safe haven.

"It's time to see your parents," Aiden said.

Leila gave a bittersweet smile. This would be the last time they saw her—if they even recognized her this time.

"You can do this."

Pushing back the rising tears, she pasted another smile onto her lips. "I can do this."

The things she'd been through since that fateful night when she'd met Aiden had shown her that she was stronger than she believed. She'd survived several attacks by demons and two attempts on her life by a Stealth Guardian. Somehow she would survive this, too, as much as it would break her heart. But she understood the importance of this and knew that for everybody's sake—the world's sake—she had to make this sacrifice. The wellbeing of billions of humans was at stake, and if giving them a fighting chance to resist the influence of the demons meant she had to take this step, then she would do it. She had no right to be selfish.

By the time they pulled up in front of her parents' house in Aiden's car, she and Aiden had gone through everything that would happen that day. She reached for the door handle when he clasped his hand over hers.

She looked back at him.

"You're the strongest woman I've ever met."

Leila smiled, his admission warming her heart. "Because you make me strong."

As they got out of the car and walked up the driveway hand in hand, she felt a prickling sensation at her back and tensed.

"Don't turn around," he murmured under his breath.

"Are they watching us?"

"Yes. Are you afraid?"

"Yes," she answered. There was no need to lie. Fear was good, Aiden had told her. It would keep her on her toes and ultimately safe.

When she reached the door, she didn't have a chance to even ring the bell. The door was torn open, and Nancy greeted her enthusiastically.

"Leila! My dear! We were all so worried about what we saw on TV. Are you all right?"

Leila forced a charming smile and gave the housekeeper a quick hug before squeezing past her into the house.

"No worries, Nancy. It was all a big misunderstanding. I'm sure the news will report in a few hours that I had nothing to do with what happened at Inter Pharma."

"Ah, that's a relief!" Nancy said as she eyed Aiden who now closed the entrance door and stood in the hallway.

"Oh, sorry, this is my boyfriend, Aiden. Aiden, this is Nancy, my parents' caregiver." She knew that half of the introduction wasn't necessary. Aiden already knew everything there was to know about Nancy.

He shook Nancy's hand, flashing a boyish grin. "So pleased to meet you. Leila talks about you all the time. You take such good care of her parents."

Nancy blushed and made a dismissive hand movement. "Oh, they're so easy to work for."

"Where are they?" Leila looked down the hallway, listening for their voices.

"In the den. Your dad is reading the paper, and your mother is watching TV."

The walk down the hallway felt longer than ever before. Would they recognize her today? Her father maybe. He often seemed more lucid than her mother. Would she know today that her daughter was visiting, or would it be like it was when she'd called from the massage parlor? Leila prayed that this was a good day for both of them.

"I'll make us some tea," Nancy chirped and headed for the kitchen.

"We can't stay long," Leila called after the caregiver.

"Your parents are due their tea anyway. It's no bother." Then she disappeared into the kitchen.

Aiden squeezed her hand in reassurance. She nodded at him, then slowly walked into the den. Her mother sat on the couch, staring at the TV, a soap blaring from it. Her father sat in his favorite armchair, folding a newspaper and putting it on a side table. He looked up and straight at her.

For a moment she stood there frozen in place, waiting. She searched her father's blue eyes for a sign of recognition.

"Leila?" he suddenly said and rose hesitantly.

She ran toward him and threw her arms around him. He hugged her to him.

"Thank you, thank you," she whispered. "Oh, Dad, it's so good to see you." She raised her head to look at him.

"You haven't visited in a long time," he admonished.

She decided not to tell him that she'd spent half a day with him and her mother only two weeks earlier. "I know, Dad. I'm sorry."

"Well, at least you're here now." Then he looked past her, releasing her from his embrace. "You brought a friend?"

Leila turned. "That's Aiden, Dad."

Her father nodded. "Hello."

"Sir, it's a pleasure meeting you."

"How is Mom?" Leila asked and cast a look at her mother who was still staring into the TV as if she hadn't even heard the conversation that was taking place not five feet away from her.

Her father shrugged. "Fine, I guess."

Leila took a few tentative steps toward the couch, then crouched down in front of her.

"Hi, Mom."

Her mother stared back at her, then moved to the side to look past her at the TV.

"Mom, it's Leila, I'm here to visit."

She gave Leila an inquisitive glance before training her eyes back onto her TV show. Leila took her hand and squeezed it, trying to hold back the tears that started to well up in her eyes.

"They said Leila disappeared," her mother suddenly said. "The TV said it."

Leila let out a sigh, half relief, half pain. At least her mother's words meant that she still grasped something. "Leila is here, Mom, I've come back. The TV was wrong."

Her mother turned her head fully back to her. "Leila is back?"

Stifling her tears, she answered, "Yes, Mom, Leila is back, and she loves you very much."

"Why doesn't she come and visit then?" Her mother's eyes stared right at her, but still there was no recognition in them.

"She will, Mom, she will very soon. Your daughter loves you. She wants you to know that."

"I love her, too."

Leila released her hands and rose, turning away in order not to show her tears. Aiden put a comforting hand on her forearm.

"She might not know who you are, but she knows you love her. Isn't that most important?" he asked.

She nodded. "Yes. It will have to be enough."

When she turned back to her father, he was sitting in his chair again, reading the paper.

"Dad?"

He didn't look up this time, almost as if he was in his own world, too engrossed to hear anything else.

"I have to go," she whispered, knowing he didn't even hear her.

As they left the house only moments later, saying their goodbyes to Nancy, Aiden took her arm and led her back to the car. She lowered the window all the way and waved at the caregiver from inside the car, making sure Nancy would later recognize the fancy Ferrari.

Leila reached for the seatbelt out of habit, but Aiden's hand stopped her.

"Maybe it's better that way," she mused, looking at Aiden who put the car in gear and drove off. "Maybe she'll never find out that I died today."

At the next intersection, the light was red.

"Time to go, baby," Aiden instructed. "Hamish is waiting on the sidewalk for you. You'll be cloaked all the way."

She nodded and heaved herself out of the car window like they'd practiced the entire week. Then she gave Aiden another look. "Be careful."

When the light turned green, he took off like a rocket. There was no other traffic. The Stealth Guardians had made sure of that. She watched as Aiden's car ran a red light at the next intersection.

The crash could be heard in the entire neighborhood. Moments later, it was followed by an explosion. Aiden's car had crashed into a gas truck that had come from the right. Everything went up in flames, the gas from the truck spilling everywhere, spreading the fire to engulf the entire intersection, incinerating Aiden's sports car.

"Be safe," she whispered. "Please be safe."

"He can't be killed by fire," Hamish murmured behind her.

"Where is he? I can't see him." Nervousness crept up her spine. What if Hamish was wrong? What if an explosion could kill a Stealth Guardian after all?

"He would have dematerialized at impact and emerged behind the gas truck," Hamish tried to calm her. "At worst he would have gotten singed a little."

"But what if—"

Bare arms closed around her, pulling her into the hard muscles of a naked man she would recognize anywhere. Naked, because the fire had burned the clothes off his body, yet left him untouched.

"I'm here, baby."

41

Deirdre had organized everything perfectly. Nobody had gotten hurt. The Stealth Guardians had made sure no innocent bystanders were anywhere close enough to the accident to get injured. Yet the demons who'd followed Aiden and Leila from her parents' house had seen what they needed to see: Aiden and Leila crashing into the gas truck and being incinerated.

A body that, thanks to dental records, would be identified as Leila's, would be found in the wreckage. Deirdre had made sure there would also be a dead body behind the wheel of the truck. She had driven it herself, but gotten out the same way Aiden had escaped the flames. To ensure that the authorities' investigations led to a dead end, the Stealth Guardians had transported a recently deceased man from a Middle Eastern war zone through the portal, guaranteeing there was no chance the charred body could ever be identified in the US. They'd placed him in the stolen gas truck and rigged it to explode when Aiden's Ferrari hit it.

There was no body for Aiden. It didn't matter what the police thought of that inconsistency, but the demons, who knew that Stealth Guardians couldn't be killed by fire, would be satisfied. Add to that the eyewitness account of Nancy seeing them get into the very recognizable sports car, and the demons' own observations, and Leila's death would be believable.

For the first time in days, Aiden felt his body relax, the tension shedding like dead skin. There was only one thing now that was still on his mind. And he would take care of it now.

He put a hand on Leila's lower back, making her turn away from his compound mates who were chatting in the great room. She smiled at him.

"Come," he murmured only for her to hear.

Interest flickered in her eyes. "Where to?"

But without waiting for his answer she accepted his hand and followed him out of the room. He led her along the corridor leading to his quarters.

"Do you remember that my father took me aside after the council meeting?"

"Yes…"

"He told me that the council knew that I had brought you to the compound. And no humans are allowed here."

He sensed her pull in a breath. "Are they going to punish you?" She gave him a concerned look.

"They will, unless I rectify the situation." Having reached his rooms, he opened the door.

Hesitantly, she stepped inside, and he closed the door behind them. He noticed worry on her face.

"It's time for that now."

She nodded, her lids lowering to hide the sadness that had crept into her eyes. "I have to go then?" She turned away from him. "I understand. I do. I knew it couldn't be like this forever." Her voice broke.

"I'm not asking you to leave. I'm asking you to stay." He moved behind her and cupped her shoulders.

She turned her face to him. "But you just said I have to leave."

He smiled. "I said I have to rectify the situation. But that doesn't mean you'll leave. I want you to stay. As my mate, my wife."

Leila's mouth dropped open, and her eyes widened. "Your… you want to…"

He stroked his knuckles over her cheek. "Yes, I want. I want very much." He pressed a kiss on her lips. "The only humans ever allowed in any of our compounds are the mates of a Stealth Guardian. The council gave me time to decide. I didn't really need all that time to know, but I wanted to give you time to get used to me, to see what life with me would be like. What life at the compound would be like, before I asked you. Leila, I love you. Will you be my mate, my wife, mine forever?"

Her eyes searched his, surprise and doubt still shining through them. "But…" She bit her lip.

His heart clenched. Did she not feel the same for him? Had he misinterpreted her loving gazes, her caring touch, the sparkle in her eyes when she looked at him? He lowered his eyes, her rejection hurting more than anything else ever had. Every time they had made love since they'd defeated the demons in the cave, their lovemaking had become more intense, deeper, more connected. He'd poured *virta* into her so many times, his compound mates had started giving him dirty looks. Hamish had even pulled him aside one day and told him to give Leila a break.

"But," she continued then, "you're immortal. I'll die in fifty years or so. I'll grow old next to you while you stay young. You won't love me then. It'll never work."

He lifted his head, relief coursing through his cells. "That's your only objection?"

"Only? Isn't that enough?"

"Tell me you love me."

She hesitated.

"Leila, if you love me, please tell me now. If you truly love me, I need to know."

"I love you, but—"

He cut her next words off by sliding his lips over hers and searing her mouth with a passionate kiss. She loved him. The confirmation of what he'd hoped for this entire time spread in his body, making it hum with pleasure.

Slowly he released her lips. "Are you sure? Absolutely sure?"

She nodded, her eyes suddenly brimming with unshed tears.

"Good, because if you aren't, the bonding ritual will kill us both."

Leila jolted physically. "What are you saying?"

Aiden brushed a strand of hair out of her face. "Remember the first time I made love to you the Stealth Guardian way?"

When she nodded, he continued, "You collected the *virta* I poured into you, and you concentrated it on me when you put your palm over my heart. It was flowing through your arm. Had it reached my heart, we would have been bonded. And when that happens between a couple that doesn't truly love each other, it kills them both. Not instantly, but within weeks or months, so they have time to regret their actions."

"Oh my God!" she gasped.

"Yes, but if our love is true, you'll feed off my immortality, you will remain young with me and age only fractionally, the same way I do."

"But that can't be. Science..." she whispered, clearly fascinated.

"It's within our powers, so we can choose our mates freely among both species. However, I still don't understand how you could have known about the bonding ritual. It's a secret."

"I didn't. I swear." Then she shook her head. "But that night, I saw inside of you. I saw a bit of your soul."

He didn't think it was possible. "Only mated couples can sense each other's souls."

"But I saw it," she insisted. "What does it mean?"

He pulled her head closer to his, looking into the depth of her ocean blue eyes, seeing his love reflected back at him. "I think it means that we were always meant for each other."

"But what if we're wrong? What if this isn't love? We've only known each other for a short time. People can't fall in love that quickly."

Aiden gazed deep into her eyes. "I'm willing to take that risk, because even a few weeks or months with you will be infinitely better than living eternity without you."

"You're willing to risk your immortality for me?"

There was only one possible answer to her question. "Yes. But I can't make this decision alone. Your life it at stake, too. So if you have any doubts about your feelings for me, you have to refuse me now."

Her hand came up to stroke her fingers over the scar above his brow, then down his cheek and along his chin, her feather-light touch leaving a trail of fire on his skin.

Then she smiled at him. "I already died once today. What are the odds of me dying again?"

He grinned. "If you put it that way…"

Aiden slanted his mouth over hers, capturing her lips. Under light pressure she parted them, allowing him to delve inside her delicious cavern, while his hands busied themselves with divesting her of her clothes. It wasn't difficult, because she was more than willing to help him in his endeavor.

"Eager?" he whispered between kisses.

Leila's hands went to the waistband of his pants, snapping the top button open, then sliding down the zipper. When her hands found his hard-on and wrapped around him, he let out a groan. Her lips twisted into a smile.

"I doubt I could be more eager than you."

He thrust into her hands. She had a point; he was positively bursting to take her, the knowledge that this time their lovemaking would culminate in a bonding ritual, making his body hum with anticipation. He'd never felt happier in his entire life.

The moment they shed their last pieces of clothing, he lifted her into his arms and carried her to the bed, laying her on the crisp sheets. She looked perfect there, because it was where she belonged: in his bed, in his life, in his heart. He swept his gaze over her curves, savoring the moment his eyes traveled over her heaving breasts down to her long and shapely legs, those powerful thighs that had held him night after night as he'd thrust into her. The pure bliss he'd found in her arms every night made him dizzy even now.

"You know I don't like to wait," Leila purred and crooked her finger.

"I made a note of that when you told me back at the farmhouse." He slid over her, bringing his raging erection to her core, her thighs spreading for him without any urging on his part. So natural, yet so exciting. So meant for him.

Aiden plunged into her slick heat, seating himself with one single thrust. All thoughts vanished from his mind as the sensation of being connected to her filled him. She bucked against him, her body welcoming him.

Without holding back, he allowed his energy to flow. The air stirred in the room, the earth trembling beneath them, quaking in the same rhythm in which their bodies moved. Mist dimmed the lights in the room, making the bedside lamps glow in a soothing orange color.

Leila's thighs tightened around him, urging him to plunge deeper and harder, her breaths irregular, her skin coated with a thin sheen of perspiration, her eyes sparkling with desire and love. He'd never seen a creature more beautiful, a woman more desirable than she. He felt honored that she had opened her heart to him, that she trusted him with her life, as he trusted her with his.

I love you, she mouthed.

"Forever mine," he murmured in response. Just as he would be forever hers.

Amidst the churning air and mist that surrounded them—the power that cocooned them—he slowed his strokes, wanting to prolong this experience. Her muscles clenched him tightly, her hands exploring him so eagerly, as if she'd never touched him before. Every touch of her fingers, every kiss of her lips felt new and more tantalizing than ever. He was on fire, and for the first time in his life he understood what it meant when people said they couldn't live without somebody. Because he couldn't live without Leila. She *was* his life.

Without her, he was incomplete, only an empty shell.

Not able to wait any longer, Aiden allowed his *virta* to flow into her. From every point that their bodies were connected, his power seeped into her, permeating her cells. As he shared himself with her, her body began to glow, the sight driving him to ecstasy.

His strokes became harder and faster, and Leila met him in the same rhythm, her arms and legs suddenly gripping him tighter. She was aware of her power now, her eyes shining with it as she looked at him.

And with every stroke, he sensed the tiny orgasms that charged through her body, making her eyes flutter and her breaths catch. He could have come with her right there and then, but the sight was too beautiful to stop. So he withdrew his cock and thrust back inside, wringing another orgasm from her glowing body. So addictive was the sight and the feeling of her muscles clenching around him that he continued until his balls tightened.

Still he held back, wanting more, wanting everything she had to give. He rolled onto his back, bringing her on top of him without dislodging his shaft from her tight channel.

"Now, Leila," he urged her.

Their gazes locked. In the depth of her blue eyes, he saw flames light up, and suddenly her entire body tensed, energy traveling through her veins. She laid her palm flat against his chest, right over his heart that beat faster than ever. He felt the approach of the *virta* that he'd poured into her, but it was different now. It was comingled with Leila's own essence, with her soul, her power, her love.

The moment it reached her fingertips and sparked against his skin, the world around him stood still. But it was only the calm before the storm that unleashed a split second later: like a blade forged of pure fire, it pierced his heart and lodged there, carving out a place for itself. The pain was as fleeting as a pinprick, yet it left behind an imprint so permanent, nothing could ever remove it.

She had claimed him, and he was now irrevocably tied to her. At that knowledge, his body dissolved into waves of pleasure, his cock exploding inside her just as Leila's orgasm crested and swept him away. Floating in an ocean of love, weightless, timeless, he pulled her face to his and captured her lips, drinking her in.

And like an endless cycle, he shared more *virta* with her as she continued to pour it back into his heart, their bodies fused in passion, their love confirmed, their lives together ahead of them.

"Mine forever," he murmured against her lips.

"For eternity."

Then another orgasm claimed her and tore him with her. He knew his ability to speak or think wouldn't come back for hours. But who needed to think and speak when he could feel instead?

EPILOGUE

Zoltan took a reluctant bow before the Great One. Before he could straighten to his full height, the leader of the Demons of Fear rose to his feet and took a step toward him.

"You've failed!" he thundered, the sound of his voice echoing in the vast, deep cave where he held court.

Zoltan clenched his jaw shut, fury coursing through him. He had already had the drug in his hands without knowing it. That knowledge gnawed at him. He'd been so close. And now, everything was lost: the scientist was dead. He'd seen it with his own eyes. Later, the medical examiner had confirmed that it was her body that had burned in the wreckage. The Stealth Guardian's body hadn't been found. It didn't surprise him. He would have been able to escape the inferno.

The sharp tips of his claws emerged from his fingertips, evidence that the anger that boiled inside him was getting stronger and would not be so easily subdued today. He wasn't in the mood to be taken to task over his failure, even less so knowing ten of the Great One's guards were watching his humiliation.

"An accident," Zoltan pressed out, even though he had his doubts about it. What if the Stealth Guardians had in the end decided to kill the scientist after all, realizing it was safer for them that way?

"There are no accidents!"

Zoltan raised his gaze. "No, there aren't."

But his leader wasn't done admonishing him. "I believed in your capabilities. You assured me that this woman would be easy pickings, that the drug would be ours. And now, Dragor, what have you got to say for yourself?"

Zoltan listened to his birth name, but didn't like the sound anymore. He had changed. He wasn't going to cower any longer. He saw himself as the new leader. And the name he'd chosen for himself, the name of a successful entrepreneur, one he'd had to kill after he'd resisted his influence, suited him fine. He'd in fact admired the man for his strength. Yes, his new name, Zoltan, reflected that strength.

"My name is Zoltan now."

The Great One advanced, bringing them within a foot of each other. "I decide what your name is, boy. I'm your leader. And your chances of becoming my heir died with that woman. Do you understand me?"

"Yes, I understand fully," Zoltan replied and pulled his dagger, driving it into his leader's stomach.

Realization flashed in the demon's eyes as Zoltan drew the dagger upwards, slicing him open. Green blood and guts spilled, and gurgles escaped his dying leader's mouth.

"I don't need you to declare me your heir anymore. I'm taking what's mine, old man."

Then he kicked him backward, dislodging the dagger from his gut. With preternatural speed he turned, witnessing as the guards stared at him in shock, ready to attack.

Zoltan squared his stance. "Are you ready to die for your dead leader, or would you rather live and serve the new Great One?"

He waited, feeling power surge in him, never taking his eyes off his opponents. They exchanged glances.

"Then bow before me!"

One by one, the demon guards lowered their swords and fell to their knees. With satisfaction, Zoltan turned to the throne and took it, molding his broad back against the cold stone.

"Things are about to change. The Stealth Guardians will feel my wrath." He stared at the demons who were now under his command and smiled to himself.

"Soon, very soon," he murmured under his breath.

ABOUT THE AUTHOR

Tina Folsom was born in Germany and has been living in English speaking countries for over 25 years, the last 14 of them in San Francisco, where she's married to an American.

Tina has always been a bit of a globe trotter: after living in Lausanne, Switzerland, she briefly worked on a cruise ship in the Mediterranean, then lived a year in Munich, before moving to London. There, she became an accountant. But after 8 years she decided to move overseas.

In New York she studied drama at the American Academy of Dramatic Arts, then moved to Los Angeles a year later to pursue studies in screenwriting. This is also where she met her husband, who she followed to San Francisco three months after first meeting him.

In San Francisco, Tina worked as a tax accountant and even opened her own firm, then went into real estate, however, she missed writing. In 2008 she wrote her first romance and never looked back.

She's always loved vampires and decided that vampire and paranormal romance was her calling. She now has over 32 novels in English and dozens in other languages (Spanish, German, and French) and continues to write, as well as have her existing novels translated.

For more about Tina Folsom:

www.tinawritesromance.com
http://www.facebook.com/TinaFolsomFans
Twitter: @Tina_Folsom
Email: tina@tinawritesromance.com

14758234R00159

Printed in Great Britain
by Amazon.co.uk, Ltd.,
Marston Gate.